THE HOUSE OF THE
VANISHING GOBLETS

THE HOUSE OF THE
VANISHING GOBLETS

THE EDINGTONS

COACHWHIP PUBLICATIONS
Greenville, Ohio

The House of the Vanishing Goblets, by the Edingtons
© 2018 Coachwhip Publications
Introduction and Afterword © Curtis Evans

Arlo Edington (1890-1953)
Carmen Ballen Edington (1894-1972)
The House of the Vanishing Goblets published 1930.
No claims made on public domain material.
Cover image: Architecture (cc) Prayitno; chalice (cc) Angelo
  Steccanella

CoachwhipBooks.com

ISBN 1-61646-463-1
ISBN-13 978-1-61646-463-9

LIGHTS, CAMERA, MURDER!
The Edingtons and *The House of the Vanishing Goblets*
Curtis Evans

I. Introduction: Mystery and the Winchesters

Old dark house mysteries, popularized in the Roaring Twenties by a menagerie of hit stage thrillers like *The Bat, The Cat and the Canary*, and *The Monster* (and the films adapted from them), were still much in vogue in books and on screens in 1930, the year that the husband-and-wife writing team of Arlo Channing and Carmen Ballen Edington published their second detective novel, *The House of the Vanishing Goblets* (*Murder to Music* in the UK), a follow-up to their extremely successful 1929 detection debut, *The Studio Murder Mystery*. The Edingtons based the titular dwelling in their second detective novel on what today remains one of the largest and eeriest old dark houses in America: the so-called Winchester Mystery House in San Jose, California, a sprawling Victorian mansion that was begun in 1884 by Sarah Winchester, widow and heiress of firearms magnate William Wirt Winchester, and still not completed at her death nearly forty years later in 1922, eight years before the publication of *The House of the Vanishing Goblets*.

According to legend, Sarah Winchester, emotionally devastated after the deaths of her husband and only child, came to believe that she must continuously build a mansion in order to house the restless aggrieved spirits of all the unfortunate people who over many years had been violently extinguished by her husband's famously deadly rifles. The result at the widow's own demise was a seemingly endless, bizarre abode of 161 rooms (spanning 24,000 square feet), 47 fireplaces, 17 chimneys, 52 skylights, over 10,000 panes of glass (including superb work by the Tiffany Company), 13 bathrooms, 6 kitchens, 2 basements, and 3 elevators. Among the more eccentric features of the house are a séance room (with only one entrance but three exits); stairs that are dead ends; a so-called "door to nowhere," which opens onto a second-story drop, and other doors that open on blank walls; windows that overlook other rooms; hidden chambers and secret passages; and designs and patterns which come in sequences of 13 throughout the structure. (For example, the 13th bathroom that was built has 13 windows and 13 steps leading up to it.) The mansion's seven-story tower toppled in the 1906 San Francisco earthquake, never to be raised again, and other parts of the house that were damaged at that time were left unrepaired, adding to the strange and unsettling appearance of the structure. It is difficult to imagine a better setting for a murder mystery than the Winchester Mystery House, which opened for tours in 1923, a year after its mistress' death and six years before the Edingtons commenced writing *The House of the Vanishing Goblets*. 95 years later the weird mansion also served as the subject and setting for the 2018 horror film *Winchester*, starring Oscar-winning British actress Dame Helen Mirren. It would seem that you just can't keep a bad hant down.

II. MYSTERY AND THE EDINGTONS

Although today in the 21st century Arlo Channing Edington and his wife Carmen Ballen Edington are almost entirely forgotten authors, the husband and wife are notable for their early

The Edingtons

Arlo Edington, 1934

depictions of California in their detective novels, the first of which was published fully a decade before Raymond Chandler's celebrated LA crime fiction debut, *The Big Sleep* (1939). Additionally, both *The Studio Murder Mystery* and *The House of the Vanishing Goblets* portray murders impacting a fictional Hollywood film studio, making them the first Hollywood crime novels of which I am aware, anticipating Ellery Queen's *The Four of Hearts* (1938) and Raymond Chandler's *The Little Sister* (1949).[1] Both Arlo and Carmen Edington were employed, appropriately enough, in the Hollywood film industry during the early years of the Roaring Twenties. Indeed, theirs was a studio romance— though the bloom had come decidedly off the rose by 1934, when Carmen successfully sued Arlo for divorce in the midst of his campaign for the lieutenant governorship of California. Thus ended for good and all what once had been a promising exercise in collaborative mystery authorship.

Arlo Channing Edington was born on September 23, 1890. Like many a fictional California starlet (including Mavis Weld in Chandler's *The Little Sister*), Arlo hailed from small-town Great Plains America, specifically the little burg of Washington, seat of Washington County, Kansas, a rural farming region bordering eastern Nebraska that in the year of Arlo's birth had reached, at nearly 23,000 souls, what would prove the peak of its population. Reflecting the optimism of a growing community, county citizens in the late 1880s constructed a grand Second Empire Courthouse in Washington, but by 1900 the population of both the county and its seat already had begun inexorably to decline. Thereafter the number of people recorded as living in the county diminished in every census, finally in 2010 reaching the current low of less than 6,000. Symbolically the ornate old courthouse, having been severely damaged by a tornado, was torn down in 1932 and replaced by a flatly rectangular grey limestone structure, of the sort too monotonously familiar today in declining small-town America.

Arlo's family had been quite familiar with the majestic old courthouse, with his father, Talfourd Channing Edington, being a land surveyor and civil engineer, his paternal grandfather, Aaron Benjamin Baumberger, sire of Alice Rebecca Baumberger Edington, District Court Clerk, and two of his aunts employees of local newspapers.[2] Grandfather Baumberger resided in Washington next door to the Edingtons, who in addition to Arlo had two sons, Claude Burton and Harry Elias, as well as a daughter, Merle. The two aunts of the Edington children who were connected with the newspaper business were Lillie Baumberger, a reporter, and Rose Edington, a linotypist and subscription canvasser for numerous newspapers in eastern Kansas and Nebraska, including the *Emporia Gazette*, the mouthpiece of celebrated Progressive Kansas journalist William Allen White, the so-called "Sage of Emporia." That Rose Edington had a confident character with a core of sound common sense—a trait she shared with the children of Talfourd and Alice Edington—is suggested by the newspaper woman's correspondence with White, who hired her to canvas subscriptions not long after he bought the *Gazette* in 1895. In her letters Rose bluntly lectured the esteemed young journalist that he needed to recruit more county correspondents. Put plainly, people paid newspapers to see their names in print:

> I am aware that you are a writer of considerable note and may labor under the impression that this correspondence must have something with brains to it. No, that isn't necessary at all. Most anyone writes good enough, and if it is only "Jim Jones butchered yesterday" and "Mrs. Smith had a quilting and Mrs. Brown and Black were there," Jones, Smith, Brown and Black will take the paper and the general public can skip such items if they don't want to read them. . . .[3]

After graduation from Washington High School and a year at Business College, Arlo qualified as a registered pharmacist in 1909. He was employed in this profession for the next eight years in the towns of Washington, Frankfort, and Marysville, Kansas, Omaha, Nebraska, and finally Springville, Utah. During the First World War, while he was still living in the Beehive State, Arlo served as a recruiting sergeant at Fort Douglas, just east of Salt Lake City. At war's end he set out for Los Angeles to join his two brothers, Claude and Harry, both of whom, with California dreams dancing in their heads, in the 1910s had entered two of the Golden State's hottest industries: crude oil and moving pictures. Arlo's elder brothers founded the Edington Gasoline and Refining Company, for which Arlo worked as a research chemist in the 1920s, again recalling Raymond Chandler, who at the same time himself was employed as a bookkeeper and auditor with the Dabney Oil Syndicate.[4] Additionally, while Claude Edington confined his efforts primarily to the family oil business in Long Beach, Harry, who was described as a "physically small man with a taste for cashmere" (all the Edington boys were short and slender of stature), quickly distinguished himself in Hollywood as an executive producer at Goldwyn Pictures Corporation and its successor company, Metro-Goldwyn-Mayer.

With MGM Harry in 1924 served as production manager in Rome on the lauded Biblical epic *Ben-Hur: A Tale of Christ* (1925), starring Latin heartthrob Ramon Navarro in the title role. *Variety* raved about the film, the most expensive silent picture ever made, calling it the "greatest achievement" in "motion picturedom," while at the behest of Italian dictator Benito Mussolini, King Victor Emmanuel III bestowed a medal upon Harry for his hard work—the latter event a more dubious distinction today, to be sure. Ironically, Il Duce in the event had the film banned in Italy after finding to his fury that the main Roman character, Messala, was the villain of the piece, and that

Barbara Kent, film star, and Harry Edington, theatrical agent, recently returned to Hollywood from their honeymoon after a surprise elopement to Yuma, Arizona. Photo shows the couple after their return.

Barbara Kent and Harry Edington

the film's titular hero, Ben-Hur, was a young Jewish convert to Christianity.

After leaving MGM, Harry became a much sought after agent to film stars. In partnership with Frank W. Vincent he represented such cinematic luminaries as Cary Grant, Greta Garbo, John Gilbert (Garbo's frequent co-star and the so-called "Great Lover" of silent film), Marlene Dietrich, Claudette Colbert, Edward G. Robinson, Basil Rathbone, Ann Harding, Nelson Eddy, Douglas Fairbanks, Jr., and Erich von Stroheim. Harry was particularly close to his client Greta Garbo, for whom he was credited with cultivating the famously enigmatic Garbo mystique. After going back into film production in the late Thirties, Harry served as the associate producer of the film *Love from a Stranger* (1937), a fine British suspense flick starring his former clients Ann Harding and Basil Rathbone that was based on Agatha Christie's classic chiller "Philomel Cottage"; and a few years later, in 1940-41, he briefly became executive in charge of "A" movies at RKO Pictures, producing *Kitty Foyle* (1940) as well as Alfred Hitchcock's screwball comedy *Mr. & Mrs. Smith* (1941) and his psychological suspense thriller *Suspicion* (1941), the latter of which was based on Francis Iles' noted crime novel *Before the Fact*. Like others before and after him, Edington found that working with (or for) the demanding Hitch could be stress-inducing indeed. "I have a raving maniac on my hands with Hitchcock!" he once lamented in a memo to a colleague. Possibly after having been worn down from such stressful film work, Harry, who wed film actress Barbara Kent in 1932, passed away after a heart attack at the age of 59 in 1949. Barbara Kent survived him by 62 years, expiring in 2011, ostensibly the last living person to have worked as an adult in Hollywood's silent films.

With such a go-getter of a brother as Harry Edington, it is not surprising that Arlo was able to find a foothold for himself in the film business as a scenarist and assistant director for Goldwyn Pictures. In 1921 Arlo assisted direction on no less than four films: *Don't Neglect Your Wife*, *The Man with Two Mothers* and, most notably, the crime dramas *The Ace of Hearts* and *The Night Rose*, both of which starred that titan of the silent, Lon Chaney, and were directed by acclaimed director Wallace Worsley. The latter film was banned by the New York State Motion Picture Commission on the grounds that it was "highly immoral" and likely not only to undermine public morality, but actually to "incite crime." Sadly, this tantalizing piece of ostensible depravity is considered a lost film.

The previous year Arlo had sold a film scenario called "Brute McGuire" to Fox Film Corporation, which developed it as a moving picture under the title "Bare Knuckles." The film was a crime melodrama which tells the story of "Brute" McGuire, a former hoodlum from the San Francisco underworld who is put in charge of a dam construction project in the Sierra Nevada Mountains, with fateful consequences. Working with Arlo on the screenplay (though she was uncredited) was Goldwyn publicity writer Carmen Ballen, a spirited 25-year-old former journalist from San Francisco. She and Arlo fell in love during the course of their collaborative scripting, and the enamored couple wed in the study of the Episcopal rectory at Long Beach on October 2, 1920. Abe Lehr of the Goldwyn Company generously presented a complete set of flat silverware to the newlyweds, Arlo being "one of the best liked men in the Goldwyn organization."

Meanwhile, a Fox film crew was busily at work constructing a replica dam up north in the Sierra Nevada as the backdrop for the exterior scenes in *Bare Knuckles*. The next year, when *Bare Knuckles* was released in theaters around the country, the evident result was, according to a notice in the *Daily Bonanza* of Tonopah, Nevada, a rousing film "full of red-blooded action." Arlo and Carmen, now man and wife, collaborated again that year (though their work was uncredited) on the script for *A Blind Bargain* (1922), another Wallace Worsley directed Lon Chaney vehicle, this time a horrific tale about the baneful side effects of experimentation with monkey glands upon humans, then a topical if outré subject. After this it is not clear what, if any, film work the couple did, either together or separately. Five years later, however, Arlo and Carmen, who gave birth to the couple's two children in 1922 and 1928, had definitely left the movie business—though the pair efficiently exploited in writing their former connections with it.

In 1927 Carmen wrote a series of film star confession stories for true confessions magazines, a new reading niche that had rapidly expanded after the launch of *True Story* in 1919. Allegedly Carmen's confessions were based upon confidences made to her "in the dressing rooms of the stars, when she was a publicity writer for the Goldwyn studios." While she frankly conceded that her stories were "pot boilers," Carmen nevertheless avowed that she was also working on a higher-browed "novel dealing with the psychological and physical problems and reactions of married life." This novel appears never actually to have been published (assuming it was even finished), Carmen together with Arlo having turned to writing something else entirely: a detective novel drawing heavily on their Hollywood experiences.

Born in Los Angeles, California, on December 31, 1894, Carmen Ballen—or, to use her christened name, Carmencita Eunicia Alicia Ursula de Ballén—was the daughter of Peruvian diplomat Alejandro de Ballén and American Virginia Garland Lewis. Carmen's Peruvian father remains an elusive individual, but by 1900 Virginia had declared herself a widow and was residing alone in San Diego with her young daughter Carmen and an unmarried sister, making her living from teaching elocution lessons. After moving to Santa Cruz and later San Francisco she became a self-professed naturalist; and for many years she wrote newspaper features on the natural world, first for the *Santa Clara Surf* and later for the *San Francisco Bulletin*, which was edited by a family friend, prominent Progressive journalist Fremont Older. Virginia's daughter Carmen, who grew up in Santa Cruz and was educated by private tutors and at convent schools in San Diego and San Jose, also worked for the *Surf* and the *Bulletin* (on the latter paper covering City Hall), as well as the *San Francisco Examiner*, before she was lured away by the lights, ever so bright and beckoning, of Hollywood.

After Goldwyn Pictures hired Carmen as a publicist in 1919, her most important task was acting as literary assistant to Anzia Yezierska, a Jewish-American immigrant writer whose 1920 book *Hungry Hearts*, a collection of short stories about immigrant life in New York City's Lower East Side, was made into a film by Goldwyn studios in 1922. Goldwyn paid Yezierska, whom their publicity department had glibly dubbed the "sweatshop Cinderella," $10,000 for the film rights to the book and brought her to Los Angeles, where she received $200 a week as a screenwriter, providing the author her first sense of financial security; yet she returned to New York after only a few months, feeling spiritually smothered in Hollywood luxury. The film version of *Hungry Hearts* was well received and today it is considered a historically significant picture on account of its portrayal of immigrant life, yet Yezierska herself was displeased with the result, her screenplay having been heavily edited and sentimentally altered by Jewish humorist and playwright Montague Glass, who received all of the writing credit.

Along with her husband Arlo, Carmen Ballen seems, in contrast with her client Anzia Yezierska, always to have kept an eye firmly affixed on the bottom line and the main chance. Mysteries had become quite the rage by the late 1920s, when Carmen and Arlo were writing the first of their detective novels, *The Studio Murder Mystery*, in the hope of getting rich quick. In 1928 mystery writer and recovering highbrow novelist and critic S. S. Van Dine had secured the number four place on the US bestselling fiction list with his third Philo Vance detective novel, *The Greene*

Murder Case, a milestone in American literary culture which Van Dine himself matched the next year, when his detective novel *The Bishop Murder Case* placed fourth among 1929 fiction best-sellers, not far behind Sinclair Lewis' *Dodsworth* and Erich Maria Remarque's *All Quiet on the Western Front*. Clearly fast money could be made from writing good mysteries—though some clever publicity work on their behalf surely would not hurt either.

III. MURDER AND SOMETHING MORE: THE SHORT MYSTERY WRITING CAREER OF ARLO AND CARMEN EDINGTON

Before Arlo and Carmen Edington had even found publishers for *The Studio Murder Mystery*, they managed to sell both the serial and film rights to the book, for the then impressive sum of $11,500 ($165,000 today), incidentally surpassing the amount which Anzia Yerzieska had made on the film rights to *Hungry Hearts*. Published in 1929 in the US by Reilly & Lee—best known for their production of the Oz children's books by L. Frank Baum and his successors—and in the UK by the Collins Crime Club, the book, though by no means the sort of Van Dineish bestseller of which all American mystery writers doubtlessly dreamed at that time, was an immediate success, propelled not only by the novelty of its setting but by its serialization, between October 1928 and April 1929, in *Photoplay* and the release in May 1929, under the same title, of the film, publicized as one of the first "all talkie" movies.

Regrettably faithful to the book only in its broadest outlines, the film, which was directed by the able Frank Tuttle (director of the Philo Vance crime films *The Canary Murder Case*, *The Greene Murder Case* and *The Benson Murder Case*, Dashiell Hammett's *The Glass Key* and Graham Greene's *This Gun for Hire*), tells the story of a caddish leading man (future two time Oscar

winner Fredric March, in one of his earliest films) who is knifed
to death on a Hollywood film set. Suspects in the dastardly murder include the leading man's director, with whose wife March's
character had recently had an ill-chosen fling (Warner Oland, in
a role predating his most famous contribution to mystery films,
Charlie Chan—one waits almost on tenterhooks for him to say,
"Thank you so much."); his long-suffering yet still quite jeal-
ously-prone wife (March's real life spouse, Florence Eldridge);
and his ingenuous young girlfriend and her war veteran night
watchman father and tippling cabdriver brother. Official investigation is provided by Captain Coffin and the oafish and much
dissed Detective Lieutenant Dirk (Eugene Palette, best known
to mystery fans as Sergeant Heath from *The Greene Murder Case*
and four other Philo Vance films), while also fitfully on hand is
Tony White, the evidently obligatory smarmily handsome and
facetious amateur sleuth (Neil Hamilton, fated to be known forever as Commissioner Gordon from the Sixties *Batman* series),
who seems to spend most of his time providing nearly intolerable "comic relief" by outrageously baiting bumbling Detective
Dirk—or "pinhead" as Tony White not so wittily dubs him.

That Fredric March's roguish yet magnetic Lothario dies in
the first 12 minutes of the film while Neil Hamilton's blithe and
blandly insipid "tennis, anyone?" hero goes on apparently forever
is symptomatic of this film's flagrant misuse of its material. Far
superior as a film, it must be admitted, is the adaptation of
S. S. Van Dine's *The Greene Murder Case*, which also was filmed
in 1929 as a talkie and directed by Frank Tuttle. Of course
the film version of *The Greene Murder Case* has the inestimable
advantage of William Powell as suave man-about-town and amateur sleuthhound Philo Vance (not to mention Eugene Palette
this time playing a cop with an IQ above room temperature), but
the film also wisely stays far truer to its respective source than
does *The Studio Murder Mystery*.

Aside from making the identity of the murderer blindingly obvious from the beginning of the film, a cardinal sin in a detective story, the film version of *The Studio Murder Mystery* is notable chiefly for having neatly excised most of the fresh character elements which favorably distinguished the novel, the fruit of the authors' several years of hard labor in the film biz. When it came to portraying itself on the screen, Hollywood, it seems, preferred to churn out standard issue clichés rather than present anything provokingly original. The climax of the film—a confrontation between Tony White and the fiendish killer—occurs during a "dark and stormy night" and at the fadeout there is the usual romantic clinch for the male and female love interest. Gone from the film are the most interesting of the book's characters: Abraham Rosenthal, the hyper-emotional yet extremely canny President of Superior Films Studio; Franz Seibert, the visionary, temperamental and monocled Teutonic director (he is replaced by Warner Oland's "Rupert Borka" in the film, a far less colorful figure); and unrelenting LA Captain of Detectives Smith, who always gets his man—or woman, as the case may be.

Grandiose film director Franz Seibert seems obviously partly inspired by Erich Von Stroheim, who had signed with the Goldwyn Company in 1922 to make his mammoth film *Greed*, which though regarded as one of cinema's greatest masterpieces today was deemed a flop and fiasco at the time; while several Hollywood film executives come to mind as the inspiration for Abraham Rosenthal, including not only Samuel Goldwyn but Louis B. Mayer of Louis B. Mayer Productions (later merged with the Goldwyn Company). Mayer's well-known concern with safeguarding the (public) morality of his stars and his preoccupation with how his films would play in not only Peoria but throughout all of Middle America are echoed in the thoughts that run through Abe Rosenthal's appalled brain when he comprehends to his utter horror that real-life murder and accompanying sex scandals have dared most indecorously to intrude upon the sacred stages of Superior Films:

> Years before, when motion pictures were only the promising embryo of the gigantic industry they now are, Abraham Rosenthal had been wise enough to see that scandal could be the danger and ruin of the industry. . . . [H]e . . . had understood and forgiven much. But one law he had always maintained in regard to his own studio. . . .
>
> "Vat you do avay from here, I cannot help. But vat you do on my lot, on *my* lot . . . that iss my business. I vill haff no scandal—no dirt! Right avay I hear about anything here, here in *my* studio, and out you go!"
>
> For years this had been the unwritten law, scrupulously obeyed. And now . . . MURDER! Murder, creeping in at night, had trailed its black garments over the unsullied record of Superior Films; had thumbed its nose at the unwritten law, and with a mocking sinister laugh had flitted away. Away? Would it return? Ah, that was the question! Once in, when would it not come again, and with it, how many companion evils?
>
> Murder is murder, even in a place where make-believe reigns. . . .

Some modern-day readers will decry the heavy-handed dialect speech, so out-of-fashion today, that is spoken in the novel by Rosenthal and his Production Manager, Isadore "Izzy" Cohen (though Lannigan, a superstitious Irish night watchman, and Yvonne Beaumont, a flirtatious French leading lady, speak in similarly exaggerated lingo), as well as some of the stereotyping sentiments that characters utter, like "A Jew knows no gratitude ven it iss a matter of business" (this voiced by Rosenthal himself). Yet Rosenthal is that rare thing in Golden Age detective fiction, whether originating either in the US or the UK: a major Jewish character, on the whole quite sympathetically presented. Typically in the detective fiction of this era, Jews appear only briefly and unflatteringly, either as scheming financiers or crazed Communists. "Rosey," as Captain Smith affectionately begins to call the movie mogul over the course of the novel, even functions as something of a co-detective figure with Smith by the conclusion of the Captain's investigation, making him one of the few Jewish sleuths from the era. (Off the top of my head I can think of merely three.) In my view the byplay between Rosenthal and Smith is, Rosey's obtrusively heavy Yiddish dialect notwithstanding, one of the most enjoyable aspects of *The Studio Murder Mystery*, making most regrettable its total loss in the film version of the book, where both of the characters have been deleted from the story. The studio head in the film is as pallid a gentile as could be imagined, while elderly and gentlemanly Captain Coffin is nearly as forgettable, his limelight having been stolen by the sparring between his idiot underling Dirk and the irritatingly insouciant amateur Tony White.

Rosenthal and Smith, along with a number of other characters from *The Studio Murder Mystery*, reappear in *The House of the Vanishing Goblets*, the Edingtons' successful follow-up to their first detective novel. The couple wrote *Goblets* in 1929, after they had moved with their two young children, six-year-old Channing Crane and one-year-old Nicida Ynez, from Los Angeles to Carmen's girlhood home, Santa Cruz (having received, on their departure from LA, a grand sendoff from their Hollywood friends at the celebrated Café Montmartre). However, in the novel, which the authors dedicated to Arlo's benevolent brother

Covers for THE STUDIO MURDER MYSTERY
Top: UK (Curtis Evans), Bottom: US

Claude, Rosenthal plays rather a smaller role than he did previously, the murders taking place "on location," as it were, during the filming in the countryside of *Souls at War*, an anti-war picture helmed by pacifistic director Ellinson Broox (Franz Seiburt being unavailable).

Having descried during the shooting of the film a massive Victorian mansion, abandoned and decaying in the countryside, Broox pronounces the strange sprawling pile the perfect place for his gloomy picture's interior footage, for the ornate house could well double on the inside as a French chateau or even, as one imaginative literary bloke on the scene suggests, Edgar Allan Poe's doomed House of Usher. Brooks and the film's hotheaded leading man, William Hoxton, depart to explore the house by night—and they do not return. The next day the two unfortunate men are found foully slain in separate rooms of the mansion: Broox fatally shot in the kitchen, Hoxton most savagely done to death in the music room, his head battered to an unlovely pulp. "God of Abraham!" dramatically exclaims the scandal-averse Rosenthal a couple of times on learning the news by telephone, before collecting himself and putting through a call to his friend Captain Smith, formerly of the LA Police Department, and requesting him to do some freelance investigation on the spot. Smith complies, bringing along his old assistants, the sober Ryan and the loutish Clancy (the latter of whom in truth does rather remind one of Eugene Palette in *The Studio Murder Mystery*); and soon he is enmeshed in a bizarre case involving disappearing guns, beautiful wandering women, a ghastly face in a Tiffany window, canned cherries, candle grease, a dozen or more vanishing goblets and—How Sherlock would approve!—a curious incident of a dog in the nighttime.

Certainly the Edingtons' selection of the Winchester Mystery House as the locale for their story was felicitous, as it makes a shuddery setting indeed for a tale of murder and its ratiocination. (One only regrets that a floor plan was not included.) Just how important the setting is to the mystery becomes increasingly clear as the tale moves along. I will leave the reader to discover what role the titular goblets play, but rest assured that they do figure significantly in the story and, indeed, are mentioned not only on the final page, but additionally in the next and final Edington mystery, *The Monkshood Murders* (1931), which sees Smith and his myrmidons investigating a slaying in the newspaper business—a field with which, as we have seen, both of the Edingtons were also familiar. As the title suggests, the killing

Five Mystery Writers Discuss the Craft

Left to right, Elizabeth Jordan, author of "The Night Club Mystery," presides over the discussion and holds out for "less blood and more mystery"; Audrey Newell, who is a newcomer in the field with "Who Killed Cavelotti?" does not mind killing off characters so long as it sustains the mystery and can be done plausibly; Janet Laing, author of "The Villa Jane," comes out frankly for the fantastic and the weird; and The Edingtons, authors of "The House of the Vanishing Goblets," get in a final word in favor of Hollywood and the movie locations as the ideal background for murder mysteries.

The Edingtons (on right) with a few of their contemporaries.
(ATLANTA CONSTITUTION, May 8, 1930)

UK cover for THE MONKSHOOD MURDERS *(CURTIS EVANS)*

agent in the novel is the deadly flowering plant *aconitum*, variously known colorfully under such folk names as monkshood, wolf's bane, and devil's helmet. To this botanical subject Arlo, a former chemist and a bulbs enthusiast and onetime President of the Southern California Gladiolus Society, and Carmen, daughter of a nature writer, brought some measure of authority.

Sadly *The Monkshood Murders* was the last detective novel which the couple would write, marital estrangement putting an end to their promising joint career as crime writers. Arlo and Carmen spent part of 1932 suing S. S. Van Dine for the massive sum of $500,000 (around $9,000,000 today), alleging that Van Dine and the Vitaphone Film Company had plagiarized the Edington novels for Vitaphone's S. S. Van Dine Mystery Series, which was composed of a dozen short films released in 1931 and 1932, one of which was suggestively titled . . . *The Studio Murder Mystery!* Coincidence? The outcome of the lawsuit is unknown to me, though had the Edingtons actually been awarded the princely sum they demanded from Van Dine and Vitaphone, I imagine that the bestselling author's lavish lifestyle would have come to a crashing close. Later that year, Arlo and Carmen permanently separated, with Arlo returning to Los Angeles to go back to work in the oil business as a Director of the Edington-Witz Refinery Company. Carmen remained in Santa Cruz with the children.

In April 1934 *Drum Madness*, a mystery set in Tahiti that is attributed to both of the Edingtons and to one Maryanne (Mary Anne Avery) Barrett, was published in England by Cassell. However, Carmen later claimed that she and Maryanne Barrett, who then was president of the Writers Club of Santa Monica, were the sole authors of the novel, which was the first of three mysteries the pair had contracted to write for Cassell. In what was perhaps a shot at Arlo, Carmen also declared that *Drum Madness* was her best book. Arlo himself spent much of 1934 campaigning for the Democratic nomination for lieutenant governor of

California. He was, it was reported, running for the office "on his record as an organizer of unemployment relief units in Los Angeles County and the work he accomplished as a representative of Independent Oil Producers of California opposing the Oil Code in Washington, D. C."

Unfortunately for Arlo, his campaign was fatally undermined when, just a few months before Election Day, Carmen hit her estranged spouse with a divorce suit, alleging on Arlo's part both intolerable cruelty and "intemperate jealously." Carmen won the suit, the judge awarding her custody of the couple's younger child, six-year-old Nicida, and ordering Arlo to pay support to his wife and daughter of $75 apiece monthly (today the equivalent, in total, of about $2750 a month). The couple's eleven-year-old son, Channing, elected to live with his father, who remarried the next year, in October 1935, to Clelah Belle Keltner Ross, a native Indianan fourteen years younger than he. Carmen's suit revealed that the couple held $25,000 worth of community property (about $460,000 today), including oil interests in southern California.

Ten days after losing the divorce action brought by his wife, Arlo was ignominiously defeated in the Democratic lieutenant governor primary, finishing seventh out of ten candidates with 27,617 votes, or merely 4% of the total tally for the race. Finishing far ahead of the rest of the pack, with 51% of the vote, was Sherwood Downey, a Progressive lawyer who was running on the EPIC ticket of the gubernatorial candidate, author and former socialist Upton Sinclair, EPIC being an acronym based on Sinclair's political platform: End Poverty in California. In the midst of the Great Depression, Downey's economic progressivism was far more in tune with Democratic aspirations than Arlo's effort to loosen federal regulation of the oil industry. After the election, Arlo, now disenchanted with the Democratic Party, became a Republican.

Arlo, who died in Los Angeles at the age of 63 on November 16, 1953, eight years after his second wife and four years after his film executive brother Harry, seems to have given up on his writing dreams, but Carmen attempted to keep her hand in the game throughout the Thirties. In 1937 she returned, after a two-year hiatus, to mystery writing, again working in collaboration with Maryanne Barrett on another novel, which was set in the Santa Cruz Mountains; however, nothing ultimately seems to have come of this effort. Aside from giving talks (recalling her elocutionist mother) on her brief life in the movie industry and teaching a class in Santa Cruz called "the craft of writing," Carmen seems to have completed no literary work from thenceforward.

In the Thirties Carmen's life became briefly shadowed, like Arlo's, by a certain amount of scandal, that of the sort which one finds in classic crime fiction, including the authors' own *Monkshood Murders*, though Arlo had nothing to do with the affair. Having separated, as we have seen, from Arlo in 1932, Carmen that same year became a fast friend of, as well as the business manager for, Mrs. Z. Kathleen Ayers, a doctor's widow of two decades' standing who was an outsize personality in Santa Cruz and formerly San Francisco. An energetic philanthropist and clubwoman, Mrs. Ayers was active in the Soroptimist International, a worldwide charitable organization of business and professional woman founded in 1921 that promoted global peace and improvement in the lives of women and girls throughout the world. She co-founded Soroptimist clubs in both San Francisco and Santa Cruz, as well as one of San Francisco's first circulating libraries, all the while making the newspapers on account of her various automobile speed exploits, including setting the record for driving from San Francisco to Portland, Oregon, at 22 hours and 34 minutes.

Near Santa Cruz she and Carmen together ran the Happy Valley Ranch, but this gratifying state of affairs abruptly ended when Mrs. Ayers died suddenly in December 1934 after a brief illness. After recovery from the initial shock and mourning, tongues began wagging locally when it was revealed that the late lamented clubwoman had made Carmen both the executor of her will and her sole heir. It had been said that the long-widowed and childless Mrs. Ayers, who was 45 years old at her death, had no close relatives, but now appearing mysteriously on the scene was a man, one J. L. Smith of Chico, California, of whom it was variously said that he was Mrs. Ayers' brother, adopted brother, or stepbrother. Further, it was claimed that Mrs. Ayers' will only had been "discovered," providentially for Carmen, after the wealthy widow's death. With scandalous talk buzzing unpleasantly about her person, Carmen, apparently doubting the adage that there is no such thing as bad publicity, composed a letter to the *Santa Cruz Evening News*, in which she vigorously countered these unflattering assertions. Carmen claimed that J. L. Smith of Chico, though admittedly Mrs. Ayers' nearest kin, was in fact merely her third cousin, and that the will had not been "discovered" as was being alleged, but rather had long resided safely in the possession of her, Carmen's, attorney. Despite the nasty talk from some Santa Cruz gossips, Carmen seems to have secured her inheritance from Mrs. Ayers and with it financial independence for the remaining 37 years of her life.

Having never remarried and, indeed, having kept her husband's surname, Carmen Edington died at the age of 77 in 1972, two decades after Arlo's demise. Her modest obituary noted only, out of her many accomplishments, that she had been a member of the Third Order of Saint Dominic, having returned in later years to the Catholic faith of her father.[5] A mass of the resurrection was celebrated for Carmen at the Resurrection Church in Aptos, California, before her mortal remains were interred in Holy Cross Cemetery. The films and the crime novels of four and five decades earlier then seemed but a distant, darkening glimmer on the far horizon; yet happily today, nearly a century after those bright young things Carmen Ballen and Arlo Edington first went to work for the Goldwyn Company in the hopeful, dawning days of the Hollywood film industry, one of the couple's amusing and intriguing mysteries has itself finally been resurrected.

ENDNOTES

[1] Both *The Film of Fear* (1917), by Arnold Fredericks (Frederic Arnold Kummer) and *The Film Mystery* (1921) by Arthur B. Reeve preceded *The Studio Murder Mystery*, but they concern the film industry in New York, before the great migration to Hollywood. Earl Derr Biggers' Charlie Chan mystery *The Black Camel* (1929) tells of the murder of a Hollywood film celebrity, though this murder takes place not in Hollywood but rather in Honululu.

[2] Oddly enough, native Pennsylvanian Aaron Benjamin Baumberger's great-grandfather, Johannes Riegel, was an ancestor of neighbors across the street of my mother in the Pennsylvania village of Gratz.

[3] Sally Foreman Griffith, *Home Town News: William Allen White and the Emporia Gazette* (New York and Oxford: Oxford University Press, 1989), 74-75.

[4] Both the Edington boys' parents and their sister Merle would move out to LA as well in the Twenties, taking

The Winchester House (ANNA FOX)

employment connected with the oil and gas business. Talfourd Edington ran an automobile service station while Merle, who never married, became an oil broker.

[5] Carmen and Arlo's daughter Nicida had become a nun in 1951, adopting the name Sister Mary Edington, although she left her order and took a husband the year following her mother's death.

THE HOUSE OF THE
VANISHING GOBLETS

TO
C. B. E.
IN APPRECIATION

Authors' Note.—Every character and every action
of this story is fictitious. The house which suggested it, which caused us to people a similar structure
with our imaginary folk, is a fact, unbelievable as
it may seem.

I

One thousand men, survivors of the World War, dim shadows in the gray dawn, surged against the iron gates of Superior Films Studio, pitiably anxious to play-act it all again for the price of a ten days'—or even a day's—meal ticket!

Inside, pandemonium! Trucks backing and filling. Wardrobe clerks rushing out of that long building, bent double under great piles of uniforms, helmets, puttees and boots, to add to the already towering stacks of them beside the graveled driveway. Property-men laboring along with heavy boxes. Others grabbing the boxes, checking their contents: rows of squat, deadly looking Colt's automatics—rows of blunt-nosed shells to fit them!

Skeets Williams, head property-man of the Ellison Broox Special Productions Unit, yelling orders to his helpers, tossing his hair out of his eyes, and the sweat with it—stopping now and then to comb it with skinny, nervous fingers, and to mutter, as he gazed wildly about: "Gees! What a mess!"

A man popped out of the small building by the gate and dashed into the scene, yelling:

"Say, what d'yu think this is? A funeral, or something? Step on it, will yu? I got to get those birds outa the road! The traffic cops'll be here in a minute!"

"Get the hell out of here! What gives you the idea we ain't stepping on it? You poor sap, d'yu think I don't know what the chief's goin' to say when he lands into this mess?"

With these pleasantries, Hank Dowling, assistant casting director, and Skeets Williams parted, Skeets to jump nervously forward as he saw Isidore Cohen, production manager, approaching. The irritable Cohen's eyes lit suspiciously upon him.

"Say, you Skeets!" he exclaimed in his habitually jibbering manner, "d' you know vat it vill cost if ye don't get into production to-morrow? How much for vone day only this bunch iss not vorking? I got it all down. Right here I got it!" He shook a sheet of paper filled with columns of figures at Skeets. "You got to get on location to-night! By to-night you got to do it . . . and give a look!"

His small black eyes rolled from side to side and he threw out his hands in a disgusted, insulting gesture.

"Yes, Mr. Cohen. We'll be shooting to-morrow, sure. . . . Yes, Mr. Cohen," yelled Skeets, and leaped upon a box in order to avoid the backing of a loaded truck.

What the head property-man said to himself was not so polite. He stood still a moment and rapidly scanned the equipment. Then he grabbed a megaphone and called shrilly:

"Let 'em come! Hey, Hank . . . shoot 'em along . . . *let's go!*"

Hank popped out of his office and over to Scot MacDougal, the gateman.

"Open 'em," he snapped, and then to the men: "Line up, you! No crowding! I'll call you by name."

Lannigan, night-watchman, on his last round before relief, stopped to look and spat noisily into the drive.

"'Tis just loike thot! Spittin' in the face of Providence . . . is the Jew!"

Scot MacDougal turned slowly and let his cool stare rest on the little Irishman. Then he said, with an edge of contempt in his deep voice: "What's biting you the noo, ye superstitious little wart?"

"Bitin' me, is it? Listen to the mon!" snorted Lannigan. "'Tis a fool I am for belavin' ye'd know the manin' av a presintmint! No, not if it wint skitterin' across the lawn, loike it did the night Dwight Harden was murthered!"

Lannigan's tone was bitter.

"And ever since that night, you've been croaking like an old woman of 'presintments' and 'signs' and 'warnings.' Because you called the turn once, Lannigan, 'tis no sign ye'll do it again! Forget it, man. You grow tiresome!"

Lannigan's bright, beady eyes flickered up resentfully at the brawny Scot.

"MacDougal, d'ye mark that bunch o' men? D'ye see thim murtherous weapons? Ye can make all the fun o' poor auld Lannigan ye've a mind to, but the Jew will rue the day he let thim killers in thot gate!"

"You old fool!" snapped MacDougal, disgusted. "Will you tell me how Mr. Rosenthal can produce a war picture without guns and men . . . to make it better . . . ex-soldiers?" He broke off to step up to the incoming line of men.

"Move along . . . move along. . . ."

They stopped their curious gazing about and quickened their steps. For a moment MacDougal and Lannigan watched them, then the latter began to moan softly under his breath: "Wurra! Wurra!"

MacDougal turned impatiently upon him.

"Shut up, or get away from the gate, you old croaking raven!"

"I'll shut up and I'll move meself whin I get good and ready, Scot MacDougal, an' not before! You'll mind me warnin' ye whin it's too late! To be sure, I'd do better to tell the Jew himself . . . he's more sinse in his head . . . and that he has!"

Lannigan made as if to step out into the studio entrance, for Rosenthal's big car had slipped up to the gate. MacDougal hissed a low-toned order:

"Keep your trap shut, you old fool!" and his bleak, blue eyes froze down on the little Irishman in a way that had made many a man obey him, and no shame to them.

"Ye dir-r-ty redcoat!" spat Lannigan, but stood aside.

The fat man with the round, genial face, who sat in the back seat of the car, leaned forward and lifted his hand in greeting to MacDougal.

"Good morning, sir," the gateman returned heartily, with a deference born of genuine liking and respect. When the car had gone on, he walked over to Lannigan.

"You'll not be worrying Mr. Rosenthal with your silly superstitions, d'you hear me?" he ordered menacingly. "Not a day goes by but you come bellyaching up here with a tale of spooks and hobgoblins, and such foolishness! Now I'm telling you once for all, Lannigan, that it's time to quit. You can't go carrying the reminder of Hardell's murder around the rest of your life. It isn't healthy. You'd better forget it. I'm telling you, man!"

"And tell me this too, you're so smart, Scot MacDougal! Why did a black cat cross me path jist at the stroke of midnight, last night? The same as it did whin Harden was murthered? And why did a pixie crawl inty me ear and bore a wee hole in me head whin I was after trying to get a bit of sleep between me rounds? And why did a beetle go clickin' against me lanthern . . . a-makin' the death rattle wid her wings . . . and ye heard the owl yerself, for ye admitted as much! 'Tis death they mane, all av thim!"

MacDougal grunted. Lannigan glared at him, then continued:

"And thin tell me why the white pigeon wint an' sat on the auld chimly av that desairted set at two o'clock this mornin' . . . wid her head cocked sidewise, a-listenin', waitin' fer the Angel of Death, she was . . . and it was that same white pigeon as flew over stage six on the dawn that Harden was murthered there! Now phwat have ye to say to all thot, Scot MacDougal?"

"Shut your trap!" snapped the gateman. "That's what I have to say! You're getting old and wandering in your wits. Better take a grip on yourself, Lannigan, my man!"

Without a word MacDougal turned his back and walked to the other side of the gate. Sometimes the little Irishman tried him sorely. He had been bad enough before, but since the affair of Dwight Hardell, when he had come up to MacDougal shivering and blabbing of ghosts and banshees and queer happenings (which later proved only too gruesomely true), he had kept up a continual testimony of other similar indications of tragedy. Remembering that shocking affair, and Lannigan's accurate prediction of it, sometimes MacDougal himself felt reminiscent and apprehensive chills. But then he would throw off these doubts and mutter angrily that Lannigan was a crazy old Irish monkey . . . and stalk away from him.

Now the night-watchman picked up his empty dinner pail and walked out the gate.

"Ye can mark me out, Scot MacDougal, and I'll be lavin', but ye can't put an end to the things I told ye, and yell live to see the day come to prove to ye I was right! 'Tis a tragic cycle things here are movin' in now . . . a bad moon . . . and she's not waned yet . . . mark me wurrds!"

Lannigan squeezed out between the files of incoming men, and MacDougal breathed a gusty sigh of relief. The nagging of the little man was like a gadfly that would not be slapped away.

The watchman's steady blue eyes picked out a shining black and white car from the boulevard traffic.

"Make a way, there, men," he called, going up to the gates. "Make way for a car!"

Ellison Broox halted his machine just inside the gates and got out. For a moment he stood looking quietly at the line of men. MacDougal stepped up to see if there was anything the director wanted.

"Those my men, Mac?"

"Yes, sir."

"What d'you think of them, Mac? How do they look to an ex-officer like yourself?"

MacDougal ran his eyes quickly down the line.

"That's a dandy lot, sir. Well set up, of a size generally, and a fine bold look in their eyes! I should say the casting office did well by you, sir!"

"For once in its life, eh, Mac?" agreed the director genially. "Yes. They're all right. I can make a picture with them."

He turned to go on, but stopped to ask:

"Is Randall on the job, Mac?"

"Yes, sir. Quite early."

"Good. When Morin and Hoxton come in . . ."

"They're in their rooms now, sir, getting ready."

"Good. Send word to them I'll take them up in my car."

Hank Dowling rushed out of the casting office. "Are they all right, Mr. Broox?" he asked anxiously.

"Capital, Hank! Capital! I couldn't have done better myself!"

"That's great! We've got your thousand, too!"

"That's fine, boy. And remember, Hank, don't send Marjorie up until I send you word."

"Right," said Hank. "There's those damned phones, Mr. Broox. I've got to get on the job. Wish you all the luck in the world, and the best war picture ever shot!"

With a wave of his hand he was gone. Broox stood watching the incoming men with keen eyes. Already he was picking the ones he would use in special bits of action, studying each face closely, marking the way each man moved forward. One of them, looking up and catching the intent stare, returned it for a moment and then turned white around the mouth. He stepped out of the ranks and up to the director.

"What do you want, my man?" asked Broox.

"I just wanted to be sure . . . first . . . *Captain Jones* . . . that it was *you!* And to give you what I've waited ten years to hand you . . . *this!*"

His fist shot out and caught the unsuspecting director on the point of the chin. He followed up his blow by flinging himself bodily upon him Immediately cries and commotion broke out all around, but before anything else could happen, the burly gateman let out a roar and hurled himself upon the director's assailant, hauled him off and shook him like a rat.

"Let go of me, damn you!" cursed the soldier, frothing in anger.

"Yes . . . let . . . him . . . go . . ." gasped Broox. He waved his hand reassuringly at the collecting crowd.

"Move along . . . everybody . . . it's nothing."

"What'll I do with him, sir?" said MacDougal.

"Just put him out, Mac. He's no doubt crazy . . . shell-shocked, poor fellow. Undoubtedly he takes me for someone he's got a grudge against. . . . Let him go. . . ."

"He's dangerous, sir! I'd have him locked up, I would!"

"Too much red tape. I'd have to appear against him. I haven't time. No . . . boot him out and start him on his way. . . ."

"Mistake you for someone! You know damned well I know you, and no mistake about it either, you . . . ! I'll get you yet . . . when you haven't a body-guard around you," yelled the man, following the promise with a string of curses.

"None of that, fellow," said MacDougal sharply. "Out you go now!"

Broox stood while MacDougal dragged the man to the gate and threw him out. When the watchman came back Broox said, with a half smile:

"Well, my fine bunch of men haven't started out so well, have they, Mac?"

MacDougal gazed bleakly off to see that the man kept going. Then:

"Lucky he didn't harm you, sir. He didn't, did he?"

"Only my pride, Mac!" returned the director as he started down the drive.

"Shall I tell the casting office you're one man shy, sir," called the gateman.

Broox shook his head.

"Doesn't matter either way. One man more or less isn't serious."

He straightened his clothing, put on his hat, that had been brushed solicitously by an aspiring extra, and moved on down the drive, where he joined Rosenthal and Cohen, who were standing in front of the wardrobe building, watching the work.

"Out early, Rosey, aren't you?" he said.

"Vat vas all that commotion up at the gate?" returned the president of Superior Films.

"Nothing to speak of. Some poor fellow went berserk and tried to murder me. MacDougal threw him out."

"Vy did he vant to murder you?" asked Rosenthal, his round eyes staring.

"Don't know. I think the chap thought I was somebody else. He acted like he had a score to clean."

"H'm," said Rosenthal, rocking back and forth on his heels, frowning. Then: "Vell, I must say, Broox, you take it very calmly! I hope some of those other fellows don't get an idea they vant to murder me! I think, maybe, it vould be more healthy for me in my office!"

Broox laughed.

"Better take Izzie in with you, too. Then I won't have to explain interminably just why it is costing the studio so much money to send me on this location!"

He winked slyly at the president.

"That's it! That's it!" cried Cohen reproachfully. "Jump on me just because I am tending to my part off the business! I tell you, Broox, vidout I make you explain efferything, ve don't haff no money left to pay your salary ven this var picture iss done . . . now vat do you think off that for explaining?"

"I'm not worrying!" said Broox. "Say, Rosey, you haven't changed your mind about Yvonne Beaumont, have you? I'd rather have her in this picture than any girl I know. She's French, and . . ."

"That iss all settled two veeks ago, I told you, Mr. Broox. Miss Beaumont vill be sailing for Europe next Monday in her first starring picture," said the president shortly.

Broox shrugged good-naturedly.

"You're the boss! Well, wish me luck . . . I'll probably not be seeing you again. We hit out tonight, and I'll be on the jump all day."

Rosenthal turned immediately to the director, his brown eyes grown solemn.

"I haff all the faith in the vorld in you, Broox, otherwise I vould not be spending five hundred thousand dollars on 'Souls at Var.' Most certainly I vish you luck! It vill be hard enough anyvays . . . so . . . I vish you the best of luck . . . and," he added naïvely, "us, too!"

He clapped the director affectionately on the back with his fat jeweled hand, gave him a firm, steady pressure with the last pat, and turned away. Someway it always went to the heart of Abraham Rosenthal to see his people leave the studio. When they were there, under his eyes, he felt better. He knew that keeping a mob of people, especially ex-service men, in hand . . . getting out of them what was wanted . . . coordinating the big mob scenes and the little, intimate close-ups of the principal characters was no easy task. He knew that Broox would come back haggard-faced and nervous . . . albeit victorious!

"Maybe it vouldn't be ten days you vill take?" said Cohen hopefully, after Rosenthal had left. "Ten t'ousand dollars a day that location vill cost us . . . t'ink off it! Ten t'ousand dollars!"

But Broox, watching Randall, his assistant, coming up the drive with brisk steps, did not answer. Instead he went out to meet him.

"How's she going, son?"

"Like a clock, boss, like a clock!" beamed Randall. "We'll be rolling to-night, sure enough!"

However, it was close to midnight when Scot MacDougal locked the gates on the buses loaded with men, now fully equipped with army regulation fighting outfits.

It will be many a day before the sight of a thousand men in U. S. khaki, oversea helmets on their heads, will cease to give Americans a sharp pain of remembrance . . . a quick, cold twitch in the vitals. Even Scot MacDougal, formerly of the Royal North-West Mounted Police, locking the gate after them, felt it. And added to it was Lannigan's doleful turning of what had happened to Broox that morning into a premonition sinister and foreboding.

"Ha, and phwat did I tell ye, Scot MacDougal, when I saw that bunch marchin' in? Perhaps now yell be mindin' phwat I say! And 'tis not the last of it!"

"Shut your trap!" snapped MacDougal, as he did so often now, but Lannigan, clumping away into the dark on his midnight round, continued to mutter and cross himself.

It was somewhere on the Cahuenga Pass, near Universal City, that a man stepped into the road in front of one of the buses. The driver, nearly running over him, jammed on the brakes and cursed volubly.

"Dowling, the assistant casting director at the studio, called me at the last minute to take the place of another man. My name's Donovan," the man in the road called, standing in the glare of the headlights. The driver looked a him a moment, and then yelled back:

"Maybe he did and maybe he didn't! You'll have to talk to the assistant director before I'll take you on!"

"Where is he?"

"In the car following the buses. Watch your step, because Red will just naturally run over you. He's that kind."

"Blow your horn, then, and give some sort of signal. . . ."

Immediately the other bus drivers, brought to a halt, and hearing the head bus tooting impatiently, set up a commotion. Red, Randall's chauffeur, turned off his gas and leaned out.

"What the . . ." he questioned the air in general, and in particular a traffic cop who had just zoomed up on his motorcycle, attracted by the noise.

A man came running past the last bus and stopped beside Red's car, panting.

"S'cuse me, sir, but the assistant casting director at the studio said you were one man short, and for me to outfit at the Western Costume Company and to catch you on the way out."

"All right. See me in the morning. I'll give you a slip then. Climb in that bus ahead," said Randall, and to Red, when they were going again:

"Hank's getting darned particular about details all at once! Can you feature the poor sap . . . holding up the whole parade for one man! That guy pulls the darnedest stunts!"

"Yeah . . . and holding up production's the best thing he does. Say, let's light out ahead of this funeral procession and make time!"

"Can't do it, Red. If anything happens, I got to tail 'em to fix it up!"

"Gosh, the assistant director's always the fall guy, ain't he?"

"You said it," replied Randall tersely, adding, under his breath: "How I hate locations!"

II

Volumes of noise bursting from one side of the mountain canyon and thundering against the opposite, hurtling off, and rocking in deafening reverberations between!

Volumes of blinding, choking, obscuring smoke, belching profanely into the sweet mountain air, accumulating in mammoth, sausage-shaped billows; rolling stiflingly down the fern-clad walls!

Earth and rocks cast up in tons. Trees uprooted. Animals running madly, with fear-distended eyes. The rattling fire of small arms. The shouting of hoarse commands.

Massed ranks of dun-colored bodies, charging forward, falling flat. Other rows stumbling over them. Destruction! Devastation! Blood . . . and murder!

A thousand men making make-believe war in frighteningly realistic fashion! And a scant handful of men that motivated it all, standing in a little group apart, yelling triumphant, excited comments to one another; gloating over every, ghastly detail of recorded tragedy . . . shell-shocked earth and prostrated men!

Until at last there was but one live space in all the cruelly laid waste land. One still softly rounded hilltop, wearing its fresh dress of tender spring green. It stood there, proud and radiant in color, slowly becoming pallid under the billows of smoke, yet smiling vernally, not knowing itself doomed.

Just under its crest lay row upon row of brown bodies, flat on their bellies, waiting the signal to inch forward over its soon to be lacerated surface; to inch forward with peering, death-dealing eyes; with silent, menacing movements.

Toward this green crest a battery of camera lenses was focused. And standing apart, waiting a signal from the little group beside the cameras—that little group which held destruction in the palms of their hands—were two men, coughing the smoke from their lungs, eyes blinking and watering from the blinding sting of the nitro fumes.

One of them, a small man with a small voice, with always a bit of apology in it, as though making excuse for his very existence, looked unhappily across the ravaged earth.

"Seems too bad to do that," he said. "It took thousands of years for those trees to grow. And look at those poor field mice . . . the rest of the animals! I saw one dying, Hoxton. His eyes held as much agony as the best trouper in a death-bed scene! It's the end of creation, the destruction of Atlantis, for these poor forest things!"

"Yeah," agreed Hoxton indifferently.

He was a gigantic man, and his big-jowled, massive face, now grimed and dirty, held no look of pity. Instead it seemed to glow with an intense, pleasurable excitement at the destruction about them.

"Say," he demanded, moving his little piglike eyes scornfully over the slender form of his companion, "how did they ever pick you for this job, anyway? You look as much at home in khaki as a white rabbit! Here we are in the middle of a bloody war, and you go raving about dying rodents and Atlantis! Make pictures, Morrill—make pictures!"

From the base of the hill came a warning rumble and ton after ton of earth and rocks shot high into the air. A sequoia at whose base had been planted a charge of TNT wavered, then up-ended in a flash of fire, and at last settled back to earth, its huge roots, blasted and raw, torn clear of the earth that had for centuries been their bed.

"Seems too bad to do that," repeated Morrill, his rather prominent, pale blue eyes watching the woods giant settle down in its last agony.

"There'd be some hope for you, fella," grunted Hoxton, unmoved, "if you weren't so damned sentimental. You can't help your size, but, by the gods, you could cultivate something besides a maudlin old maid's viewpoint."

The top of the hill blew off like a green cap in the wind and settled in a thundering rain of spring-damp clods about them. Hoxton leaped forward with a curse. Morrill took a hasty, startled glance, then seemed frozen where he stood. With an air of extreme distaste, he removed some gravel from his ear, and was wiping that member thoroughly with a clean white handkerchief, when a third man charged up the slope, roaring as he came:

"What d'you think this is, Morrill? A tea party? Who asked you to fly that flag of truce? Where the hell would you get a white handkerchief on a battlefield? D'you suppose you'd take time to doll up if the Jerries were after you? My God, *will* you forget you're a society dame for long enough to register as a soldier?"

"As I protested to Mr. Rosenthal, Randall," said Morrill, showing a bit of fire, "I'm entirely miscast in this picture! I never had any aspirations to be a fighting man . . . except once in my life . . . and then they wouldn't have me!"

"That's once the army showed sense!" snapped the harassed assistant director, and leaped off the hill just in time to escape a small explosion.

Morrill sat down suddenly, with his mouth full of debris. Hoxton, safely out of range, watched the fastidious little man removing it, shuddering with distaste at each gritty ejection, and roared delightedly:

"I guess that will hold you for a spell, Morrill! I told you not to be so damned fussy. You know what Sammy said to Abie: 'Pictures, pictures, Abie, not gloffs!' This is war, brother, war . . . not music recitals!"

"You may go on insulting me indefinitely, Hoxton," said Morrill, with a plaintive positiveness, "but you cannot contaminate me!"

Randall charged up the slope again.

"Say, *will* you two guys get out of the picture? Can't you hear the boss? He's yelling his guts out!"

"You mean we are finished for the day?" called Morrill hopefully.

Hoxton heaved to his feet, grunting,

"Suits me, Randall. How about that gully? Would a fellow be safe taking a nap, or are you guys going to blow her to hell?"

"Naw. G'wan and sleep."

Hoxton ambled out of camera range and was soon snoring blissfully, the battle-line roaring on both sides of him. Morrill, however, did not sleep. Hunched up on a rock, he watched the spectacle. Patriotism, in the time of the big war, had lifted him out of his innate physical cowardice. It was the only time in his life he had experienced bravery . . . could talk man to man with the big fellows. With an almost unbalanced passion he had wanted to get into the army, but he could not make it.

Several persons had heard him say, with that plaintive, belligerent peevishness:

"I feel really vindictive against that man who turned me down! Really vindictive! It was the dream of my life to lead my countrymen into battle!"

An unrealized dream, but none the less ingrowing in the regret it carried. When Morrill referred to it, people looked at him a bit startled because of the bitter passion under his small voiced protest.

More earth blew up, and blew up again. The thousand men were begrimed with it, worn and irritable.

Ellison Broox, making "Souls at War," was no lily-fingered, light-tempo man. He knew what a war picture called for and he knew how to get it. Most of the time he was out in the field with the men, calling encouragement, painting with fired words an even more vivid picture than the riddling of cannonading etched upon the land itself.

He reached out and down into the memory of every one of those thousand men, holding them by the compelling force of his brain, throwing them back again, willfully, into those terrible, soul-tortured days at the front, following up each exhortation with the roar of the guns and the explosion of mines.

Until at last he got what he wanted! Haggard, burning eyes, and drawn, twitching faces, fainting bodies carried forward by that strange, unnamable strength that enters into men in battle long after their natural physical and mental powers have weakened and given up.

"God! Look at 'em!" Broox exulted to his cameraman. "Look at 'em! That's what I wanted to get into it . . . the real thing! Show these chair-warmers and one-minute men. . . ."

He stopped himself suddenly.

"But that's old stuff now, eh, Serge? People have almost forgotten. But the people must never forget the horror of war, Serge. That's the only hope! Keep showing the mothers how their sons suffered . . . show 'em and show 'em again! If we can keep the frightful, utter, criminal waste and uselessness of war before the world, perhaps . . . perhaps . . ." he stopped, and Serge was

amazed to hear the customarily stern and unemotional Broox
catch his breath in a gusty sigh.

"We never had pictures to do it with before, Serge. Maybe it
will be different this time. There's some hope they won't forget.
Well, boy, better call it a day pretty soon. We've got some great
stuff . . . great stuff!"

Shortly after, the elements, as if outraged by this wanton, stupid destruction, made audible protest. A roar of thunder like the
Furies let loose, vibrated from heaven to earth. Against it, like
lesser chords in a gigantic military march, burst the reverberations of exploded mines. Wicked, menacing streaks of lightning,
jagged across the sky, drove down to the ground with intent to
split it in twain.

"She's going to rain!" said Skeets Williams, and began gathering up the "props."

Serge, the strange Russian cameraman, with his big head and
pale face, stood leaning against his camera, gazing at the spectacle.

"There's that place up there," he suggested carelessly. "We
can move a big bunch inside and go on shooting . . ."

Broox wheeled around and followed the man's bright gaze.

"Looks not unlike a French village. What is it? Who owns it?"

"The spirits. It was a legacy to them," said Serge.

"Bosh! Talk sense, man! None of your foreign nuances for
me! If we shoot it, we'll have to get permission. It's a good out,
though!"

"We've been holding it in all afternoon. It looks like a million
dollars in the camera."

Serge threw down his cigarette and went to peer again through
his lens at the odd, many turreted group of buildings on the hill.
He peered at various angles, jumping backward and forward as
he shifted his camera, in leaps that were astonishingly high and
agile. Once, Broox, drawn by this activity to turn his gaze from
its moody contemplation of the horizon, smiled, and said:

"Ever think of going back into the Russian ballet, Serge?"

"Never! I find making pictures much more adventuresome, but it is not good to let the muscles get soft. Also I find it very convenient at times to be able to do . . . this. . . ." and he went into the air like a rubber ball and landed neatly back of his camera, as he flashed his sudden, brilliant smile. But Broox had again turned to look at the sky. A frown gathered his forehead in knots. His hand went up and pulled reflectively at his chin. Serge said, in his soft, unhurried, precise diction:

"Certainly. You can do it. If you do it now!"

"You're a queer fellow. You always get my thoughts. You mean that Hoxton stunt?"

"Exactly. That finishes the sequence. I mean, it could. If it rains hard enough to ruin the field, you can do a little rewriting and throw the rest of the action inside the place up there. A retreat . . . men trapped in that château . . . the assault . . . the hand-to-hand struggle . . . the place blown clear to hell!"

"You're too damned occult, Serge. You'll be telling me my own past next. But you hit the nail on the head. I can do it. How about the light for Hoxton. Can we make it?"

"If we shoot her right now!"

"Let's go! You know the action. Hoxton charging straight into the camera . . . shell exploding right behind him, which gives us the background of thrown up earth and rocks," said Broox. Then, raising his voice:

"Skeets! Hey! . . . Skeets! All set with that battery? Where the hell is that hidden mine, anyway?"

"Right over here, sitting pretty, boss. All I need is the word!"

"All right, boy." He turned to Serge.

"Set your camera just far enough so you won't be blown up. Randall, get Hoxton and bring him back over that rise there! Remember your side-lines. Keep him in. Make it snappy now. Our light's going!"

Then when the assistant director and the actor appeared over the hill, Broox raised his megaphone and roared, while Randall scooted out of camera range:

"Hoxton! You're charging a machine gun . . . come a-running . . . straight into the camera . . . big close-up now . . . do your stuff. Don't stop for anything! Smack into the camera! Let's go!"

Dropping his megaphone, he put a whistle to his lips and blew a shrill blast.

Skeets bent instantly to the switch at his feet. Hoxton, body crouched, head and shoulders forward, face twisted into a ferocious, murderous mask, broke into a rush that would have carried him past the camera. Simultaneously the meeting line of earth and sky behind him was obliterated by a mass of clods and stones, the fringe of which threw the actor prone and covered him with small lacerations. The effect in the camera was that of Hoxton having literally been blown off the hill. Serge cranked triumphantly, chuckling the while, but Broox's face was intense. He was waiting the last act of the little drama, for he knew it would come!

Slowly the huge man began to get up, rubbing his limbs and examining his anatomy tenderly. He had been so utterly astounded by the unexpected explosion behind him, and his subsequent slamming down on the ground, that he appeared to have completely forgotten the camera. The picture he presented in his amazement was unconsciously and actually ludicrous. Serge began to grind again, calling out impishly:

"Keystone Komedies, please witness. This man is good for a starring contract any time! Sennett please write!"

With a roar of rage Hoxton reared to his feet and came at Serge, his manner not far different from the one in which he had rushed the imaginary machine gun nest. Serge, undaunted, continued:

"And we now have the famous charge of Bill Farnum in that never to be equaled hand to hand combat in 'The Spoilers.'"

"Damn you, you dirty Russian monkey!" yelled Hoxton furiously, his great fists balling menacingly. Broox stepped quickly between the two.

"Keep your shirt on, Hoxton! You're not hurt!" he said sternly.

For a moment the actor's eyes, now bloodshot from sand and rage, wavered between the director and cameraman, as if he were undecided which to attack. Catching sight of Morrill looking on, he roared belligerently:

"What the hell are *you* grinning about?"

The small man immediately straightened his countenance, but Serge said, coolly:

"The shoe, it is on the other foot, my dear chap! You've been razzing Morrill all day. Now it's his turn. How do you like it? Not so well, eh?"

"None of your damned business. You keep out of this anyway. My fight's with Broox!" Hoxton swung his smoldering eyes upon the director and the muscles in his neck swelled and grew purple.

"You're a hell of a fine director, you are! Can't get your stuff unless you pull a dirty trick like that! If you think you can get away with that sort of thing with me, you're just crazy, that's all! I don't have to risk my neck for anybody's damned picture! I can walk out of here right now and get more money than Superior Films is paying me!"

He stopped, panting, his big body tensed for an attack. Broox looked at him coldly:

"That's a bit strong, Hoxton." His tone was held down, but the spectators, of whom there were now quite a number, felt the promise of explosion in the gritty undertone of his voice.

"In the first place, Hoxton," he continued, standing his ground, "I'm not fool enough to take a chance of really hurting you . . . risking your neck, as you say. It wouldn't be worth my while—for a picture. You'd be surprised to know I tried out that stunt with a double first, to be sure it could be done with safety to you! In the second place, the only thing that's the matter with you is extreme laceration to your pride! Those bruises and scratches will heal up in a couple of days. If you can walk into any physician's office and make out a case against me, you're welcome to do so . . . incidentally, you'll be the first one to get a kick out of the fact that you've just had the best close-ups you ever saw on the screen . . . bar none! It's got a punch worth a million dollars. If you were the kind of a good sport you expect everybody else to be, you'd take it for what it was worth . . . and forget it!"

The director had jumped verbally on every attempt of Hoxton's to interrupt. His words had snapped out with all the authority with which a motion-picture director is vested. Enraged as Hoxton was, he was held silent from well-trained habit, until his director ceased. Then he burst forth:

"That's all bushwah, and you know it, Broox! You know damned well you might have shot me to hell! As for calling me a bum sport, you can't get away with that! Nobody can! And you needn't stand there looking so damned superior just because you're directing this show." His eyes, rolling redly, showed his control was slipping. Broox saw it too late, for with a bellow Hoxton was on him.

There was a streak of something from back of the camera and the actor's legs were imprisoned as in a vice. He was thrown to the ground and pinned there. Broox stepped aside and looked down at him and the man who held him.

"Thanks, Serge," he said. "You can let him up."

Serge twisted around to face the actor, still gripping his trunk with those queer, knotty legs of his.

"What do you say, my friend—do you feel peaceable, or will you go berserk again?"

"Let go of me, or I'll kick your guts out!" roared Hoxton.

Serge promptly sat down on the actor's legs, and then, squeezing in upon his ribs with his knees, and with his long arms twisted back of him, gripping Hoxton's toes and twisting them, he watched his victim with his thin-lipped smile. Not long, and Hoxton grunted for release. Then only did the cameraman get up. Broox went over and pulled the actor to his feet.

"Come on, old man. It was a surprise. I grant you that. But what's on the film is worth it. It'll put you in the lights. I'll admit it was a mean trick, looking at it one way, but I didn't mean it the way you're taking it. You'll be hollering for joy when you see it yourself. . . . Man, I tell you that close-up is worth *a million dollars!*"

It was this last enthusiastic outburst that put the quietus on Hoxton. Here was something he could understand and cotton to—praise of himself.

"Was I good—honest?" he asked, with that sudden change of mood, cultivated through a thousand occasions when, at the call of "camera," the actor snaps into comedy or tragedy, or drops it as quickly.

"*Good!* Say, it's a knock-out! Marvelous!" exclaimed Randall, quick to get his director's hint. All the way back to camp he told Hoxton just how marvelous it was.

Seated at mess that night they heard the deluge of rain descend on the tent roof. For a moment no one spoke . . . listening. In every mind was the realization that picture-making for the morrow was washed out. Randall's brain became instantly a turmoil of the innumerable details attending a change of shooting schedule. Broox mentally climbed the hill and stood looking speculatively at the old pile there, picking out possible interiors.

Hoxton, who had slumped into a sullen silence after the pleasure of his "million-dollar close-up" had worn off, glared at his plate and gulped his food as though he had a personal grudge against it. Morrill spoke first, in his hesitant voice, and everyone laughed when he finished.

"I'm not a bit sorry," he said, with that little sidewise, slightly petulant uptilting of his head. "No, sir. I'm not a bit sorry. I'm not crazy about chasing over that damned explosive! That last mine nearly blew the back seat off me!"

Hoxton exploded a "Ha! Ha!" through a tremendous mouthful of meat and potatoes, and then, remembering how near he had come to losing his own back seat, relapsed into black-browed silence again.

"Say, boss, this rain means we lose a day anyway, no matter how you look at it!" exclaimed Randall. "Whew! And when Izzie gets wind of it! Salaries for one thousand extras, not to mention ourselves . . . expenses ten thousand dollars a day, and . . . *she rains!* Holy cats!"

Broox passed him a cigarette.

"Keep your shirt on, son. We're going to shoot interiors to-morrow. The rain won't stop production." The director drained his cup of coffee unperturbed. Randall stared at him stupidly, and then exclaimed:

"*Interiors!* Say, did I hear you right? Quit kidding me, chief! Where we going to get interiors big enough to house a thousand men? You aren't going to try to shoot inside the tents, are you?"

"No, no, Larry, nothing like that," Broox laughed. He pushed back his chair and looked at the rest.

"Did you notice that big place over on the hill?" he asked.

"Sure. Looked like a village. You haven't got it in your head to shoot *that*, have you, Chief?" Randall's voice was tragic. Silently he was thinking, "How am I going to fix that up, now? Who owns the dump, and where do I find 'em, and probably they'll want to hold us up for shooting the place, and then I've got just one more expense account to fight out with Izzie. . . ."

His train of thought was side-tracked by the director's asking for a Coleman lantern.

"You're not going up there to-night, Broox," protested Morrill, peering upward at the canvas roof which was sagging down in water-filled hollows.

"I'm not made of sugar, Morrill, and it isn't the first time I've had a good wetting. Of course I'm going . . . and . . . you're going with me!"

Blank consternation froze on the little actor's features.

Randall snickered, and Hoxton's wide mouth started to spread, but was stopped by Broox saying:

"Hoxton, you too! Step on it, Larry, and get Skeets to dig out three flash-lights and that lantern. I expect he's got one."

"But, Chief, it's late now, and she's still pouring," said Randall in a last useless protest.

"And we'll want army slickers," continued Broox, unheeding.

Randall knew when to talk and when to act. He turned immediately to what he was bidden.

Morrill by now had recovered his voice.

"But, Brooxie, old man, we can't go snooping around up there! They might . . . they might . . . er . . . take us for marauders and shoot us, you know!"

"The place is deserted. Skeets told me a lot about it this afternoon. The boy grew up around here somewhere. Furthermore, it's not a village but one huge building. . . . Ideal! Ideal! We'll shoot her, then duplicate her in miniature, and blow her to hell!"

"How you going to light her?" asked Hoxton.

"Run the power plant up. Thank God, for once we came prepared for any eventuality. It's going to be great stuff!"

"Well . . . anyway, no more wading through the muck. I suppose you're through with the outdoor stuff?"

"Yes. Got some great stuff. More than enough to carry. We'll simply transfer the action of our principals to the interior and entrances of that old place. Marvelous! Looks just like an old château . . . with a few story changes to fit it, it'll punch the picture up splendidly."

"I understand you are going up to-night, to work out the changes, Broox," said Hoxton.

"That's it. May be at it all night, but what's the odds? That bit where you and the girl have your scene together, you know . . . I'll just put that in the house, and . . ."

Morrill broke in plaintively:

"But, Broox, I cannot understand, really, why you should want *me* up there to-night! Old chap, I'm pretty well done in, you know, plowing over that rough ground!"

"Us matinée idols must get our beauty sleep, you know," smirked Hoxton, with an exaggerated wink at Broox.

For just an instant something like bitter resentment flashed and was gone in the little actor's pale eyes. Then he said, apologetically:

"I'm no good unless I sleep, Broox. Hoxton is quite right."

"A little thing like a night out doesn't faze me. I'll go with you, Broox." With which declaration Hoxton swaggered to his feet.

"It's like this, boys," Broox explained. "I'm no set builder. It takes a fellow like Giddy to do that. Sets have to be built in proportions. That is, to match up with the actors in the camera. I've never seen that house. I'm taking a chance, anyway, even though it looks like a good bet. Now here I've got a couple of extremes . . . no offense, Morrill, but you're undersize. Hoxton, here, is the opposite. You're both principals. I want to get you boys up there and stand you up against the places I pick out for sets, and put you through your stuff. I want to see how she's going to stack up in the camera. . . ."

"I should think that Serge would know better," said Morrill.

"He would. But Serge will have to work all day to-morrow. I am going to let him and Larry handle a lot of mob stuff in the mud in the morning. And mob stuff around that house up there. That'll give us a chance to sleep in, and pick up our stuff after lunch. I know it's tough on you boys, but we're in a hole because of the rain, and we've got it to do."

Skeets and Larry came in, both loaded.

"Don't you want me along, Chief?" asked Randall solicitously, as he helped Broox into his slicker.

"I should say not, son! You've got to stay here and run this camp. Remember, we've got a bunch of unknown fellows here . . . shell-shocked, some of them, at that. A lot of hell could happen around here if anyone went off his head. Did you put those two fellows on guard? Fine. Did you get it over to everyone that this camp is run the same as the army? Lights out at ten, and nobody leaving grounds? O.K. Look for me when you see me. I may work all night."

"I'll send a man up with hot coffee and sandwiches later, shall I?"

"Better let the cook get his sleep. Cooks are queer cattle . . . got more temperament than movie stars, and I don't blame 'em."

The director picked up his lantern and started out. Morrill indulged an anticipatory shivering as he got into his slicker. Skeets, who had been standing by silently, now went up to the director.

"Say, Mr. Broox, please don't go up there tonight!" he pleaded. The director looked down into the lad's concerned, freckled face.

"Why, Skeets, there's nothing to worry about. It's just an old, empty house, son."

Skeets shook his head,

"It's more than that, sir. Honest! Men have disappeared that went up there! Honest! It's . . . it's *haunted!*"

Broox laughed and patted the boy's shoulder.

"You were brought up on old wives' tales about that place, Skeets, and you can't get over the fear of it. We'll be all right. You turn in and get your rest, because I'm going to work you for all there's in you to-morrow."

When the three had left, the assistant director and prop boy stood silent a moment. Then Skeets shivered.

"Oh, B-oy! Say, you couldn't dr-a-a-ag me up there on a night like this!"

"Why?"

But Skeets shook his head stubbornly.

"Say, big boy, if I told you *all* I know about that place you'd be chasing whiffiedings and whangdoodles all night long. That place is *dangerous!* I'll bet something happens to them," he added dolefully.

"Get out of here, you wet blanket," yelled Randall.

"Suits me," said Skeets promptly, adding impudently, "Speaking of wet blankets. Here's where I have my innings. No wet ones for the prop man—no siree! Not when I got a stack of extras in my tent! What d'ya think of that, big boy?"

"I think you're going to part with 'em, right now! You put a couple of dry ones in Mr. Broox's tent, and one on Hoxton's and one on Morrill's bed, and . . . the rest on mine! Step on it!"

For an hour after the director and his actors passed through the camp and by the guard there was laughter and singing from the tents. Through their damp sides showed black silhouettes as the men moved about. This was a lark to them, who had enjoyed no such warm and well-fed aftermath of the long bitter days Over There.

Then one by one the lights went out. Only the guards kept their vigil, and even they grew lax-eyed.

"Say, this is the bunk!" said one to the other, as they met and took shelter for a moment from the downpouring rain.

"Ain't it, though. You'd think a bunch of Jerries was creepin' up on us! I've a good mind to go to bed. Nobody's going to leave camp. The lights are all out, and you can't hear a sound. They're all asleep."

"Uh-huh, pretty near there myself. Got a light?"

They chatted for more than overtime, reviewing the events of the day.

"Say, this director knows his stuff! Acts like he was over across himself."

"Him? Hell, no!" the second man burst out laughing. "Say, when you've been around these picture nuts as long as I have, you'll know they know about everything! It's their business! That guy could direct a birth scene and act just like a mother!"

They parted chuckling. The rain poured down. Now and again a muffled roar of thunder came from behind the mountains. Black night, slashed through with lightning, claimed everything for her own.

Skeets Williams, snug under two extra blankets he had not given to Randall, shivered and muttered:

"I'm getting as crazy as Lannigan, maybe, but I got a *queer feeling* something's goin' to happen!"

III

A bugle blowing reveille awakened Larry Randall from a sound sleep. He glanced at his watch. Six fifteen. He tumbled out of his cot, dressed hastily, and made his way down the long canvas-lined street toward the mess tent.

All about him the camp was astir with the miscellaneous activities of a thousand men making their simple preparations for the day. From all sides came laughter, ribald jests, the rough horseplay of men to whom soldiering had once been serious business, but who were now reenacting old scenes in a spirit of revelry.

"Thank God, the rain's over," said Randall.

Skeets Williams was the only other person at the director's table. On camp locations Skeets rated that privilege.

"Skeets, did you call Broox?" asked Randall, as the kitchen flunky slid a platter of ham and eggs in front of him.

"Yeah, sure! I sang out it was six fifteen as I came by. Clear day. Does that mean we shoot in this mud, or do we do a lot of stuff up in that old house?"

"Can't say until Broox gets here. Where's Hoxton and Morrill? Did you call them?"

"Yeah, same time I called his nibs. Morrill crabbed about being called when it was too muddy to work, but I told him to dig out anyway. What's the orders?" he added.

"Sit tight until the boss comes in and I'll ask him. I've a hunch we take a power plant up to that old house and shoot interiors. Here comes Morrill now."

There was a petulant frown on the little actor's face as he made his way toward them.

"Ungodly hour to get a fellow up," he said peevishly. "We can't work in this mud."

From long custom Randall let his eyes go rapidly over Morrill's equipment. He had long since learned that he could never trust an actor to have any costume complete or correct. And what was more to the point, Broox was a demon for spotting little details, and if Randall let anything slip by, the bawling out he would get was something to be avoided. So, instead of answering Morrill directly, he said:

"Where's your revolver? Why'n Hades you fellows can't remember to dress is more'n I can understand! And when you make up don't forget that wound on your temple . . . you've got close-ups today, so make her look convincing! If I didn't wet-nurse you fellows, you'd come on the set with nothing on that matched up. Don't you remember you had a gun on yesterday?"

"Most certainly I remember I carried a gun. I was waiting for you to halt your irate tirade before I explained. Mr. Broox gave Hoxton my gun last night. That's why I haven't got it!"

Randall eyed Morrill thoughtfully a moment. Then he said:

"What for? Hoxton's supposed to have his own gun!"

"Well, it's sort of a long story, and not exactly to my credit," said Morrill, flushing a little. "You see, I thought I saw a what-you-call-'em . . . and I fired at it. I broke a perfectly good window. If it was a haunt, I'm sure the nasty thing got quite a shock."

"Say, you mean you really *saw something*, Mr. Morrill?"

Skeets leaned over the table eagerly, his eyes big. Not waiting for the actor to answer, he added breathlessly:

"Was it . . . was it . . . sort of like a woman's face?"

Morrill thought a moment.

"Well, really . . . I . . . yes . . . it might have been. You see the thing was so . . . gigantic . . . quite as big as an umbrella top I should say, that . . ."

"For crying out loud, are you trying to tell me that you saw a face as big as an umbrella top!" exclaimed Randall in disgust.

Morrill raised hopeless eyes to him.

"I'm perfectly well aware that no one . . . *no one* . . . is going to believe me, so there isn't any use talking about it. That blustering Hoxton merely guffawed most insultingly! Nevertheless, Randall, I am positive I saw a face as big as an umbrella top!"

"All right, Morrill, I believe you, if that makes you feel any better," said Randall, grinning. "But say, how does the old dump look for interiors?"

"The house is positively outlandish. The very sight of it, close up, gives a person the horrors. Have you ever read Poe's 'The Fall of the House of Usher'? 'I looked upon the scene before me—upon the mere house—upon the bleak walls, upon the vacant eye-like windows, upon a few rank sedges, and upon a few white trunks of decayed trees, with an utter depression of soul. I reined my horse to the precipitous brink of a black and lurid tarn that lay in unruffled luster by the dwelling, and gazed down, but with a shudder even more thrilling than before—upon the remodeled and inverted images of the gray sedge. . . .'"

Morrill stopped quoting and looked up, his eyes fear-filled. "Only," he said earnestly, "the image I saw was in one of those eye-like windows."

"Yeah," said Randall unmoved, "and you never had no horse, either, buddy. Go on about the house and forget the socketless windows."

"I won't work in it, or go into it again after dark," said Morrill positively, as if following out some train of thought of his own, "not if I never put on greasepaint again."

There was unusual decision in the little actor's quavering words, belied by the trembling of the coffee-cup he held hastily to his lips.

"Come down to earth, Morrill," snapped the assistant director. "You and this Poe guy both sure got it bad! What I want to know is the boss going to use the place, and did you get anything doped out?"

"I . . . really . . . couldn't say as to that. I merely gave you my feelings in the matter," returned the actor exasperatingly.

Randall sat looking at him a moment, and then shrugged and kept some unflattering comment to himself.

The cook came in and looked at the two empty seats.

"Say, is the boss coming to eat, and that fat guy . . . where's he? This ain't no buffet, meals-at-all-hours, lunch counter!"

"You'll get Mr. Broox a meal whenever he wants it, understand that, fellow?" snapped Randall promptly, and to Morrill:

"Now listen here, Morrill, no more side-tracking. What time did you get through up there last night?"

"I was in bed about . . . well . . . some time before morning, I think. I cannot say about Hoxton and Mr. Broox. They stayed up there!"

"You never came back here alone!" exclaimed Randall unthinkingly, but Morrill smiled his self-demeaning smile and admitted:

"No, indeed. Not little Percy! After I got excited and shot a hole in the window, Mr. Broox thought I'd be shooting one of them next, or myself, so he sent us both back to camp. He gave Hoxton my gun for safe-keeping. When we got here, Hoxton decided he wanted to go back and play the organ some more. So he went!"

"Play the organ! What are you talking about!"

"The organ. Hoxton was playing it, and he said he wanted to go back and do it some more. The fellow's not half bad at it either. I was quite pleasurably surprised!"

"Huh . . . well, so he went back. Then what?"

"My dear Randall, what is this, a questionnaire, or something?" Morrill protested mildly, after repeatedly trying to consume his coffee, and having to set it down each time before it touched his lips.

"No . . . go ahead and eat, Morrill. I just wanted to know if the boss spent the night in the dump, or came back. As for that, I guess the guard would know more than you about it. Skeets, chase out and ask those two fellows that were on duty last night. Say, never mind, go peek in the boss's tent. If he's asleep, and you wake him up, I'll fire you. If he's not, and speaks to you, ask him if you can bring him a tray, and what he wants me to do with this mob until he gets up."

Skeets came back looking serious.

"He ain't there!" he said solemnly.

"Well, for God's sake don't look like a funeral. That means he's up and around camp somewhere, and, we better snap into it, or something'll pop. Go rout out Hoxton and tell him to dress."

"Say, Randall, I forgot to mention it . . . dear me! How stupid, I might have been slumbering sweetly all this time. Now isn't that too bad!" Morrill registered a look of extreme regret and sadly stirred his third cup of coffee.

"Well . . . rave on! I'd like to know what's the matter with you this morning. Honest to God, Morrill, you act like you're full of dope! What did you forget to mention?"

"That Mr. Broox told us before he went up there he was going to let you handle the shooting of the mob scenes this morning, and that Hoxton and I could sleep in . . . he said he would also sleep in, and get on the job after lunch!"

"Is . . . that . . . so!" said Randall, half angered, half aghast at the prospect. "Well . . . I'll be damned! So *I'm* to handle the mob stuff, and will you please go on with your pretty little tale and tell me *how* . . . and *where* . . . I'm to handle it?"

"I really couldn't say; that's all I know," said Morrill.

"What a sweet dish . . . this turned out to be!" muttered Randall gloomily. "Listen, Skeets . . . Where is that kid now?"

"You sent him after Hoxton," reminded Morrill.

"Oh, hell!"

Serge came in and slid into his chair.

"'Lo every one! Ham and eggs!" he shouted to the cook. "And bring me a gallon of Java . . . black as sin and thick as murder. Well, my esteemed co-workers, what's the dope? Do we shoot the old manse on the hill?"

"God, I don't know, Serge. The schedule's all shot to pieces. Say, did you see the boss anywhere this morning?"

"I did not. However, I see the little old merry sunshine is on the job again. I expect that means we work. We better get this picture on the film quick, with all these extras, or Izzie will just naturally have nervous prostration. Heigho for the life of a picture man . . . eats rotten grub and sleeps when he can. . . ."

"Say, bozo," yelled the cook from the open doorway, "if you don't like this grub, you can starve . . . get me?"

"Or eat it and starve! It's all the same, cookee!" retorted the irrepressible Serge, who stood in fear of no man or woman, no matter what or how important their station. When the rest went softly on the cook's toes, for fear of being served a tough steak or a burned egg, Serge tramped all over them and got the best "eats" in camp. Now he cleaned his plate rapidly and thoroughly, and then said:

"I say . . . what'd you ask me about Broox for . . . isn't he in his tent . . . done a Houdini or something?"

"I just asked you, that's all," snapped Randall, who was getting peevish under the weight the load of his duties had begun to assume. "Well, it's about time you showed. What you been doing? Playing nursemaid to that lazy tub Hoxton?" This last addressed to Skeets, who had come back and was looking more serious than before.

"Say!" Randall yelled before the boy had time to answer, *"will* you quit looking that way! What's the matter with you? Look natural, will you? Where's Hoxton?"

"I . . . don't know . . . that's why I'm looking funny, I guess," chattered Skeets. "I've asked everybody around, and nobody's seen either the boss or Hoxton, and their beds weren't slept in, and I'll bet anything something's happened to them up at that house!"

"You poor ninny! They probably spent the night there. It stormed to beat the band until this morning."

"Mystery in a crumbling manse . . . famous picture men disappear," intoned Serge's impish voice. "Who made off with the stern director and heavy-jowled villain? When last seen the two were turning down a secret passage, and their remains . . ."

"I say, stop it!" called Morrill suddenly, in a high, squeaky tone, and began to shiver violently.

Randall and Serge eyed him in amazement, then Serge chuckled.

"Either you are very clever, Morrill, or you really are a coward," he said slowly.

"I'm not at all clever, Serge. I admit to being a craven. The very memory of that place gives me chills! I assure you, I mean it. Something terrible has happened there and left its impression! Of that I am sure. Voices seem to hiss at you from the walls . . ."

"Voices?"

"Well, I mean unheard voices, if you understand me."

Randall got to his feet.

"We've had enough of this monkey business. I'm going up there. You probably got the creeps because you're afraid of the dark! I hate to wake Broox, but, by the gods, it's eight o'clock now, and not a foot of film ground. Serge, you stick here and get your equipment ready to move up there if I give the word. Have Slim tune up that engine, and figure some way to pull that power plant through the muck up that hill in case the boss wants to light her. Skeets, kick out and tell those grips to get everybody fully equipped for action. Give the men all a round of blanks for their revolvers, but no one leaves camp until I get back. After you see to that, Skeets, follow us up to the place. And cook . . . no back talk now . . . you stand ready to get a good hot meal for the boss if he wants it. C'mon, everybody. Let's go!"

He rose and gave Morrill a look that brought the little man to his feet after him. On the way through camp he picked up a man to send down for the boss's tray if he wanted breakfast brought up.

"Holy cats! What a place!" exclaimed Randall. He stood in the weed-grown drive and gazed upward, trying to encompass the strange structure quickly and entirely. Turrets rose behind turrets. Windows swelled out like bloated stomachs, queerly shaped and rounded, adding to the disquieting effect of personality in the place. Towers with small watch-outs rose at intervals, some with outside, twisted stairs that began twenty feet from the ground, and apparently had no entrance negotiable to human feet. The entire north presentation of the huge monstrosity had been left unfinished . . . rooms without outer walls gaped like yawning, snag-toothed mouths; plaster lay in heaps of crumbled debris on their floors. Contrasting this they saw great doors, worked with most intricate and delicate skill . . . carved, ornamented with metal, and finished to the last fine detail.

"'I looked upon the scene before me . . . upon the mere house, and the simple landscape features of the domain, upon the bleak walls, upon the vacant eye-like windows . . . and . . . There was an iciness, a sinking, a sickening of the heart, an unredeemed dreariness of thought which no goading of the imagination could torture into aught of the sublime,'" quoted Morrill, and shivered violently. "I . . . I . . . it's a terrible, foreboding monstrosity," he said.

"It's a damned funny looking shack, and no mistake, Morrill. No wonder it's deserted."

"Yet not a speck of dust, Randall! The windows fairly shine, and the polished floor of the big ballroom! I ran my fingers over them to see!"

"You would!" said Randall. "You're sure the typical old maid, Morrill. But say, how do you account for it?"

"I tell you, Randall, that place is occupied! I did not see any-one, but I felt presences. Distinctly I felt presences!"

"Well, there's plenty of room, Lord knows. She must cover five or six acres! *Holy* cats! Six acres of one house. Well, come on. We can't stand here gawping. Which way did you fellows go in last night? And for God's sake quit shivering!"

"That . . . that big door. It opens directly into a huge ballroom."

"All right, we've wasted enough time looking at the dump, now let's get the boss."

Randall led the way, entered through the big door, and, with-out so much as a look about the gigantic Space, cupped his hands about his mouth and started calling.

"Hey! Broox! Broox! Broox!"

After a moment he stopped to say to Morrill: "Light out, like a good fellow, and help, will you?"

"But, my dear chap, where will I light out to? You can see for yourself there are thirteen entrances to this room!"

"Well, go where Broox went last!"

"You must remember, Randall, I wasn't here! Hoxton was un-doubtedly the last to see him!"

Randall stopped and dropped his hands and looked at the actor strangely.

"Say, why did you put it just that way? Has anything hap-pened to him?"

"Why . . . er . . . I meant that I wasn't here when he finished, Randall. He might be anywhere around this old pile. If he was in the south end, say, he couldn't hear us if we yelled our lungs out! Really, you should have brought about a dozen men up here to search."

"Hot time to tell me that! Well, there are only two of us and we're going to find him . . . get me? You start going!"

"Hey! Broox! Broox! Broox!"

Randall left the ballroom and followed a long hallway, stopping at each of its offshoots to call loudly. His voice echoed back to him spookily from the great empty rooms. Soon he became conscious of another sound. He stopped calling to listen. Silence! He had a consciousness of someone waiting, of held breath.

"Hey! Broox! Broox! Broox!"

And again that other wailing voice!

It joined in with his, giving him the feeling of being mimicked, and with that thought the always unexplainable uneasiness and lack of surety that mimicry creates.

"Dammit! Shut up, will you!" he yelled.

"Hey, Broox! Broox! Broox!"

"What a hell of a place to look for anyone. I could go yelping through this old dump for a week and never meet myself once!" he muttered, impatiently, his one thought being to locate his director, his eyes unseeing of the strange passages and angles and weird corners. There it was! That wail again! It was closer!

It followed right on his call, and he could distinctly get a word—

"Ca—l—a—mity! C—a—l—a—mity!"

Calamity!

For a moment Randall felt the skin on his head prickle; a cold shiver ran down his spinal nerves.

"Ca—l—am—ity!"

The voice rose and fell, and the echo of its first syllables caught up with and mingled dismally with the last, so it seemed he was being beset with innumerable voices, cautioning him against going farther . . . holding out warning menace of untold terrors.

For a moment Randall let it get him, looking wide-eyed about the vast hallways and rooms, that stretched emptily away and away—and then he shook himself angrily.

"Ca—l—l—a—mmy. . . . C—a—l— l—a—mity!"

"Gosh, it's getting worse. *Clammy* Calamity this time!"

Randall muttered. Then an upwelling of indignation seized him.

"Who the hell are you?" he bellowed, and head down, shoulders set in a catapulting angle, he charged ahead, down a hall, through a tier of rooms, around a corner . . .

A scream, the jolting impact of another body, a faint whiff of fragrance, and a hysterically laughing . . . no . . . a sobbing girl, tight in the arms with which he instinctively gripped her!

"Were you calling, or was I hearing things?" he demanded instantly.

"You were hearing me, I guess," she gasped. "I was calling our dog!" Then with a little cry of relief:

"Oh, I'm so glad you're a . . . normal . . . human being . . . a man!" She shivered a little against him.

"I am too . . . but why . . . especially?"

"I heard a voice roaring like a bull . . . and I was scared to death anyway. Then I told myself I was a silly, and kept on going . . ."

"Just what I did. Only I thought you were . . . well, I don't know . . . some weird spook, I guess. But say, what the deuce were you saying anyway?"

"I was only calling our dog," she started, and then stopped and laughed shakily.

"Oh, no wonder you thought I was a bad spirit! Our dog's name is Calamity. We call him 'Clammy' for short. We named him that because he's always getting into trouble, or lost, or something. As he is now. . . ."

"Are you living here . . . Miss . . . Miss . . ."

"My name's Love," she said, "Beatrice Love," and immediately blushed, because Randall was looking at her very seriously and approvingly, with his nice brown eyes. She began talking hurriedly to cover her confusion.

"Mercy, no, I don't live here. I don't see how anyone could live in this crazy house! We got caught in the storm. Then Clammy got lost some place in this insane building, and . . ."

"Poor little tike. I expect he's locked in, or fallen down something. Easy enough in this da— in this dump!"

All the time Randall was wondering if he were not still asleep down in his tent, with the worrisome thought on his brain of having to arrange to shoot this strange old house, and only dreaming of this beautiful girl, with her fresh and vibrant loveliness, so radiantly contrasting the deliberate, artificially aided charm of picture girls. Surely she was an alluring dream lady . . . and he himself wandering without beginning or end, through some sleep-induced fantasy! Then he realized she was sobbing, leaning against the wall.

"Oh, don't do that!" he protested, coming back to realities. "Maybe he's all right! Come on. We'll find him . . . !"

"It isn't really Clammy. It's Aloysius! He's lost too!" she confessed. "I've been trying to pretend it was only Clammy, because I'm afraid. I'm afraid to think what might happen to Loish!"

"Aloysius! That means a man," he thought. Of course there *would* be a man. Anything so lovely as this girl . . . whose beauty seemed to him like a flower flaming delicately in the old dusky place, would be mixed up with a man someway! How could she escape? Probably dozens of men! He had found her too late, that was all! Randall was startled to find himself experiencing the bitter jealousy of long-known love and ownership! It bewildered him, so that her words came to him as through a mist.

"Won't you help me find Loish? Maybe the two of us . . ."

"Of course! Let's go. In union there is strength!" he returned rather foolishly, but she smiled up at him gratefully.

"Thank you so much. But aren't you looking for someone too?"

"I'll say I am! My director!"

"Well, there's no use going back that way, because I've been all over those rooms. They're empty."

"And I've been through that end. How about striking off to the west, here?"

"All right. Oh, I hope Loish hasn't gotten into trouble! He's so . . . well, he acts on impulse and thinks afterward. In a place like this he'd be likely to do anything . . . and he had a gun."

"Say, would you mind telling me who this Aloysius person is?"

His tone was ludicrously stiff, as a young man's tone is likely to be when he is attempting to be very formal and camouflage his real feelings. Beatrice Love laughed.

"He's only my brother," she said demurely.

Then they both laughed. But underneath their ensuing burst of gaiety there was a sense of pervading gloom. Each was conscious of the other's realization of it and determined to attempt to throw it off. Randall said presently, speaking for both of them as they stood and peered silently down a boxed-in hole, whose dim bottom was, after all, reassuringly empty:

"Shucks, we've both let this old dump get us! I'll bet your brother and my director have met up and are having a powwow some place, all the time we're working ourselves into brain-storms!"

"Perhaps," she agreed doubtfully. "But you know, there *are* dangerous places in this house! I got locked in the oddest little room, myself, and it was a long time before I found which one of the thirteen panels in it was a door!

"*Holy* cats! Don't jump, now, I'm going to call again."

"Hey! Broox! Broox! Broox!"

"I'm going to call Clammy," Beatrice announced when the echoes had stopped.

"C—a—l—a—m—ity!"

Only silence answered them. For a time they refused to heed it. Then the continued stillness began to depress them. It gave back such a hopeless finality to their eager searching—clamped down on them so irrevocably!

"Gee, I hope this is the last door we go through," said Randall. "We must have opened a hundred!"

He pushed on a strangely carved panel and stepped through the opening. Immediately the door, which had upon its face the grinning malicious outlines of a malignant-featured visage, pressed back against his hand.

"It's going to close!" exclaimed Beatrice. "I found one like that. Go on through, quick!"

She gave him a brisk shove. The door closed after him with a metallic click.

"Say, that was silly. Why didn't we both come through?" he called, lips against the closed panel. Then, more loudly, "Are you all right?"

"We couldn't," she called back reassuringly. "It wasn't wide enough, goose! Of course I'm all right. I'm coming right after you."

He heard her exclamation of distress.

"Why . . . it won't open again!"

Randall tried in vain to pry the door open from his side.

"Listen," he called. "It's some sort of trick affair. I'm going to see if I can get out. You stay right there where you are. Don't move! Hear me?"

"Yes . . . maybe it will open again in a minute . . ."

Randall turned to look about for some exit, took a step forward, backed against the door, with his hand thrown up across his eyes. But he could not shut out the shocking object he had seen.

For there, pitilessly revealed by a brilliant pencil of light from a window far up on the wall, lay the crumpled body of Ellison Broox!

IV

The dead man's brow, chilled with a ghastly pallor, the only light object in that dank, dark place, threw back the cruel shaft of sunlight like a reflector.

Randall did not know that he was chattering, over and over, mindlessly, "My God! My God! My God!" or that his body was trembling against the door as with a palsy, until he heard the girl's voice, high and hysterical, and her fists pounding on the door.

"*What* is it! What's the matter! *Speak* to me! *Speak to me!*"

With that instant, accurate intuition of a sensitive woman, she had sensed his horror and shock. By a tremendous effort Randall got hold of his reeling senses.

"Wait . . . wait . . . wait a minute," he articulated thickly.

"But what is it? *Tell me!*"

He could hear her breath coming and going in terrified gasps, and that helped to steady him. He must keep her away. . . . He must do something . . . not stand there shaking like a poor fool!

And now the realization came to him that whatever thing it was, or person, who had done this crime, might be crouching, hidden in one of those shadowy corners . . . might any moment attack him . . . or the girl, standing outside there alone! Again his brain went reeling away from him, and he labored to draw it back to balance.

He pressed his lips close to the door jamb. "Listen! You must get out . . . clear away! Do you understand?"

"What has happened?" she insisted.

"Nothing . . . you can help! Do you know where that big ballroom is?"

"Yes."

"Then hurry there! You'll find two men there. Bring them back here . . . but don't be alone an instant! Don't be alone . . . do you hear?"

"Yes . . . but . . ."

"For God's sake . . . *go!*"

His fear to have her passing through those echoing, untenanted rooms alone was only second to his fear to have her remain where she was! When he was satisfied she was going, he turned back to the room. Slowly, caught in the gripping terror of his imagination, that put watching eyes and listening ears in every corner, he went to touch Broox's body.

Immediately he did this, all thought of personal fear left him . . . obliterated by the regret that came upon him. Big, genial, splendid Broox! Alive only last night! Alive and giving orders . . . even patting his shoulder, and now, struck down, in his prime!

In this moment Larry Randall realized how much he had liked and admired his director—who lay here dead; and in his death . . . so sorry . . . so helpless an object! Pity for the poor corpse . . . for the soul that had left it and was wandering, lost, who knows where . . . engulfed him. Tears came into his eyes as he thought of their years of working together—when Broox had treated him almost as a son.

"I'm sorry . . . Chief . . . I'm sorry!" he muttered brokenly, choking over the words. For a moment longer he knelt there, trying to give to the dead man a measure of comfort just by his presence . . . by holding his cold hand. Then he laid it gently down and got to his feet. There were too many things to be done! How was he going to get out of this place! He revolved slowly, peering into the room's dim corners . . . his eyes bewildered because of that one piercing beam of light coming from the single window, set close up under the ceiling . . . and no way to reach it.

Then once more he was repulsed by shock. Another figure, prone and motionless, lay across the room!

And again Randall made himself get down and feel for life . . . or death. This man's head was bloody . . . and he clutched a revolver in his outflung hand. When Randall saw that, he said, slowly, through white, tense lips:

"If you've killed my boss . . . God help you. You'd better go on and die . . . right now!"

For he saw the man was still breathing, and that his breath, seemingly suspended, renewed itself with stertorous outpuffings through pale, lax lips that pressed against the floor.

Who was this man? He had never seen him before. Why, why . . . this must be her brother! Aloysius!

"Oh, God!" He brought himself up abruptly.

Her brother! And help must be gotten to him. Medical aid at once. Once more he looked about for escape and found none, except the door through which he had come, and which again refused to open. How was he going to tell her?

"Hey, Randall!"

With a hastily breathed, "Thank God!" he recognized the voice of the man he had brought up with him, and then Skeets's voice, high pitched with excitement.

"The door won't open. Shall we break her in?"

"Sure! Bust her!" he ordered immediately.

He waited while both men assaulted the panel. He watched the boards bending in, and thought with satisfaction that they must have splintered that grinning, ugly face to bits by now.

Then unexpectedly, as though with personal irony, the door swung open on its broken, gaping frame.

"Can you feature that!" Skeets exclaimed, big-eyed. Randall grabbed his arm.

"Never mind that door. *Where is she?*"

"You mean that girl? She's out in front. She's okay."

Randall sighed with relief. Skeets stared about.

"What happened? Oh, good God! . . . is that the chief?"

"Shut up, will you. Listen. You duck back to camp and get Serge. Tell him to come a-running with ten men. Give them guns and real shells. Tell him to put guards all around this place, and to take this wounded man around to the room where that girl is staying . . ."

He stepped aside, disclosing Aloysius Love's body.

"Oh, good God!" said Skeets, eyes bulging and teeth chattering. "I told you this house . . ."

"Go on," interrupted Randall roughly, giving him a shove. "Don't stand there shivering. And listen. Bring Red's car back on the run. Hurry! Here, you," addressing the man with Skeets. "You stand right here by this door. Don't let anybody in . . . any one . . . understand?"

"I get you!"

"And you tell Serge, when he comes to take this injured man out, not to touch anything. That gun, or anything in the room. Tell him he'd better outline that man before he moves him. Got it?"

"Yes, sir!"

"All right, I'm off . . . Oh, say." He stopped as he thought of another detail. "That girl up front is this fellow's sister. Tell Serge. He'll know how to handle everything!"

"Yes, sir."

"Have you a gun?"

"No, I haven't . . . not here."

"Well, keep everybody away, anyhow, until Serge brings someone to relieve you. I'm off."

He stopped for just a moment to say hurriedly to Beatrice Love:

"Your brother has been hurt. I've sent for Serge, who will take you to him and help you with him. I'm going now to get a doctor."

Red's car swung into the drive to meet him. Randall jumped on the running-board and waved Red back into the highway.

"What's up?" demanded the driver.

"Murder . . . the boss's dead! Do you know the nearest phone?"

"Yep. Sit tight!"

Wordless they sat, bending forward in strained attitudes, their minds racing ahead of the machine. The miles piled up behind them. Once Red spoke.

"Hope the damned speed cop doesn't catch me, he said nervously.

"'Sall right. Tell him it's murder, and take him on the running-board. Be a good thing."

But no cop followed them, and Red finally brought the car to a swerving stop at the first corner of Camillio, the small town to which they had driven. Randall was out and into the store like a torpedo. "Where's your phone?"

"In the corner, mister. What's your hurry?"

But he was already there.

"Long distance. Hollywood . . . Superior Films Studio . . . Mr. Rosenthal," he said, and hung up for the operator to call him back.

"Where's a doctor?" he called over his shoulder to the store-keeper.

"One right at the end of this block. He's the coroner too, in case you need one," said the man, and laughed at his own joke.

"I do!"

He tossed a bill to the storekeeper.

"I've got a car outside. Take it and go get him here. Make it snappy."

"Keep your money, son. I guess you're in trouble the way you're actin'. I'll get him."

"Thanks," said Randall and hastened back to the now ringing telephone.

Five minutes previous to Randall's call the door to Abraham Rosenthal's private office was thrown open and a wild-looking production manager burst into the room. In one hand he clutched the morning paper.

"Oi!" he groaned, tossing it down in front of Rosenthal. "Haff you *seen* it?"

Abraham Rosenthal glanced from the paper to the over-wrought Cohen.

"Haff I seen vat? I haff seen nothings except a crazy man making off my office a place to shout and tear his hair. Vill you to please calm down, Izzie?" He again turned to the paper.

"Vill I to calm down! Mine Gott, vait until you see vat I saw in that paper, and maybe you will tear your hair also! Read it. I esk you. *Read* it!"

He jabbed at the open page with a long, trembling finger.

Abraham Rosenthal's brown eyes, filled with resentment, followed the pointing finger. As he read, his fat lips drew in and he heaved a deep sigh of anguish.

"Rain in northern California," he moaned. "*Rain!*"

"Yess, rain!" yelled Izzie. "End you esk me vy I should come busting into your office? Oi . . . ten t'ousand dollars a day that costs us . . . ten t'ousand dollars going up in smoke . . . just like that . . ." He snapped his fingers under the president's nose.

"Not in smoke, Izzie," said Rosenthal sharply. "In the mud . . ."

Izzie tore his hair frantically. "Vat iss the difference, I esk you, vedder it iss up in smoke, or down in the mud? Ve lose it, don't ye? I *told* you not to make that picture. Didn't I? End now look at it. Oi!"

"Vill you to stop moaning, vonce, and let me think . . ."

"Shure . . . shure. . . . It iss time somebody around here began thinking . . . Oi . . . ten t'ousand . . ."

"Shut up!" ordered Rosenthal sharply and inelegantly. "Vy do you alvays haff to spoil my days vid bad news? Ain't you effer going to find somethings pleasant to talk about?"

"How should I?" retorted Izzie sarcastically, "ven you do efferything I esk you not to? Some vone hass to look after the business . . ."

"Maybe it vasn't raining up there and you haff made us both miserable for nothings," said Rosenthal hopefully.

"Read it! I esk you. . . . It *iss* raining *all offer*. . . . Better ve bring them all back here and stop the picture . . ."

"Better ve find out first vat it iss really like up there," said his employer. "Vait!"

He reached a fat hand for the telephone, only to have it ring under his touch.

"Long distance, Mr. Rosenthal. Mr. Randall on the wire," came the voice of his secretary.

"All right, I vill speak to him," and to Izzie, "Randall. Now maybe ve get somethings besides your belly-achings. Hello. . . . Hello, Larry . . . is it raining . . . vat! Vat! . . . Oh, Mine *Gott* . . . !"

"Vat iss it? Vat iss it?" demanded Cohen in a shrill voice at sight of his employer's ashen countenance, reaching out and trying to take the receiver away from him.

Rosenthal removed him with a sweep of his big arm, and the terse command:

"Ged out! Shut up!" and into the transmitter, "Yes, yes . . . Randall, go on!"

Cohen backed away, but stood with bulging eyes and trembling hands, forcing himself to keep from interrupting. He knew from Rosenthal's face that something terrible had happened.

"Oi . . . Oi . . ." he groaned.

"Yess . . . yess," said Rosenthal, and raised distended eyes to his production manager.

Then, pulling the telephone closer to his fat lips, he spoke rapidly, in a voice of authority:

"That iss right. Now, you go back vid the coroner and guard efferything. Alvays put guards right away. I will haff Captain Smith up there in an aeroplane right away. Don't touch anythings. Vait for him! Don't say nothings to the local police. I vill haff Los Angeles do that. Go back now . . . and vait!"

With an almost nerveless hand he let the receiver sink slowly back into place, lay back in his chair with a groan. Trembling, he reached for his voluminous purple-bordered handkerchief and wiped his damp forehead.

"*Vatt* iss it?" demanded Izzy shrilly. "*Vatt* hass happened? For vy should Captain Smith go up there? *Enswer* me, vill you, *Abie!*"

Rosenthal heaved himself to his feet.

"Ged out!" he roared. "Ged out!" He brought his big fist down on his desk.

Cohen cast a reproachful look at his employer, opened his mouth to speak, then, without a word, turned and obeyed.

"God off Abraham!" said Rosenthal slowly, looking about him dazedly. "God off Abraham!"

His big brown eyes were filled with anguish and he stared about him as if unseeing. Finally he reached out a still trembling hand for the telephone and told his secretary to get him Captain Smith, formerly of the Los Angeles Police Department.

Larry Randall turned from the telephone to find a rotund little man, with bright, beady eyes looking at him.

"You wanted me?" he asked. "I'm the coroner, Doctor Gittles."

"Good God, yes!"

"What is it?"

"My boss's been killed. I'm Randall, assistant director with this picture company up here a few miles."

"Lead me to the place of slaughter, young man," said the coroner, and turned immediately facing the door.

As Red drove them madly back, Randall rapidly sketched what he knew concerning the tragedy. Dr. Gittles remained silent until he had finished the gruesome account.

"This other man, Love, is not dead, then?" he asked.

"No. At least he was alive when I left. I had them carry him around to the south wing, where his wife and sister are. Then I came down here and phoned my boss at the studio. He said he would send up Captain Smith, and for me to get you, but to say nothing to the local police."

"Just as well," said the coroner dryly. "Amos Lake—that's our local watch-dog—isn't what I'd call an asset in a murder case. However, he'll be out here. Los Angeles will have to notify 'em. Maybe by then your own man will be on the job. I know this man Smith. Good man! He'll stir up something. How did your director happen to be in that old house?"

Randall explained.

The coroner shook his head.

"Queer dump. Anything might have happened."

With which cryptic remark he again settled into silence. Randall, his mind seething, did not disturb him. As the car pulled into the weed-grown drive, the little coroner came out of his reverie.

"Better come with me and have your guards let me inside. Might save complications."

Then as they started toward the house, he looked back down the road and grinned.

"Here comes the local law! Never mind. Let's get in with the body. When they show up, you pilot them in. After that you can leave 'em to me. I'll handle 'em."

As they approached the broken paneled door letting into the room where Broox lay, Randall got the impression that the man Serge had placed on guard there had just come out of the room. However, when they came up to him he was standing in position in the opening.

"Were you in that room just now?" demanded Randall, eying him sternly.

The guard shook his head emphatically.

"No, sir. I've been right like this ever since your cameraman put me here, except to help them take out that other feller."

Randall had a fleeting thought he'd heard the man's voice before, but could not place it.

"What's your name?" he demanded sharply.

"Donovan, sir, John Donovan."

"All right, Donovan. You stick here. This is the coroner. I'll send a man up here to run errands in case Doctor Gittles needs him. Is there anything else I can do, Doctor?"

"Not a thing! Except send Amos and Dud back here to me. I'll take a look at the body, then I'll go around and look that Love chap over and patch him up so they can hang him properly! Tell Captain Smith, when he comes, I'll be here waiting him."

The little coroner stepped into the dim-lit room and Larry Randall, after another sorrowing look at the crumpled body of his director, turned heavily away.

Dr. Gittles called him back again.

"It's blacker than a bat's wing in here, except in that one place there. Do you suppose you can dig up a lamp of some kind . . . anything?"

"We've got another Coleman lantern in camp, I think."

"That'll do fine. Send it up to me!"

V

Randall paced up and down the strange winding walks. The dead stalks of plants stretched out toward him like clawing, menacing talons. Everything about this strange place seemed to breathe a sense of personal menace.

Accustomed to having ten dozen more things to do at one time than any ordinary human being could customarily attend to, the assistant director now fretted impatiently under his role of simply waiting until former Captain of Detectives Smith, that famous, and deservedly so, criminologist arrived.

Up to now Randall had been too shocked to consider his own status as a result of the murder. Now he did so, and admitted ruefully that Broox's death left him high and dry . . . without a director, in a studio where every director had his old and trusted assistant. He did not want to leave Superior Films. He liked the way it was run . . . and he knew, too, that it was not going to be an easy matter tying up with another director. Motion pictures was no easy business to keep busy in. Every man and his dog wanted to get into the game, and for every ordinary—and even extraordinary—position there were a dozen applicants.

He looked up from these depressing thoughts to see Beatrice Love walking toward him. Her head was bent, and she was twisting her handkerchief nervously in her hands. She would have passed him, had he not spoken.

"Oh . . . Miss Love! Miss Love!"

"Oh . . . I did not see you!"

"You look worried. Is your brother badly hurt?"

Her eyes were resting on him with a dull look, as though her mind was still functioning in some far place. She said, answering him, and yet not answering him:

"I . . . don't know."

"Why, I thought Doctor Gittles went in to see him. Couldn't he tell?"

"Oh, he did. I mean, he did come in to see him. Thank you so much! He said Aloysius would be all right, but he might remain unconscious for some time yet. He could not tell exactly. He said it would be better not to move him until he regains consciousness."

"And your sister? Is she all right? Is there anything you need that I can have sent up for you?"

"You are very kind, but we have everything. The things that were brought from your emergency supplies will do nicely. All Aloysius really needs is care, and fortunately I can give him that. I am a nurse. This strange place, mad as it is, is splendidly planned as to conveniences. We have running water, and with our camp gas stove we are quite comfortable."

"Well, when you need things . . . eggs, or milk, or anything like that, send that man down. He's supposed to guard your rooms and to attend to errands. I think it wiser to have him there until we know . . . just what conditions are around here . . . until we are sure there isn't some wild-eyed murderer loose about the place!"

They were both silent, for they both knew that they had been talking of extraneous matters, to keep from speaking the ugly thing shouting itself in their minds. Now an awkward silence fell. Out of it Beatrice spoke suddenly, and her eyes refused to meet his . . .

"Mr. Randall . . . you don't know my sister-in-law. I . . . wish you did . . . I mean, I wish you had met her before this thing happened! She is a very peculiar woman. She says astonishing things. Please promise me you won't pay any attention to her . . . no matter how she acts!"

Randall was a bit bewildered by this confession and did not know how to meet it. Again silence came between them, silence and that ugly specter in their minds. Beatrice spoke again, as though she must say something to break the unity of their thoughts, that were almost articulate in their similarity and force.

"You know there are some women who just chatter on and say awfully silly things, but in a time like this . . . why, the things they say can have such pointed application! I'm afraid . . ." she stopped because he was looking at her hands locked together now, the slender fingers twisting and turning. . . .

"Isn't it . . . silly of me? And there really isn't any reason why I should have a fit of 'nerves.' Aloysius . . . is really . . . all right!"

Randall was afraid of hidden things. He knew that repression gathers proud flesh. He had to clear this doubt that lay between them, even though she resented it . . . for he felt he must be prepared to help her . . . if he could, and if she needed him. He said abruptly:

"Tell me . . . was there any reason for your brother to kill Mr. Broox?"

He had time only to get the startled, fear-filled look in her eyes, when to them both came the roar of an approaching aeroplane making straight for the open space at the left of the house.

"That's Smith," he said hastily. "Please pardon me, but I must go to meet him . . . Beatrice . . . Miss Love . . . don't . . . worry! I don't know that you are, but . . . if you are . . . try not to . . ." he ended incoherently, and turned to dash across the tangled, overgrown garden to the field. He thought that her eyes had filled with tears, and that her mouth was trying pitifully not to tremble.

Randall followed the taxiing plane on a run and arrived beside it almost as its third passenger stepped on the ground. The tall, lean man of the three stepped forward with outstretched hand.

"You're Randall, I take it?" he said, and Randall's hand was clasped in Captain of Detectives Smith's slender, sinewy fingers, and he looked up into a pair of disconcertingly keen gray eyes.

"These are my assistants, Ryan and Clancy," Smith continued.

"Pleased to meet cha," said Clancy.

"Flat-foot," thought Randall silently.

"Haven't I seen you before, partner?"

Randall got the impression of a swagger from this big, burly sergeant, but he grinned and answered good-naturedly:

"I think so. During the Hardell case. I was coming out of the hospital on the lot . . . and you were going in, armed with a big bunch of flowers!"

Clancy turned red.

"*Touché!*" said Captain Smith, smiling. "Then you and Ryan probably have met also."

"How-de-do, Randall," said Ryan. He was much like Smith in his quiet manner, but Randall guessed that he also could be dynamite when he once got into action.

"Gad, I'm glad to get out of that thing. I don't like 'em," Ryan admitted, "but that fellow certainly burned up the air getting here!"

"And believe me, I'm glad he did! Gosh, I'm glad to see you!"

"Well, here we are, brother. Take a good look at us. Where's the murder?"

"Just a moment, Clancy," said Smith with a look at his eager assistant. "Is there anything or any message you want to send back to the studio, Randall?"

"No . . . I guess not. But I'll just keep the plane here. We might need it. We might want it . . . in a hurry, you know. Hello, Clarke!"

"'Lo Larry. Got any idea who did it?"

"No. Did Rosenthal tell you to come right back?"

"Nix."

"All right. Then you stay. Go down there to camp and tell Skeets Williams to fix you up with a tent and everything." He turned to Smith.

"I'm here to take orders, Captain. This is your job, and all I can do is to stand by and help. What do you want first?"

Smith reached into his pocket and brought out a handful of cigars and passed them around.

"Rosey's best imported," he said, and the habitually rather taut lean features relaxed in a whimsical grin. Randall remembered that Smith got a great kick out of being generous with these rare pets of the president's. Smith waited until every man was puffing appreciatively, then he drew in a deep breath, and when he spoke his tone had snapped up.

"Mr. Rosenthal told me that your director, Broox, had been found by yourself, murdered, this morning, in an old house. I take it that's the place over there?"

"Yes. There was another man in the same room. But he was not killed. Only injured. He will live, they think."

"Who was this man?"

"I never saw him before. His name is Aloysius Love."

"How do you know that? One of your picture people . . . extras?"

"No. A San Francisco man. His sister told me that they had started out . . . he and his wife and herself . . . to go to the Big Basin, and that the storm came on them, and that they took shelter in the house."

"H'm," said Smith, and Randall got the impression he did not think much of the story. Retelling it, and thinking how Aloysius

Love and Broox were found together, really acres (considering that the house actually did cover nearly six) from the wing in which Beatrice Love had told him they were located, he did not think much of the story himself. Yet he must not let Smith know his own doubts . . . or fears. . . .

"Where did you meet the sister?" Smith said suddenly.

"She was looking for their . . . dog Calamity!"

"That's a hell of a name!" Clancy burst out derisively, simultaneously with Smith's next question. "Did she find it?"

"They named the dog Calamity because he had a habit of getting into trouble. No, I don't believe she found it," returned Randall, very stiffly to Clancy and courteously to Smith.

"It looks as though the animal's name brought its own fulfilment, eh, Randall?" said Smith quietly, adding, "What's in a name . . . a rose by any other name . . ." and looking off into the distance. Randall walked on silently, waiting for him to continue his questioning.

"Who's up there . . . with the body?" he asked next. Randall was relieved that the conversation had turned from the Love family.

"Why, the coroner, Doctor Gittles. Also the local police. But Doctor Gittles said he'd handle them. He told me to tell you, too, that he'd wait there for you himself."

"Gittles . . . Gittles . . . oh . . . yes! A little fat blob, bald as a bat?"

"That's him," said Randall emphatically, if inelegantly.

"That's the first good news you've told me, young man!" Smith's tone was hearty. "I know that little badger. I like him! Now let's get into a straight chronicle of everything that happened from the time you left the studio until you found your director. Don't leave out anything. C'mon, boys, let's get on the job!"

The two other men moved closer to Smith and listened quietly as Randall told his story. Smith stopped him when he came to Broox's decision to change the shooting schedule.

"Was that general knowledge, or did only a few of you know of it?" he asked.

"Let's see. Well . . . as far as I know, only Serge, Skeets, myself, and maybe the cook and the man who waited on the table, but I think he had gone out . . . and Morrill and . . . oh, good God!"

Randall stopped dead in his tracks.

"What's wrong, son?" asked Smith kindly, noting his agitation.

"I'd forgotten all about Hoxton!" exclaimed Randall, aghast.

"What about him?"

"Why he's . . . disappeared . . . lost! Ever since I found the chief . . . that way . . . I guess I've been kind of goofy . . . I . . ."

"That's natural, my boy. No need to apologize. You say Hoxton has not been found, and he went to the house with Broox . . . is that it?"

"Yes. He and Broox were alone, as Morrill was back in camp. I'd better get someone on the job looking for him pronto!"

"Might be a good thing, yes," agreed Smith, "and when you find him, just corroborate the story of Morrill's about the gun . . . no . . . I'll do that myself. Just simply keep an eye on him. . . ."

"Say, Chief, would those fellows be using blanks or real shells . . . this Hoxton and Morrill?" interrupted Ryan.

"The gun that Morrill says he gave to Hoxton . . . his gun . . . had real bullets," said Randall slowly. "But say, you don't think . . ."

"I don't think anything yet, Randall. Well, here we are. So . . . this is the place. Very queer. Very queer," Smith said quietly.

Clancy, who had been coming along silently, suddenly shivered violently all over his fat body and let out a "Brrr!" through chattering teeth. Smith turned to look at him in amazement.

"What's biting you," he asked sharply.

"I dunno. I just felt that way when I looked at that place. It looks goofy!"

If Smith were deeply impressed by his customarily phlegmatic sergeant's reaction, he kept that to himself . . . to add to the numerous convictions that the place was "goofy" which he accumulated later. Now he said only:

"Places of tragedy always have a definite feel about them, Clancy. You just realized suddenly that inside those walls lay two men . . . one murdered and the other shot in the head . . . the head was the place, wasn't it, Randall? Merely a subconscious reaction, Clancy!"

"Huh!" snorted Clancy. "They ain't nothing subconscious about the chill that chased itself up my spine. I don't like this dump!"

"Anyway, you and Randall seem to be agreed on its being a 'dump,'" said Smith, smiling. "As a matter of fact, boys, it's the most amazing and interesting structure I have ever beheld!"

"I wish I'd never beheld it at all!" said Randall, with a depth of feeling back of his careless words.

"Did Broox carry a gun?" Smith asked.

"No . . . at least, I don't think so. There wouldn't be any reason for his carrying one. . . ."

"H'm, was this Hoxton in the war?"

"Say, that's funny. They were talking about that last night!"

"Who?" Smith demanded sharply.

"Hoxton and Morrill. Morrill's a funny little duck. He couldn't get into the army . . . undersize, and he seems to pack a grouch about it. Hoxton razzed him, and it looked to me like he didn't take it very well. Seemed to hit him on a sore place, if you know what I mean."

"So Hoxton *was* in the army?"

"Beg pardon . . . yes. He was."

"So Hoxton and Morrill were rather at outs . . . and, from what you've told me about Morrill, he isn't usually a man to resent kidding. I mean, he takes it well, usually?"

"Yes. I don't think he was angry enough to . . ."

Randall started to protest, regretting his admissions. Smith patted his arm.

"Don't get worked up, boy. My questions at this stage of the game aren't going to fix the guilt on anyone. You're like Rosenthal . . . you'd like to think this murder has been committed by some agency outside. I'd like to be able to say all murders are committed that way . . . better, that murder is never done! But it is done, Randall . . . and sometimes even I can hardly believe the brutal ways in which it is done! One more question, and don't hesitate to answer it fully, please. Did Hoxton and Broox quarrel yesterday?"

"Holy cats! You sure get at things," Randall murmured, wonderingly, "Yes, sir. They did . . . I mean . . . they . . ."

"What over?"

Randall told him.

"You are certain nothing was said about the past . . . no reference to any time in the army together? What I am trying to get at is, do you think they could have had some quarrel lasting over from their army life . . . perhaps, together?"

"Nothing like that," said Randall positively. "Nope! It was just over that fool Skeets getting excited and pulling the switch too soon, and Hoxton not knowing anything about the explosion coming, anyway. Made him pretty mad . . . but he got over it."

"Are you sure he did?"

"Why . . . I think so," said Randall. Then he burst out, "God, it's too bad! It's too bad! He was a fine fellow . . . and . . . and he was making the best war picture that's ever been made! Not just to be making a good picture, Mr. Smith, but he had an idea back of it . . . something about showing the world how horrible war is . . . the real thing . . . and trying to educate people to where there wouldn't be any more wars! Then he had to be killed . . . it doesn't seem right. He was getting *everything* on that film. I felt like I'd been to war myself!"

"Yes. He would know how. He should! He must have seen some pretty bad times Over There."

"Oh, that wasn't the reason. He was just one of the few *real* directors. He wasn't in the army . . . just a genius at getting what he wanted. . . ."

"That's only a half truth, son. And Broox was only part of his name. His full title was Captain Ellison Broox Jones. The soldiers . . . some of them . . . called him 'Hard Boiled Jones' because he was a military martinet. Some of them, too, thought they had a grudge against him because of this."

He went on, not heeding Randall's blank look . . . for Randall was putting a lot of twos and twos together in his mind.

"Get out your note-book, Ryan, and take this wire to the Adjutant-General's office, Washington, D. C.

"'Request information concerning one William W. Hoxton. Was he ever in Captain Ellison Broox Jones command, World War? Appreciate all and any information. Murder.—Smith, Captain Detectives.' Go down to the camp. He can get a car there, can't he, Randall? Good. Take that telegram to the nearest telegraph office."

Ryan started off. Randall had not moved a step since getting the information of Broox's army record. He could not help putting a sinister interpretation on the fact that Broox had never revealed it . . . for he felt that secrecy always went hand in hand with shady doings. All his picture-making story training had taught him that!

When Ryan was a ways off, Smith called to him. He stopped and the captain of detectives went to him.

"Add this, and keep your trap shut," he said. "'Also, was man named Aloysius Love, assigned, or member of same outfit? Important.'"

"Nice mix-up, eh, Chief?" said Ryan.

"Looks nasty. I'm going in, and I'll be with the coroner when you get back."

Joining Clancy and Randall, he said to Clancy: "Take a look about, will you, Clancy!"

"Sure—I get you!" said Clancy, with a knowing grin.

VI

"Welcome to the party!"

Captain Smith enveloped the coroner's pudgy little hand in his and his face lit up.

"Glad to have you with me again, doctor. What have you fellows been trying to do to our picture company, anyway?"

"Might ask you the same. Your Los Angeles outfit has certainly caused considerable rumpus with the peace and quiet of our little country-side . . . to say nothing of playing the devil with my rest."

Smith grinned. Dr. Gittles would joke in the face of Gabriel. He knew the little fellow was really tickled to pieces to have something to shatter the deadly monotony of a small-town doctor's practice.

"And besides which, this old place didn't have a bad enough name, but you fellows had to add another spirit to the old-timers that are supposed to haunt it! Untidy mess. Quite! Hey, Amos!"

He turned to a lean, heavily mustached man lolling indolently against the far wall.

"C'mon over and meet a real detective. Do you good!"

Amos Lake pushed himself off the wall and sauntered up to them.

"This is our local bloodhound, Smith. Amos, meet Captain of Detectives Smith."

"I've heard tell of you," said Lake, thrusting out a horny hand. Smith gripped it heartily.

"This here is Dud Pelly," said Lake.

"How do you do," said Smith. Then turning back to Lake:

"I hope you fellows won't let us interfere with your investigations. I handled a case for Mr. Rosenthal before, and he thought he'd feel better if I was up here . . . you know how folks are when they know a man's work . . . sometimes the confidence is entirely misplaced, eh? You understand we will cooperate with you and the doctor here, and haven't any idea of getting in your way."

"Oh, that's all right. You won't get in my way," said Lake leisurely, and then immediately explained his own statement. "'Cause why? 'Cause I ain't goin' to be around here for you to mix up with! No, sir . . . no, sir. . . ."

He stopped to guffaw loudly in appreciation of his own wit and Smith's politely exaggerated look of inquiry.

"Why, say, I got plenty of things to do right now to keep me busy for a month of Sundays! Ain't no use Dud and me sticking round any longer. We wuz jest waitin' till you showed up so's we could turn the hull thing right over, and amble along back."

For a moment Smith was nonplussed, wondering whether this was only a bit of rural humor. In any sense, he felt it called for a polite protest from him, and he proceeded to make it, but Dr. Gittles rudely interrupted:

"You ramble right along, Amos. We've got work to do. Just stir your stumps to dig me up a half-dozen good men and true from off them cracker boxes down to Simpkins' store, for a jury, and I'll be obliged."

"All right, Git," agreed Lake placidly. "Well, so long, Cap. Gimme a ring if you need the local law. C'mon, Dud!"

"Queer duck!" said Smith.

"Nobody's fool!" snapped Gittles promptly. "He's the man I told you got the dope on that kidnapping case. Remember?"

"H'm . . . then he does know his way about. Well, Doc, what have we got here . . . murder?"

"Yep!" said Gittles briefly.

Smith had gone over and was looking down at Broox's body. All the time he had been chatting, seemingly carelessly, his eyes had shifted from corner to corner, aspect to aspect, of the odd room.

He judged that it had been designed for some sort of kitchen. The ceiling was high, and there in a kind of alcove or recess to the south was a hooded vent meant to carry off the gases and odors of the cooking. What struck him as odd was the fact that there was no window to break the paneled surface of the four walls, save the one high up in the south wall, near the ceiling.

Broox's body lay on the floor almost midway of the west wall, and out just far enough to allow for the sink and a sort of sink drain table made of tile, which were the only pieces of furniture in the room, if one discounted the faucets for hot and cold water above the sink.

The room was rectangular in shape, about twenty-five feet the long way, which was north and south, and about eighteen feet wide. At the north side, breaking the wall, was another alcove, set in to the west of the center. Two polished beams of some sort rose out of the intricately inlaid floor about midway of this alcove, and were imbedded in the ceiling, which was also of the finest woods, in inlaid patterns.

All about the four walls, to a height of at least ten feet, were carved panels, of some rare wood Smith could not name, and each panel was set off with a beaded molding of some other wood of lighter color. Subconsciously he had counted the large patterns into which the smaller blocks of the floors were set. They numbered thirteen. What an immense amount of meticulous designing had been necessary to execute such a pattern!

"What a queer room!" he said.

"Queer is right," said the coroner. "The whole place is queer. You haven't seen anything yet!"

"And I understand that door we came through was some sort of trick thing, they had to break in?"

"Yep . . . time spring of some sort."

Then, as Captain Smith again took up his rambling talk, Gittles waited. He knew that the words that came from the detective's mouth, and the deductions that were piling up in that trained, analytical brain, were far from matching. He was silently enjoying the chance to watch this famous man from the start of a case. Himself a keen psychologist . . . one of the first of the coast medical fraternity to add the science of psychiatry to the practice of medicine, Dr. Gittles hoped to learn from watching a master of the game at work.

Smith finally turned away from his survey of the room to ask:

"How's the other chap . . . Love?"

"Oh, he'll live," said Gittles. "If he'd been an inch taller, he'd be conversing with St. Peter by now."

"Meaning?"

"Meaning he was shot across the top of the cranium. The bullet struck the frontal bone just in front of the coronal suture, and plowed a gouge along the parietal bone, quite deep in front, and shallow as it progressed on back. Which means that the bullet was going up. Going down, it would have killed him deader'n a mackerel."

"H'm . . . can you give me any idea of which way he was facing . . . was it directly toward Broox?"

"Can't say positive. Most likely he was. It's a cinch he was facing whoever shot him . . . square on."

"Can you tell me how long a time elapsed between the two shots . . . the one that killed Broox and the one that wounded this man Love?"

"Might have been simultaneous. Love must have shot before being wounded. He couldn't have afterward. That shot might have hit Broox, just as he was aiming to shoot Love. Shock of Love's bullet caused Broox's muscles to jerk . . . result . . . bullet goes high of mark, and skins Love's cranium. Broox falls dead."

"Very concise. Thanks. Then you think both shots occurred at approximately the same time? A life may depend on your answer, Doctor!"

"Heck, don't I know it!" exploded the little coroner testily. "I've said my say! Shots might not have been exactly simultaneous . . . but mighty close to it. Couldn't have been over five minutes or so apart. I can place the time of Broox's death to the minute, almost, but he's a corpse. With a wounded man it's a little harder. The exact timing of his wound is a question."

"H'm. Thanks. Then your theory is that these two men met here, fought, and shot it out?"

"Looks that way. This man Love's gun lies there, as it was when I came in. Broox's clothes tell the story of a tussle before they took to their guns."

"Yes . . . they do," said Captain Smith. "Two buttons gone, collar torn, coat ripped, raw gash across the forehead . . . yep, that shows fight. But now, Gittles, how about Love? What evidence of a tussle there, and where is Broox's gun?"

The little coroner's mouth fell agape.

"Heck," he said disgustedly. "Come to think of it, I never noticed; but seems to me Love's clothes were all of a piece, only dampish."

"And Broox's gun?" prompted Smith.

"Never touched it! Never saw it! He didn't have one."

"Must have had! Lord, Doc, he's got to have had, if your theory is correct."

"Then where *is* the damned thing? It's a cinch it couldn't get up and walk off!"

"No . . . not by *itself* . . . *that's* a cinch," said Smith, vainly probing the door for some sight of it. He was rather upset.

"What a *sweet* dish!" he said finally.

"Nix," said Gittles. "What we've got here is a mess, Captain. A *mess!*"

Captain Smith took a silk handkerchief from his pocket, carefully picked up the one gun, released the catch, and emptied it.

"One shell gone . . . shot recently . . . forty-five caliber."

"And from the looks of Broox's wound he was shot with that same," said Gittles.

"Where's the bullet? Got it yet?"

"Went clear through him."

Smith walked over and after a search located the spot where the bullet had buried itself in the wall. He dug it out with his knife and brought it back to Gittles.

"Forty-five calibre," exclaimed both men immediately.

"So you think that establishes Love shot Broox, eh, Gittles?"

"What do you think? Doesn't it look that way?"

Smith remained silent. The coroner watched him a little annoyed, but was jarred out of his pique by a sudden chuckle from the detective, who had gone to where Love had fallen and was looking down at a chalked outline of the wounded man's body, drawn on the floor.

"I can see that Serge has been in here," he said.

"Very impudent fellow, goes rarin' around like a leaping orang-outang? Is that your Serge?"

"That's Serge!"

"Yep. He was here. Rather he had been, before I got here. That young Randall had him take this wounded chap around to where the family was stopping. He informed me he could give me the exact distances of everything, where Love was from Broox, and everything."

"Yes, that would be Serge," said Smith chuckling. "And he could! Great fellow. Did he try to jump over you, Doctor?"

"Heck, no . . . why?"

"Oh, just another one of his funny little mannerisms." Then seriously, "I'm darn glad he was on the job. He'll know whether Broox's gun was here, and a lot of other little details. Must talk to him later. Feel better. Well, let's get back to our problem: Two shots . . . one gun . . . one shell exploded. . . . Let's see if we can find the empty shells."

He walked about swiftly, and then amended . . . "The shell," and bent to pick up the only one he could locate. "See the other one anywhere, Gittles?" he asked.

"Nope."

"Well, well, well," said Smith reflectively. "Our goulash gets a couple more ingredients." He still walked about, his eyes on the floor.

"Now that shell there, it could have come from nowhere save from Love's gun. Distance just right if we allow a little for its rolling."

"That's right."

"Now where in Tophet is that other shell . . . and the other gun?"

"Search me."

"Well, then, let's go on to the next thing." Captain Smith turned his attention to where, on the floor, scattered and mud-stained, were some loose sheets of motion-picture typewritten script.

Gittles said, watching him

"Tromped 'em up considerable. Shows there was a fight."

Smith picked up several sheets, muddied with footprints. For a moment he held one in his hand. A piece of it had been ground off, or torn away. He looked about for the missing segment, but did not find it. He then folded that sheet carefully and put it in his pocket.

"Have you walked around on these papers?" he demanded.

"Nope!" indignantly.

"Mind letting me see the bottoms of your shoes."

Sputtering, the coroner held up first one foot, then the other.

"No, you're not guilty," said Smith. "H'm . . ."

He crossed to the body and stood looking down at a sort of table in front of which the dead director lay. But his eyes were not for the dead man's body. Instead they centered on the little pile of sheets lying in disorder on the top of the table. The fact that there were here more of the papers which Broox had brought with him did not interest Captain Smith. But what did bring a gleam to his eyes was the fact that on the top of the pile were a half dozen sheets, mud-stained, crumpled, but showing plainly the marks of muddy shoes, as did those that were scattered about the floor. And again one with a segment missing!

"Now how did those dirty sheets get up here!" he said softly. "It's a cinch they didn't do it by themselves. H'm . . ."

The sun, striking down through the high window, had moved from the body and was now shining directly on this table and the sink adjoining it. Captain Smith leaned over the sink as his eyes were caught by a red gleam. It was a preserved cherry. He wrapped that carefully in a bit of paper. It also went into his pocket. He noted the place was bare, as far at least as he could discern, either of food or food cupboards.

Once more he stared down at the table. A little blob it was this time. Smith touched it with a tentative finger nail, turned, and stared off at where a Coleman lantern, extinguished, lay on its side some distance south of the body. Then, very carefully with his penknife, he removed the drop of melted wax, wrapped, and tucked it away.

Dr. Gittles stood close by, watching, but refraining from questions. He realized he was at last seeing this master of his craft digging out intangible and overlooked bits of evidence, apparently from nowhere. What these unrelated, seemingly inconsequential things could have to do with what had happened here, Gittles did not know.

Once more Captain Smith bent over the body—bent closer to look at a darkish stain, that was not blood, on Broox's vest.

"Just keep that vest where it won't be touched until I want it, Doc, will you?" he said.

"Sure!"

"What do you know about this house, Doc?"

The little coroner hesitated, then he said:

"It's a long tale. I could give you a few things, but you'd better have the whole story."

"All right—I'll see you at your office later. Do you know if this room has another entrance?"

"That I couldn't say. There're doors and traps in this place everywhere, and lots of them are concealed."

"H'm . . . then it's a case of examine this room thoroughly for other exits. Well, that will have to wait also."

He crossed to the extinct Coleman lantern, a mate to the one that was now furnishing them light, and bent down to examine it.

"This must be the lantern Broox brought up last night," he said. Being careful to use a handkerchief, he seemed to be interested only in testing the valves that controlled the fuel supply to the mantle. Finally he seemed to reach a conclusion.

"H'm . . ." he muttered.

Dr. Gittles knew that in some manner that lantern had added another confusing link in the chain of clues.

"How many people, actually, have been in this room since you have been here, Gittles?"

"That fellow that made those chalk-marks, Randall, who came with me, Amos, and Dud. That's all. Of course, I don't know who was in here before I came."

"Did any you have mentioned . . . were they under your observation all the time?"

"Yep. All in the clear, every way . . . as far as messing with anything. Even Amos refused to do a thing. Said he had promised to hold everything for you fellers."

Captain Smith crossed to the door and said to the man on guard in the passageway:

"Who has been in this room or near it, since you came on guard here? Serge put you here, I understand."

"Yes, sir . . . the cameraman. Well, let's see. There was a man here when we came up. I relieved him. One of the men from camp. Then Serge and a fellow named Duke and myself took out that feller that was hurt. That's all, mister."

"Didn't Love's sister . . . or wife . . . come in to help?"

"The sister came as far as the door. I wouldn't let her come in. Serge sent her to git a place ready for her brother."

"Did you or that other man walk anywhere near Broox's body?"

"Nope—" positively.

"Didn't pick up Broox's gun, or anything?"

"Nope."

"You're sure, my man!"

"Yes, sir. I been here all the time. No one else's been in there except just what I've told you."

Smith turned to Gittles. "Is that right? Was this man on guard all the time you were here?"

"Yep. He was here when I came and he was still here when I came back from looking after Love later. He's been right there ever since, far as I know."

They both had the same thought. Rather, Dr. Gittles's mind made a leap and caught up with Smith's deductions. Their eyes met. Gittles said:

"Of course, Smith, he could easily have stepped into this room while I was with Love . . . and back out again, and no one have been any the wiser. But what would he want to do it for?"

"I don't know that he did, Gittles. But every possibility must be chased down for its possible motive. Unless one of your supposed spirits flew off with Broox's gun, *somebody* got it. That somebody *had* to be in this room. Question, when . . . and also, who? But there's somebody else mixed up in this affair somewhere, of that I'm certain. On the other hand, Randall says Broox didn't have a gun. The gun is not here . . . that is a fact. If he didn't, then what the hell *did* happen?"

"Shucks! If a man was going to carry a gun for any purpose like this here . . . he wouldn't go telling anyone he had it. I wouldn't bank too strong on that assistant director's statement."

Smith smiled

"Now you've brought up something else again, Gittles. Premeditated murder! You think Broox might have come into this place with the idea of meeting someone here and shooting it out with him?"

"Well, if he didn't customarily carry a gun, and he shot Love, it looks that way, doesn't it?"

"There's a lot of 'looks' around here, Gittles, that don't match up."

Both men had reached a temporary stopping-place in their deductions, when the clear threads of the thing were beginning to snarl together in a befuddling maze. It was then they were startled out of their transitory mental whirlpool by unmistakable sounds of a scuffle . . . thumps . . . loud-voiced protests . . . bumps . . . that seemed to come from behind the solid east wall.

"What's that?" exclaimed Gittles, and was answered immediately by Clancy's voice shouting:

"Shut up! You can't explain a damned thing to me! I caught you red-handed!" and the smack of a blow, feet clumping down what were evidently steps, and then the wall shook to the blows of Clancy's heavy fist.

"Hey . . . open up! Chief! You there?"

In two strides Captain Smith was across the room and attempting to find some way to open a panel that was one of three
in a row.

"Wait a minit. I'll bust her!" roared Clancy.

"What is it, Clancy?" demanded Captain Smith sharply.

"Aw, nothing!" came Clancy's drawled words with triumphant
deliberateness. "I just got your murderer, Chief . . . that's all!"

VII

Smith and Gittles exchanged looks of surprise. Before either of them could speak, Clancy found the catch and released it. The door swung open to disclose the burly sergeant with his captive clutched by the shoulder. With a heave of his big arm, he swung the man round facing his superior.

"Here's the guilty party!" It was impossible for Clancy to keep the gloating triumph from his voice. His whole manner shouted: "While you've been chewing the fat down here, look what I've gone and done!"

"So, you've found the guilty party, eh, Clancy? And what makes you think that?"

"Hell's fire, Chief! Didn't I catch him just now—red-handed, by the side of the dead man?"

"*What?*"

Captain Smith's rather ironically careless acceptance of Clancy's claim snapped into a puzzled, sharp inquiry.

"Sure! Standing right beside Broox! Wasn't that his name?"

Smith stepped aside, and Clancy's eyes, taking in the dead director, bulged twice their size.

"Huh! Who's *that feller?*" he demanded.

"Broox!" said Smith laconically.

Clancy stared, and his fat features screwed into a grimace of amazement.

"Well . . . if *he's* Broox, then who's that guy upstairs?"

"Upstairs?"

"Yeah . . . upstairs!"

"I don't know," said Captain Smith who was momentarily jarred out of his usual calm, "but I'm going to see right now."

He took the stairs three at a time, with Gittles puffing speedily after. Half-way up, Smith paused to call down:

"Hang on to your man, Clancy."

"Don't get funny, now," Clancy instantly cautioned his catch, who had not made one move toward escape. At this admonition, however, he assumed an expression and posture of such ferocious and murderous intent that Clancy let out a roar and started back, listening, hypnotized, to the words which hissed melodramatically from his captive's lips:

"Murders have been perform'd,
  Too terrible for the ear: the times have been,
  That, when the brains were out the man would die.

"Murder most foul, as in the best it is;
  But this, most foul, strange and unnatural!"

"Shut up! Ain't it bad enough for you to do a thing like that without making poetry about it?"

Clancy's shock was genuine, and sincere loathing rasped in his voice. "You . . . you . . . why, you . . . say, ain't you got no feelings at all?"

He stared in honest confoundment at the man, whose collar he had again clutched tightly.

His prisoner dropped his pose as quickly as he had assumed it. His slight person sagged heavily under Clancy's beefy hand.

With a shudder he lifted his well-kept hand and shielded his eyes from the sorry figure on the floor.

Clancy, believing he had found the fellow out, jerked him upright. "Quit your play-acting! Nobody around here yelled camera!" he snarled.

"You missed your cue, my friend. That was your line when I attempted to quote Shakespeare. Is my art . . . so great then, that you cannot tell the real . . . from the unreal? I assure you I am . . . quite . . . ill . . . I had . . . no love for Hoxton. . . . poor buffoon . . . but Broox . . . too bad . . . too bad!"

To Clancy's further astonishment the man in his grasp turned quite green and slumped, a dead weight, to the floor.

"Now what the hell?" asked Clancy of the world at large. "What the hell?"

As Smith and Gittles reached the top of the stairs, their eyes focused simultaneously on a huddled form lying in a strangely prolapsed posture.

Without a word they crossed the floor space of the room they found themselves in, and stood by the side of the body.

There were times in Dr. Gittles's rich experience of dealing with cadavers that bereft him of words. In these times he puckered up his pursy mouth in a soft, long-drawn whistle and teetered a bit on his short legs. He did this now. After a moment he said, his voice soft, but his words stark:

"Brain's scrambled!"

Smith did not speak at all, and the little coroner shoved him unceremoniously aside.

"Let me get at this fellow, Smith."

"Lord, yes. Help yourself," replied the detective, momentarily sickened. "Good God, what a deed! Fiendish!"

"Just mangled his head . . . that's all," agreed Gittles, lifting it from the floor, and peering intently at the pool of blood underneath. While he continued his examination, Smith looked about the room curiously.

It was unfurnished, except for thirteen musical instruments. An organ, a harp, drum, bass viol, bass trombone, and an assortment of others Smith could not name, making up the unlucky number.

"Organ . . . that matches up with Randall's retelling Morrill's story. 'Hoxton came back to play the organ again.' Lord, what a queer place! Thirteen . . . and the silver and gold on that harp shining like new . . ." Suddenly he turned to Gittles.

"Doc, where's the caretaker of this place?"

"There isn't any that I know of."

"Who guards these things? They are valuable. Even I, who am no musician, can see that!"

"The fact is, Smith," said Gittles a little shamedly, "folks around here think this place is haunted. A ton of gold bricks would be perfectly safe here. Nobody'd come near them. I . . . I . . . er . . . wouldn't set foot in the goofy old shack myself, if I hadn't been called on this case!"

"Someone must be here. These things have been polished recently!" Smith persisted.

"Sure. Spirits, I tell you! And listen to me, son, there's more truth than fiction in a lot of things we can't understand!"

Smith saw that he was not going to get anything more out of the little doctor until he was ready to sit down with him and hear the story from beginning to end. He walked about examining everything minutely, having recourse more than once to a pocket magnifying-glass, until he saw that the coroner had completed his work. Then he went back to him.

"Murder, of course?"

"Plain as the nose on your face. Better pick up that gun."

"Will you lend me your handkerchief? I've got mine around Love's gun." And when he had received the cloth, and taken up the revolver:

"Forty-five Colt's. Same as the other . . . one bullet shot . . . recently . . . now for the shell." He looked about, and so did Gittles, fruitlessly. Their eyes met, acknowledging their failure. Smith shrugged.

"The plot thickens, Gittles! Well, my friend, it looks like a great deal of the why and how of this lies in your technical knowledge. Tell me all you can about this . . . murder . . . and don't miss . . . because my case will be built on your findings." Smith awaited the answer impatiently.

"Killed instantly by a blow on the back of the head from some blunt, heavy instrument. The skull was smashed first . . . like an eggshell . . . a second blow messed the head up considerably . . . mashed the bone down into the brain. Time of demise, between eleven-thirty and midnight. Same time those two downstairs got it."

"Did he move after he was hit—I mean walk forward, or turn?"

"Never wriggled. Just flopped . . . blooie!"

"Do you think there was a struggle . . . that he was fighting with an assailant when he met his death?"

"I do not," stated Gittles positively. "I think he was hit, unexpectedly, from behind. There are no signs about his clothing of a struggle—no bruises on his body I can see."

"Could he have been facing the other way—say just have come up those stairs from the kitchen, and been struck down?"

"No, my son . . . *no* . . . *no!* He fell where he stood, and the way he was facing . . . which was *toward* the stairs from the kitchen. His assailant attacked him directly from behind. I see what you're driving at. Your idea is that he and Broox fought. He escaped to here, and the Broox pursued and killed him?"

"Something like that. You say he fell dead when he was hit by such a blow as you see positive evidence of. Well, here's another one, then. Could he not have been moved over there, afterward, making it appear that he was struck down there?"

For a moment the doctor's bright eyes twinkled silent over this suggestion. Then he said, with a chuckle:

"I've heard that a man had to know a lot, have a great deal of general knowledge, to be a motion-picture director. I doubt very much, however, if he would have knowledge enough of the peculiarly characteristic posture a body assumes when a man is struck down by such a blow as this man received, to be able to duplicate it perfectly. I doubt it! No, sir, the body tells its own tale . . . bears mute evidence of the place of its fatality!"

"I . . . suppose . . . so," said Smith, speaking slowly and ruefully. "Come to think of it, there would be a trail of blood, too. A wound like that would bleed some."

"Yes . . . some," agreed the doctor dryly. Getting down, he again lifted the man's head and disclosed the blood underneath. "*Some!*" he repeated significantly.

"All right, Doctor . . . I give that up. But I am curious to know about this 'characteristic posture' that tells so certainly he dropped dead as he is now! I can learn something here!"

"Right-o. Here goes. Having received a blow of this kind, our man, any man, is dead . . . dead standing up, or in whatever position he occupies at that time. His brain has been literally killed. Now here's something you may not know about death. It won't hurt to repeat it, even if you do.

"A man can be shot through the heart and he may be able to move about, carry on, as it were, provided at the time of his wound there is sufficiently strong impulse of some major emotion *in his brain* for it to dominate his muscular impulses up to the point where the brain faculty finally accepts the fact which his heart nerves are sending it . . . that is, that he is *dead*. He is dead, you understand, in one sense, the moment he is shot through the heart . . . in another sense he is alive and still able to function until the brain actually accepts *as a fact* what *is* true.

"For example, let me give you an illustration. It is reported that Rasputin, that Russian monk, was shot through the heart while coming down a stairway in a Russian house. But in his mind, at that time, was a firm belief that he *could not be killed*. He had survived poisons strong enough to kill an ox! Result, after being shot through the heart; after he was killed, from a strict medical point of view, he made his way clear down those stairs, and in spite of the fact other shots were entering his body. He even stood a blow and was able to grapple with one of his assailants; able to turn and climb back up those stairs before his mind finally accepted the facts as they existed. Then, and not till then, did he die. Does that tell you anything?"

"A lot," said Captain Smith, who had listened with the closest attention.

"All right. So shot, or wounded, such a man, with such a powerful impulse to complete some thought action, might move, might even have climbed these stairs in an extreme example. Broox down there might, under such emotion, have moved, taken a step, or more than one. Wait . . ." as Captain Smith was about to interrupt . . . "I'll give you my reasons for saying Broox didn't, later. Let me finish with this fellow.

"Now in cases like this, where the brain has been literally reduced to a pulp by an immediate and violent blow, the whole thought impulse, or, to use a better term, the whole involuntary reaction of the nerves is exactly reversed from the example I have just given.

"The brain is dead and the nerve centers down the spine get word of it immediately. The seat of emotion in this man's brain was literally blotted clear out of commission. Result, the brain container—his head—did a dive . . . immediately. The rest of his body followed suit, following the arc of motion set into being by the head. In other words, the body slumped forward, with the head falling first. Almost invariably we find men thus killed, lying in such a position as to give the impression the head and shoulders have fallen under the torso. As a matter of cold fact, they have done just that, in so far as this is physically possible. Now if you will notice carefully, that's exactly the way this man is lying. Hence, when he was struck down he was standing facing the kitchen stairs, with his back to this door."

"That makes the case . . . sweet," said Captain Smith, frowning.

"Can't help that," said Gittles. "You've either got to accept that fact, regardless of your other evidence, or you've got to hunt for someone around here clever enough, who has also had sufficient experience with violent death and the handling of dead and dying people, to have moved him and replaced him correctly so as to give us just the impression we have outlined. Someone with medical experience . . ."

"Look out, Doc," said Smith, with his first touch of levity, "or I'll be looking up your record next."

The little coroner grinned.

Smith was silent a moment. Then he said:

"Doc, you say there's a possibility Broox, having been shot through the heart, could have moved afterward . . . like Rasputin, you know. How do you know he did not?"

"Very simple. You'll know yourself if you stop to think "'

"H'm . . . oh . . . certainly . . . blood!"

"Rasputin left a ghastly, gory trail, I'm told," Gittles commented.

"Yes . . . yes," Smith agreed in an absentminded tone. Already his mind had left that idea and was intent, with a concentration that was almost painful, on picking out some key to unlock this tragedy.

Of one thing he was positive at this time. Somewhere in the actions of the three motion-picture men . . . in yesterday's work, or in Hoxton's unmerciful kidding of the smaller man, or in

Broox's near-killing of the gigantic heavy, lay the impulses that had culminated in the death of two of them.

Where Love fitted in he could not guess; but fit in he certainly did. In some way the four of them had become involved in a set of circumstances . . . if he could only know what had gone on in this uncanny building during the dark hours of the night before!

One ray of hope penetrated. He was anxious to talk to Morrill. He thanked his good fortune for past experience with motion-picture people. He would be better able to tell if Morrill, splendid trouper as Randall had said he was . . . were lying and acting out the part of the lie! The vivid imagination of the actor, fed through years of dramatic interpretation, could quickly invent the fantastic story that Morrill had told Randall, of faces as big as umbrellas, uncanny presences.

Gittles had gone back and was again looking at the dead man's head. Then he stepped to the door back of him and opened it, revealing another flight of stairs.

"The blow was struck from behind and to the left side. That means his murderer came up those stairs from down there."

"Wait a minute," Smith exclaimed, and ran down the steps. They led into a short tunnel, which, after about ten feet, debouched through a square stone opening. Smith found himself standing in one of the fireplaces of the huge ballroom.

He stepped out and into the room, and looked back. He saw that the back of the fireplace was movable and had been lifted in some way, leaving the entrance to the stairs. For a moment he felt about, trying to find the spring or latch to regulate it, and then gave it up. Going back to Gittles, he said briefly:

"One of the trick affairs you've been telling me about. Those stairs go down to the ballroom through a fake fireplace."

"Huh . . . *just like her!*" Gittles grunted.

"Who?"

"Well, Captain, if you're ready to go, I am," replied Gittles, evasively. Smith began to be curious over the way the little coroner evidently disliked discussing the house while in it.

"Doc, I can't put my finger on why I ask the question, but there's an impression lurking around in my mind somewhere, and I can't down it . . . could a *woman* have struck that blow?" Smith was plainly worried.

Gittles pursed out his round mouth and teetered a moment before he answered. Then he said:

"Yes. Under the grip of tremendous emotion . . . passion . . . fear even."

"Well, that's that," said Smith. "Downstairs we have two men shot, presumably in a duel of some sort . . . and presumably necessitating the use of two revolvers and two bullets, and leaving two empty shells. What do we find? One gun and one shell . . . and our two bullets! Up here we have one man killed, presumably by a blunt instrument, and we find one gun, with one shot and one shell missing! Match that up for me, will you?"

"Not me," said Gittles laconically.

"Very sweet. Very sweet . . . come now, Doc, do me a good turn and add another clue to that very *lucid* . . . list!"

But the other shook his head and grinned. "Death at the hand of person or persons unknown, and I've said my say!"

"Which lets you out!" Smith agreed enviously.

They turned to go back to the kitchen and were met on the stairs by Randall, who grabbed Smith's arms.

"Say, Smith, Clancy just told me . . ." he started excitedly. Smith stepped aside and gave him a view of the room and what it contained.

"Good God! Hoxton, too!"

"I presumed this was your missing actor."

"Yes . . . yes . . . but how . . . what?" Randall said bewilderedly.

"Brain mashed . . . that's how," said Gittles dryly. "Cap'll have to tell you why."

Randall turned wide, inquiring eyes to Smith. "Give me time, Randall, give me time . . . this isn't any ordinary crime!"

"Yes, sir . . . certainly! Say, you haven't seen or heard anything of that little dog, have you?"

"No . . . and his name was Calamity, you say? It's to be hoped the poor little pup doesn't bear out the meaning of that tag, or we'll find him laid out too!"

VIII

Smith stood looking down at the pale face of Clancy's unconscious prisoner. He could not decide whether the man's mouth, fine and delicately molded as a woman's, was indicative of a similarly fine and sensitive nature, or merely of weakness, inclined to peevishness. He had known men with such mouths to turn nasty.

"What happened?" he asked sharply.

"Damfino! He just went and did a brodie all at once, after spouting a lot of highfalutin stuff about murderin' these bozos!"

"Take a look at this man!" Smith said to Gittles, who was just coming down the stairs.

"Fainted!" the coroner reported laconically. He then proceeded to administer the simple but efficacious old first-aid method of soaking him thoroughly.

"He'll be all right in a few minutes."

"Clancy, since there's no chair, prop him up against the wall there. That's fine. Now . . . what's all this about his confessing? Sure you weren't imagining things?" Smith asked.

"I'll say I didn't imagine it! You sh'd have heard him! Soon as I got him down here, and he sees Broox . . . he spills the works . . . just like that!"

Clancy opened his big hand wide and made a sidewise sweeping gesture.

"What did he say, *exactly*, Clancy?" asked his superior, his eyes fixed on the slight figure against the wall.

"Just what I said he said!"

"But you haven't said," reminded Smith with a slight edge to his tone that Clancy knew well. The sergeant got a little red.

"Well, he said . . . let's see . . . Oh, well, I can't repeat it all, but it was something about his having performed a murder too terrible to listen to! He said he just knocked the brains out of that feller and when he did the feller died! And a lot more hooie! That guy's as goofy as this whole damned dump!" Clancy was uncomfortable.

Captain Smith looked at his subordinate, frowning.

"Go on," he said. "What else did he say?"

"That's all, except something about murder being foul and this one especially being most foul and strange and unnatural. Just about then I slapped him down. He's bughouse, I tell you!"

Captain Smith, looking intently at the small man, now showing signs of recovery, was frowning over Clancy's words. "Said he'd performed a murder 'too terrible for the ear . . . when the brains are out the man would die,'" he corrected softly, unconsciously grouping the words in some familiar phrasing. Hearing himself, the look in his face quickened toward understanding.

"Did he say anything else goofy, Clancy?"

"Ain't that enough? C'n you feature a feller standing there and lookin' you right in the eye and *braggin'* about killing a couple of guys?"

"Did he say anything about 'murder most foul, but this most foul'?"

"Gawd! That's just what he said, lookin' right at Broox there, that the murder was especially rotten and dirty and funny, only he used different words . . . *strange* and *unnatural*, he says."

"Are you trying to repeat Shakespeare, Clancy?" asked Smith with whimsical dryness.

"I'm not *trying* to repeat *nothin'*, only just what you asked for! I'm telling you what this gink said when he confessed, that's all."

"Listen, Clancy, and I'll give you his exact words," Smith said, after a moment's hard thought. "Wasn't this it?

"Murders have been perform'd,
  Too terrible, for the ear: the times have been,
  That, when the brains were out, the man would die!

"Murder most foul, as in the best it is;
  But this, most foul, strange and unnatural!"

"Sure, *that's it!* Ain't that just what I been telling you?"

Smith's intent face relaxed into his whimsical smile.

"Well, I know what you meant, anyway, Clancy. Now tell me *exactly* what happened next. Did you say anything, or do anything to him? I want to know what made this man go dead on you."

"I never did nothin'," declared Clancy in an aggrieved tone. "Gosh, I was too surprised to do anything but hang on to him and listen, except when he up and brags like that about bashing a man's head in! Then I was so damned disgusted I smacked him and shook the liver out of him . . . the dirty, cold- blooded little wart!"

"Did you *say* anything?" prompted Smith a little wearily.

"You bet I said something! I told him he was rotten enough anyway, doing a thing like that, without bragging about it! Then he gives me a dirty look that nasty-mean I pretty near let go of him! I tell you, Chief, honest, I wisht you could have seen his face! Showed his teeth . . . looked just like a mad gopher, and his eyes, golly! Then what d'ya think he says? Some fool stuff about my missing my cue, and he wants to know if he's such a fine actor as all that . . ."

Clancy was stopped by Captain Smith's exclamation:

"Now I know him! Morrill, of course. Go on, Clancy."

"Well, then he looks at Broox again, and he goes nuts. Says he loved Broox and hated that guy Hoxton. Called him a baboon, or somethin'. Then, just as I was all set to smack his dirty mouth, he goes limp on me. Gawd, c'n you feature a guy being *tickled* over a mess like that upstairs?"

Smith saw that Clancy was really repulsed to the depths of his beefy being.

"So that's all he said, then?"

"Yeah. Darn good thing, too. I was just getting set to smack him down *right!*"

Smith stood, repeating softly:

> "Murder most foul, as in the best it is;
> But this, most foul, strange and unnatural!

"Clancy, did you ever read 'Hamlet'?"

"No . . . and if that's a sample of it, I don't want to."

"I am beginning to wish I never did," interrupted a new voice. "Murder is horrible enough without adding to its horror graphic descriptions that return shrieking gruesomely in the ears."

The three men whirled to look at the speaker, as they did so Morrill put his hands over his face and shuddered violently.

"All the lines that have to do with murder keep whirling madly in my brain . . . so that I could go on saying them for hours, and never once repeat! That line of *Lady Macbeth's*, 'Out, damned spot!' and this, 'The bloodiest shame, the wildest savagery, the vilest stroke!' And again, 'Not afraid to kill him, having a warrant for it; but to be damned for killing him, from which no warrant can defend me!' 'Will all great Neptune's ocean wash this blood clean from my hand? No, this my hand will rather the multitudinous seas incarnadine!'"

"Whatdida tell you? He's as goofy and cold-blooded as hell!" Clancy exclaimed contemptuously.

Captain Smith stood looking quietly down at the man, letting him rave . . . trying to pierce with his gaze those slender hands that covered his face, and to see what the face was registering. But he could not. Failing, he concentrated on the tones of the voice, but all his straining ears could detect was a moaning remorse, that wailed dramatically as Morrill changed the immortal melancholy lines.

Clancy stood with his mouth agape. The little coroner watched Smith. It seemed Morrill would go on interminably, holding them all in this spell. Suddenly a thought came to Smith. The man was marking time . . . stalling to invent an alibi!

"That's enough, my man!" he rasped out, stepping nearer.

Morrill's hands dropped away slowly, and his mild blue eyes rose to Smith's.

"I must apologize. I have never looked at a murdered man before. I find that the screen murders I have seen . . . that looked so real on the film . . . are not at all . . . like . . . this!"

He shivered again, and his head jerked spasmodically in his effort to keep his eyes from the corpse, so close to him.

"You make a very good show of an aversion to dead men, but my sergeant found you standing over the body of Hoxton upstairs. Can you explain that?" Smith said sternly, determined not to let the actor in this man pull the wool over his eyes.

For a moment Morrill hesitated, then he said with his shy, disparaging smile:

"I am quite positive you will not believe me. I was not looking at him from choice. I had no idea that . . . that . . . Hoxton's body . . . was there . . . until just then . . . really!"

"Why were you there at all?" Smith snapped.

Morrill seemed about to explain, and then, looking into Smith's eyes, said:

"I really prefer not to talk about it! It's something I . . . it really has nothing to do with this murder, I assure you."

"Your assuring me does not convince me. Come, now, what were you doing there, and why were you there?"

Morrill's small face grew shrimpy pink.

"My great dream was to have been a musician," he stammered. "I cannot resist . . . the keys when I see them . . . last night Horton monopolized the organ, and . . . in any event, I would not have played if I thought anyone was about. . . ."

"H'm . . . you seem to be given to dreaming, my man! Another of your dreams was to lead your countrymen into battle, I understand."

Morrill's pale eyes flashed, and then dulled, but Smith saw his shoulders stiffen and his jaw muscles quiver as he said:

"It was! Cannot a man, then, have more than one dream? Would you limit his aspirations?"

"Oh, for crying out loud!"

Clancy's disgusted voice broke the invisible line of communication between his chief and the actor. For each man had been silently measuring the other's mental depths . . . sounding out the other's credulity.

"Didn't I *tell* you what he said, Chief? Didn't I find him standing there looking down at Hoxton, and the gun just dropped out of his hand? What more do you want?"

Smith said sarcastically:

"Did you intend to play that organ with a revolver?"

Morrill looked reproachfully at Clancy.

"I wish, really, that you'd go and take a walk," he said. "Your remarks are extremely disconcerting."

Smith, determined that this man was not going to get his goat, turned to his sergeant

"That's a good idea, Clancy. Go take a walk, and while you're doing it, get the shoes off this guard out here, and Love's shoes, and Randall's. I'll want Broox's and Hoxton's, but we'll get them later. By the way, just remove Morrill's before you go."

"I really cannot endure that fellow's hands on me! I will remove them myself," Morrill protested immediately, and began unlacing his boots. Clancy growled something insulting, but kept it down in his throat at Smith's quick look. When Morrill had taken off his shoes, Smith picked them up himself. He walked with Clancy to the door.

"Ain't you afraid he'll bolt?"

"No. And don't get a brain-storm, Clancy. I'm just letting him work out whatever's in his system . . . playing his little game until he gets tired and comes clean. Take all these boots down to Lake and have him lock 'em up for me. Also get finger prints of Hoxton, Broox, Love, that guard there, Randall, and later Morrill. Oh, yes, get Love's sister's too, and the wife's. Lake will get 'em developed for you."

"Gosh, I see where I got to hump myself!"

"Get everything, and make it snappy!"

Smith then went back to Morrill and stood looking down at him. The man's face had fallen into a blank of horror. Left alone for a moment, the realization of being in the same room with a murdered man . . . a corpse . . . seemed to have mesmerized him. Smith saw he would get nothing here.

"Get up, Morrill. We'll get out of here. Doc . . . will you stay until I get through with this man?"

As they passed out the broken door, Smith heard the guard remonstrating angrily over removing his shoes, and Clancy threatening to "bust" him in the face unless he "got a move on." Smith smiled. After all, Clancy had his uses!

"We'll go into the ballroom, Morrill, and you can tell me the exact action of all three of you last night."

"Ever read Poe?" asked Morrill in a weak voice.

"Some."

"'The room in which I found myself was large and lofty. The windows were long, narrow and pointed, and at so vast a distance from the black oaken floor, as to be altogether inaccessible from within . . . feeble gleams of encrimsoned light made their way through the trellised panes, and served to render sufficiently distinct the more prominent objects around. The eye, however, struggled in vain to reach the remoter angles of the chamber . . . dark draperies hung upon the walls . . . musical instruments lay scattered about, but failed to give any vitality to the scene. I felt I breathed an atmosphere of sorrow! An air of stern, deep and irredeemable gloom hung over and pervaded all.'"

Morrill's voice rose on high-gasped tones of horror and fell back in cadences of despair. Smith could but listen, and experienced a strange excitement to see how the actor's words fitted the scene. Yet he was totally unprepared for Morrill's suddenly throwing himself against the wall and staring about, wild-eyed.

IX

"Can't you feel it?" he implored hysterically. "Can't you hear things . . . all but see . . . evil spirits . . . in this place? And they laughed at me . . . they laughed . . . when I shot, in terror . . . at what I saw last night! They would not listen! They made sport of me! Ah . . . poor . . . insensate fools! Perhaps they know in death what their material, obtuse brains could not sense in life!

"Coward, they called me, coward . . . and weakling. And they laughed! *He* laughed! The imbecile chortling of a great hairy *Caliban!*"

"What was it you felt, Morrill?" interjected Smith sharply.

"The terror of this place!" Morrill's eyes rolled about from side to side. "Is there any shame in being a coward in a place where things like . . . like those two fiendish murders . . . can be done? Is there any shame to running away from evil influences that creep into a man's very vitals, and possess him? Is there any shame . . . I ask you . . . in escaping from a place where foul fiends crouch, ready to leap into your soul, take possession of it . . . and make it do their bidding? I tell you I was afraid! I was terror-stricken! I had only to look at this place . . . this strange, perverted monstrosity, to know it for what it is! They laughed at me! I warned them! And even when, in desperation, I shot at the thing that grinned so frightfully in upon me . . . even then they

133

laughed! Place of damnation! Possessed of foul fiends! I hear you chuckling . . . I feel your frightful, ghoulish triumph!"

Morrill's voice wailed off into a shuddering gasp, and he threw his hands across his face. Smith struck them away.

"If this is a show you are putting on for my benefit, Morrill, forget it! The best it will do is to postpone things . . . and . . . why man alive, a little more of that and we'll lock you up in a psychopathic ward!"

Morrill's head lifted slowly. He seemed to be making a great effort to pull himself together. Smith waited silently while he took out an immaculate, fine linen handkerchief and wiped away the beads of cold sweat that drenched his brow and upper lip. His hand quivered in such minute and speedy vibrations as to make Smith wonder if this were only acting. At last Morrill spoke.

"I admit to possessing an extremely . . . impressionable nature. I go to pieces. You have seen that. I become unreasonably worked up. Perhaps it is from years of throwing myself into highly emotional roles. Last night, coming up here in the rain and the thunder—into the reverberating, reaching corridors of this menacing monstrosity . . . seeing a dark form slipping down that passageway"—he painted to a hallway leading into the ballroom to the left of them—"seeing that wild face at the window . . . I felt my sanity slipping! But worse than that—more frightful—was the presage of death—chilling my vitals—insidiously terrorizing me so I could not shake it off! Have you never felt a premonition of things about to happen? It is not uncommon."

"Yes, I have experienced such feelings," Smith was forced to admit.

Morrill went on.

"I expect that murder . . . men brutally forced out of this life . . . their bodies mangled . . . is an ordinary thing to you. You have become calloused to it. You, perhaps, can stand beside a dead man and discuss the means that brought him to his end. The ordinary human being could only stand beside him, filled with horror . . . filled with fear of that stark thing . . . seeing in it his own irrevocable end . . . death!

"I cannot blot out that bloody head . . . poor Broox's stricken body. I cannot shake off the grip of this house! I am powerless to hold my own against the force of the influences I contact here. I feel that I shall go mad!"

Morrill's voice was shrill. The words had come rapidly, in rising crescendo. Smith saw he was about to go to pieces through the very intensity of the emotions that swayed him. He was either a consummate actor, or he was close on the verge of complete irrational frenzy.

Smith's impulse was to say, "Morrill, are you trying to tell me that while you were in this house last night you felt an impulse, through some alien influence, to commit murder?"

But he silenced that question. He would never get his man that way.

Instead he gripped Morrill's arm and started him over to a high-backed, carved wood seat, that formed part of the wall. He felt the man's body trembling as with an ague, and he saw that his smallish face had retained its greenish pallor. He sat the actor down, took a slender silver flask from his pocket, opened it, and held it out, saying quietly:

"You need a drink, Morrill. I want you to take a good stiff one! Go on! Take a big jolt!"

Obediently Morrill swallowed. After a moment, his color began to grow normal, and he looked up more calmly and said:

"I presume you are an officer of the law, and I am arrested?"

"Why presume that?" said Smith, thinking to dig deeper into the man's mental processes . . . perhaps surprise into expression some withheld knowledge of the crime.

The answer came glibly:

"Because you carry liquor with such a licensed air, and be-cause, having been here with Hoxton and poor Broox last night, I am logically a suspect."

"I am Captain Smith, and I think I am right in taking you for Mr. Morrill, the actor?"

"Yes, I am Morrill. How do you do, Mr. Smith. I cannot say under the circumstances I am charmed to meet you."

Smith noticed that a little smile accompanied the words. That liquor had been a happy thought.

"Oh, it may not be as bad as you expect. All I want Morrill, is the true story of what happened from the time you, Broox, and Hoxton left camp last night. Up to that time I have an account from Randall."

Smith watched the little actor's face closely. After a moment, when Morrill did not speak, Smith said, insinuatingly:

"I understand that Hoxton was in a bad mood . . . and that Broox was the cause of it."

"Oh, yes. Hoxton was in a blacker mood than anyone real-ized, except, perhaps, myself."

"And how did you come to realize this?"

"After we were here . . . I was sitting right on this seat here, and Hoxton made some remark to Broox about using this ball-room, and bringing in the extras . . . the sort of thing we are supposed to believe took place during the war . . . the young ladies of the house outraged . . . soldiers drunken, and the place despoiled. Well . . . it's the usual thing, and it usually goes over big with the audience . . . but Broox turned contemptuously on Hoxton and said: 'There's enough misery to put in a war picture, without going into the shameful sex angle of it! I want to forget that men committed deeds more dastardly than taking life!'

"I thought it was a queer thing for a man to say, spoken, it seemed, from out some regretted personal experience. But

Hoxton got out of it only the scorn Broox had for his suggestion. Hoxton prided himself as somewhat of a connoisseur on story construction . . . situations . . . which he most decidedly was not."

"How do you know Hoxton resented this?"

"Oh, it was quite noticeable! When Broox turned to walk away, I saw the look Hoxton gave him. It was indicative of his hidden animosity. People reveal themselves like that sometimes in unguarded moments."

Morrill lifted his pale eyes to look blandly at Smith.

"I am told I sometimes show a similar bitter resentment on certain subjects, which is really quite frightening, to people who believe me to be . . . always . . . a timid soul!"

"H'm. . . . But let's get back to your leaving camp. Start with the three of you walking out of the mess tent."

"Broox took the lead, carrying the lantern. I walked in the middle. Hoxton brought up the rear . . . Indian file. It was very nasty walking. Raining and muddy. We came straight here, almost without a word. What was spoken is not worth repeating. When we turned in the drive, and the gaunt, huge contours of the place loomed up before us in the flashes of lightning, I felt immediately that premonition of disaster of which I have told you. So strongly did it possess me that it was as though something clamped down around my limbs and made it impossible, for a time, for me to move. Hoxton said: 'Get on, you little white-livered rabbit!'" Morrill paused a moment, then went on:

"Broox called him on that. Broox wasn't a bad sort, you know, and they had something of an altercation. We walked to the front door. The lantern showed it to be a beautiful work of art. Although I am a lover of beautiful things, I got only a great depression from it. We opened the door easily and entered this room. Immediately Broox was in a transport! You see how parts of this structure have the appearance of having been shelled? That corner over there . . . the statue fallen to the floor . . . broken . . . the walls cracked . . . in parts reduced to debris? Of course, that made it an ideal set for a war picture.

"Broox planned to shoot scenes here, and then duplicate the place, in perfect condition, in miniature at the studio, and blow it up . . . matching it all up. Marvelous stuff. It was while Bronx was walking around, making notes, talking enthusiastically about this, that Hoxton made his suggestion."

"Do you know why this place is, and was left, in this condition?" Smith asked.

"No. I feel something strange about it, though! See how exquisitely this seat is carved . . . what workmanship . . . and see, right beside that shattered portion of wall, that beautiful Tiffany window! Set with moonstones and crystal . . . even a small window like that would cost, easily, a thousand dollars!"

"How do you know that is a Tiffany window?"

Morrill smiled as if in apology for displaying knowledge.

"I have seen such windows . . . at Tiffany's . . . my father purchased such a window for a landing in the stairway of our old home."

"Did Broox see Hoxton's expression of hatred . . . if such it was?"

"If he did, he made no sign. After that, Broox said he would look about elsewhere for additional sets. Hoxton said he'd poke about here, and that he'd appreciate Broox getting through with us as soon as possible. Hoxton was a great sleeper, and, too, he was naturally tired after a strenuous day of plowing over those dynamited fields . . . dirty . . . and scratched up from that exploded mine He really, you know, was most uncomfortable, and so was I. In fact, quite fatigued . . . both of us. Broox said he'd not be long. He wanted to get the idea of the main floor here. We both sat down on this seat at first."

"Did you have lanterns? It must have been very dark," said Smith.

"We had only flash-lights. It was very dark. It was horrible! Try sitting in an ordinary dark room that is strange to you . . . and then imagine sitting here . . . with this insidious atmosphere of menace! I really felt, you know, that the place was inhabited by some horrible being . . . or beings! I could see eyes, and feel things breathing against me . . . I spoke of this to Hoxton and he ridiculed me . . . in the insulting, coarse way he had. I had stood a great deal from him . . . and I resolved to make him try out his boasted bravery. I said:

"'If you are so scornful of the impressions I am experiencing, why do you not display some of your own great courage?'"

"How did you expect him to do that?" asked Smith dryly.

Morrill thought a moment.

"I don't know. It was just one of the things people say, you know . . . just a retort that sprang to my tongue through anger."

"What did Hoxton do?"

"He got up and began walking away from me, and said: 'I'm fed up with you, Morrill! There's something rotten about you. You act too much like a woman. I don't like Broox, but I'll be damned if I can stick it with you any longer!'

"I started up after him. I did not want to be left alone in the dark . . . but with one of his behemothan, devilish roars of laughter he snapped off his flash-light and disappeared. I could hear him moving, but when I attempted to find him with my flash, I could not locate him. I came back to this bench and sat. I dared not hold my flash on, for fear of its burning out, and being left without light, except a few matches. I sat here, it seemed for hours . . . scarcely daring to breathe . . . feeling monsters creeping closer and closer."

"You had your gun, Morrill?"

"Yes. I was gripping it. My hands began to drip cold sweat, so that it became uncomfortable to hold it, but I clung to it. Then the lightning commenced again. The thunder reverberated through this malebolge a hundred times magnavoxed like mighty roarings from another world! The lightning flashed so brilliantly through these scintillant windows, I was all but blinded! Then, during one of the flashes I saw a monster . . . a creature with great bristling hairs . . . flaming eyes . . . a mouth as big as a hammock. . . ."

"Oh, come, come, Morrill!"

The actor sighed,

"I do not expect you to believe me. What I saw cannot be described in ordinary language. It was an extraordinary apparition, and I must use words befitting it."

"All right, then . . . go on."

"For a space I stared back at this veritable evil-spirited Chalbroth! Then, with a scream of terror, I jerked up my hand with the revolver and shot!"

Morrill drew out his handkerchief and pressed it against his trembling, perspiration wet mouth.

"That beautiful window was ruined!" he finished naïvely.

Smith looked a moment at the shattered pane and realized that at least this much of his story was true. Someone had certainly shot through the window.

"You said something about Hoxton's playing the organ," he prompted.

"I did not know at first it was Hoxton. Right after I had shot, the chords of Chopin's Funeral March rolled out . . . I heard them between the claps of thunder. . . . It came to me that some supernatural gathering was mourning the passing of one of their kind . . . I had killed it . . . I felt that they would be after me soon. . . .

"After that I sat in a cold sweat of fear in the darkness. Finally Broox and Hoxton returned. I told them of the creature I had seen, and they laughed at me. I showed them the broken window to prove that I must have seen something or I would not have shot. Then Mr. Broox insisted that I give my gun to Hoxton. He said I was nervous and overwrought, and would do myself, or them, an injury. He rehearsed us a little . . . working out certain story situations. Then he said we might go. He wanted to look around a bit more, and write out his script. I refused to return alone."

Morrill seemed to have no embarrassment at this admission, and looked at Smith frankly when he made it. Smith nodded, understanding.

"Hoxton accompanied me back to camp, but would not give me my gun! He wanted to come back here. . . . He said the organ . . . a splendid instrument . . . intrigued him. He desired to play it again."

"I thought you said Hoxton was tired, anxious to go to bed?"

"He was. The only reason I can give for his change of mind is that there must have been a peculiarly exhilarating effect from sitting up in that little room, thundering back in gigantic chords to the thundering storm outside! I can understand that . . . a man with those huge hands . . . powerful muscles, who could encompass those tremendous, majestic chords, might get a great exultation from thus interpreting the masters of the pianoforte!"

Morrill smiled his wistful smile . . . spread his own slender, delicate hands before him, and said regretfully, with his eyes lifted to Smith's:

"That is a pleasure I have never been able to experience."

He was silent a moment and then ended his tale with the simple statement:

"After Hoxton returned I do not know what happened."

"What time did you return to camp?"

"I do not know. I thought I sat here for hours. I did not look at my watch. I went straight to bed."

"You accompanied Randall here this morning, did you not?"

"Yes."

"Where were you between the time Randall left you in this room and the time Clancy found you in the music room upstairs?"

"I was curious to know how Hoxton had gotten out of here so quickly. He would not tell me. Took occasion to make a play upon my own remark about strange beings in the house, and said that the witches took him there! This morning I spent a long time trying to find how he left me so suddenly. How he discovered the trick opening I do not know. I think it must have been by accident."

"Show me," said Smith briefly.

"Certainly." Morrill got up and together they walked to the right wall and toward the great fireplace. It was of Italian marble, beautiful in texture and exquisitely carved.

"I think it was Hoxton's original idea to hide in the fireplace and spring out at me. The fireplace was closed when Randall and I got here this morning. I finally opened it . . . that carved lotus bud there does it . . . I went up the stairway, and found myself in the music room."

Morrill shuddered violently at the memory. Captain Smith saw that the little man's face was gray and tired-looking. It indicated he had been laboring under a tremendous strain. Facing him directly, he said:

"Morrill, there's a gap in your story. What were you doing in this place for hours this morning? Surely you do not expect me to believe you were all that time looking for that lotus bud. It is quite obtrusive . . . one would suspect it almost immediately!"

"Again I feel I will not be understood. Truth sometimes appears so illogical! You will pardon me if I say that I do not think you are the type to understand how I could spend several hours doing what I *was* doing! If you were . . . an artist . . . a musician . . . yes . . . but . . . a detective . . ."

"Never mind whether you think I shall understand or not! *What were you doing?*"

"I was looking at the many beautiful things in this house! Last night I was afraid to do so. To-day, in broad daylight, I felt braver! You know, a person could spend an entire day studying that fireplace alone! I do not mean the hidden doorway, but the remarkable workmanship! The things in this house, Mr. Smith, are not just expensive things. They are masterpieces!"

"H'm . . . it seems to me that your fears for Broox and Hoxton's safety, which were so intense last night, did not impel you to assist in locating the two men this morning, when Randall asked you to help him!"

Morrill's manner became a bit agitated under the cutting sarcasm of Smith's tone.

"Perhaps my nature is a vacillating one. It may be, also, that because I feel things very strongly, I cannot maintain emotions for very long. I do not know. Put it down any way you will. Last night I was horribly upset. This morning I was carried away with the magnificence and artistry of the things I saw here . . . why look, Mr. Smith . . . examine that chandelier . . . it is of gold! The prisms are crystal! Touch them, and they will feel like ice to the hand . . . that is the test! And the exquisite workmanship in those windows . . . the floor upon which you are standing! Have you seen how the woods are mosaicked together? A queer thing, too . . . so many thirteens in the place. Even this great ballroom floor, made up of tiny bits of wood, is laid in a pattern composed of thirteen large designs. I can take you to a room with thirteen fireplaces . . . all in a row . . . and each one a perfect example of its kind! Austrian pipe clay one . . . the bricks of which are joined together so perfectly no jointure is visible to the eye . . . I forgot all about my fears of last night in my joy over these beautiful things. Then . . . when I came across Hoxton . . . and was discovered by your Sir Giblets!"

"Well, it is evident you did do a bit of scouting around, Morrill," Smith admitted slowly. Then, abruptly:

"Where was Hoxton's gun? Didn't he also have a gun when he was working yesterday?"

"Yes. He took it off just before dinner, and it is still in his gun belt down at camp, I believe."

"How did it happen your gun had real bullets?"

"For purposes of close-ups. Mr. Broox wanted to show the bullets striking. We could have tricked it, but it was simple to make this way. Hoxton was an excellent shot, you know."

"And yourself?"

"I've done a bit of target practice," said Morrill, after a hesitation.

"Would you recognize the face you saw last night . . . if you saw it again?"

"Oh . . . certainly . . . but I do not desire to see it again! Not that one! The other . . ." he stopped. He seemed suddenly to be embarrassed. "I should be glad to answer any other question, Captain," he evaded. But Smith pounced verbally on his unfinished sentence.

"What about the other?" he snapped.

"I am quite sure I saw another . . . another . . ."

"Come, come . . . stop hedging and describe this other creature . . . or person, in detail."

"I cannot. I have never seen any human being similar!"

Mentally Smith was tearing his hair and damning this little actor to perdition. But he forced himself to be patient.

"Did Broox or Hoxton see this second apparition?" he asked.

Morrill glanced up with his timid, apologetic look . . . under which Smith sensed a repressed resentment.

"I am accustomed to being ridiculed, Captain. It seems that some of us humans are put on this earth into such inferior molds, and then led into such strange and fantastic situations, that the rest of humanity is continually poking the finger of scorn and contumely at us. I could not invent, did I strain my imagination to the utmost, a tale more fantastic than the one I have just told you. Therefore, I will stay with it. . . ."

He stopped and looked directly into the detective's level gray eyes.

"I assure you that what I saw was neither the abnormal imaginings of a neurotic, neither was I under the influence of an intoxicant . . . nor looking at an extraordinarily projected creation of my own brain. . . ."

"*What . . . did . . . you . . . see . . . and where did you see it?*" demanded Smith, in a voice that was held down to a compelling monotone, and exerting his entire thought influence to will this man into explicitness.

Morrill got up and walked forward several steps. His eyes assumed a fixed gaze as one in a trance. He lifted his arm, stretched it out before him, not pointing, but with the hand opened in an arresting, wondering gesture. He began speaking slowly.

"There . . . passing down that corridor . . . I saw . . . a woman. A glorious woman . . . with face so fair as to be shiningly radiant . . . with countenance so marvelously fashioned and hued, as to seem iridescent. She was going . . . in the direction of the room . . . that room . . . where Broox . . . now lies dead! When I found my voice to call to her . . . she had vanished!"

"Did you see this woman again?"

"No, she did not return."

"*When* did you see her?"

"Just after Hoxton played."

"She was alone?"

"Alone!"

"Morrill, how could you see her in the dark?"

"She carried tapers . . . I saw the wavering gules of light in which she walked . . . she walked in beauty . . . reverently . . . as though to some mystic sacrament!"

"Rot!" Smith exploded, his patience deserting him.

Morrill's voice went down to a wondering whisper.

"Do . . . you . . . believe such a . . . glorious creature could . . . *murder?*" he asked, with his pale eyes pleadingly on Smith.

"I don't know a thing about your heavenly houri, Morrill, except that she's . . . *the bunk!*"

"Come here," said Morrill simply, and showed him where small, daintily shaped foot-tracks had been made on the floor of the passageway.

X

Smith stood just outside the beautifully carved doorway, thinking. Dr. Gittles joined him. For a bit they stood there in understanding silence. Then Smith sighed and said:

"Sometimes, Doc, a fellow does not know which lead to follow! Invariably something turns up, but I dread these still places in the hunt."

"I expect there are times when you don't know whether to sit down, the clues spread out on a table in front of you, all nicely catalogued, as per the fiction detective, or to jab a gun in some one's ribs and shout, 'When did you do the bloody deed?' . . . also as per Diamond Dick!"

"Exactly. Well, I'm hungry. Suppose we take this little bypath down to camp."

As they turned down the shorter path, Smith asked suddenly:

"How soon can you get me the analysis of the stains on Broox's vest?"

"Soon as I can get the vest up to the University of California and back . . . to-morrow maybe, or the day after."

"Will you attend to that right off? Thanks. I suppose you'll want to remove the bodies as soon as possible?"

"When you're through with them, Captain."

"Take 'em along any time. When can I talk to Love?"

The little coroner frowned.

"Got to do it right away? Well . . . sure . . . you would . . . take a look at him after I eat and let you know."

"I just wanted to ask him a couple of questions . . . won't get him worked up, if that's what you're afraid of."

"That's all right. If he lies to you, why don't keep at him . . . and he'll probably lie, you know."

"What makes you think so?"

"Just the funny way that little sister of his kept hovering over him . . . thought maybe he'd get delirious, I think, and say something."

"H'm . . . glad you told me that. What's the wife like?"

The little coroner looked puzzled, then exclaimed perplexedly:

"Damned if I know! The sister was doing the nursing, of course, and every once in a while she'd whisper something to Love's wife about keeping still until she could explain things to her. It struck me you'd like to know that. It seemed to me a bit funny."

"It is," agreed Smith dryly. "Also, I'm mighty glad to know it. Mighty glad!"

The little doctor said, unexpectedly, with a shivery shrug of his shoulders:

"Don't like that place. Gives me the creeps. If I ever was going to have a belief in spirits, that place would inspire it."

"You have made several remarks of that kind, Gittles. You are not, by any chance, trying to sell me an idea there was anything supernatural in the death of those two men?"

The coroner stood still, looked levelly at the other, and said:

"Of course not! The manner in which they were killed precludes such reasoning. Yet one does get impressions, heightened of course by the generally prevalent thought of the little town . . . the belief in a 'haunt' . . . and those impressions sometimes overcome a man's common sense. I was just talking. The place there is empty. Had stood empty for years. The woman who lived in it was . . . well, come on down to my place to-night and I'll give you the whole thing. Come early."

"Thanks. I'll be there if I can possibly make it," he said.

Again they walked on in silence, coming to a spot densely overgrown. It had a dank, unhealthful smell. The doctor commented on this. Smith had to double his tall lean frame as he approached a turn in the path. Before he could straighten he was bumped into forcibly by a red-faced and puffing Clancy, who careened around a turn muttering unintelligibly. Not apologizing, or giving Smith time to speak, he exploded into verbal skyrockets that threatened to gag him.

"D'you know what that little wart is doing? Marching down the hill to camp, like he was Napoleon leading an army! Roaming free as the daisies . . . that dirty little snoop . . . the rotten little blood-letter! And he's got his socks off too, like he was a ballet-dancer or somethin'! And when I . . ."

"Clancy, what is that you are trying to wipe my face with?"

Smith caught the burly sergeant's excitedly gesticulating fat hand and the object it contained, in a firm grip.

"Yeah . . . I was just getting to that. And he was holding that thing in his hand, like it was a posey . . . looking down at it, and telling a story to himself! When I lamps him, I let out a roar . . ."

"Of course you did," interrupted Smith blandly.

Clancy came out of his tale and shot his superior a reproachful glare. His fat jowls quivered a moment, and then he went on:

"I lets out a . . . roar . . . and grabs him. Did he look surprised? I'll say he didn't. You'd think he was just strolling about waiting for me to come along. He starts to shove this here in his pocket, but I was too quick for him. I grabbed it, and I says:

"'None of that! If you've got a gun in there, Morrill, hand it over.'

"What d'you think he does? Looks up at me like an innocent baby with those pop eyes of his, and says:

"'You do not resemble Mr. Smith in the least . . . not in the least . . . do you?' Who the hell ever said I did?"

Dr. Gittles at this point folded up and presented the fat back of his short neck while he shook and chuckled like the famous Br'er Rabbit.

Smith repressed a smile and snapped sternly: "Are you trying to tell me that Morrill attempted to secrete this when you came up to him?"

"Sure. Shoved it in his picket, like I said. So, then, after he makes his speech about me not being a dead ringer for you, I demands, 'Hand it over!' and shoved my gun in his ribs. He hops sidewise, and damn near gets shot in doin' it, then makes me a bow, and says, 'Certainly . . . certainly . . . take this to your master!' . . . your *master*, mind you! . . . 'and say that Mr. Morrill sends him a sign!' Can you beat it? That guy can't button his shirt without making a speech about it!"

"Go on, Clancy," said Smith quietly.

"Then I tells him to come along, that he's been arrested for murder, and he tells me he's as free as the breezes or something like that . . . and knowing you ain't the man to let a prisoner go, if you don't want him to, I barged right up here to see if you was still in your right mind, or not!"

"Clancy!"

Clancy looked down and shuffled his feet, and got red. Then he looked up and burst out earnestly:

"But hell, Chief. Didn't I catch him right over the body! What more could you want? And didn't he tell me in so many words just how he done it?"

Clancy's round blue eyes were fixed on Smith with growing reproach and amazement. He simply could not understand his chief's action, and he was almost tearful in his sincerity that his superior had pulled a bloomer. Smith patted him on the shoulder.

"Listen, son, maybe you don't know that Hoxton was not killed this morning. I thought not. He was killed last night, at approximately the same time Broox was shot! No . . . the solution of the crime, Clancy, is not as simple as you've got it figured. I'm not saying Morrill isn't guilty, or at least involved . . . but what you must understand is that he is just where I want him . . . running around loose. You keep your eye on him from now on, and, *no matter what he does*, let him do it! Get me?"

"Sure . . . yes, sir. Gosh . . . and I thought he was the guy all right! But say, what was he doing up in that room, then?"

"That's a long story, Clancy, and I don't know yet if it's a true one. Did Morrill tell you where he got this bunch of black hair? Did you ask him?"

Clancy's fat face spread into a smile of beaming complacency. Here was once he could deliver the goods.

"I sure did! It was the first thing I demands when I see what it is. I says, 'No back talk or side-stepping now, my man! Where did you get this?' He smiles that cuckoo grin of his and yips like a little lady:

"'You deposited me squarely on top of it, my good fellow, when you so tenderly propped me up against the wall this morning'!"

Clancy stopped, chewed his lips, and then went on slowly, evidently remembering Morrill's exact words with great effort.

"'While I sat there, my head drooped in a swoon, my sad eyes unhappily upon the floor, I observed this . . . like a small, black, and menacing creature from the nether world . . . crouching, bristling, between my quaking knees!'"

Clancy finished with a rush and let out a gusty sigh.

"Gosh, I been saying that over and over all the way up the hill for fear I'd forget it!"

Smith and Gittles laughed in sympathy, and Clancy himself grinned broadly.

"I'm not much on the book-learnin'," he admitted, a little shamefaced; "but that guy's crazy!"

"That's all right, Clancy. You delivered the goods, and that's all I care about," said Smith heartily. The sergeant's round blue eyes glowed happily at the praise.

"Now beat it, and follow Morrill . . . and report to me when he settles somewhere."

"Sure! You betcha!" and Clancy was on his way.

"I take it that fellow's loquacity is only second to his loyalty," said Dr. Gittles, who had gotten pleasure out of the sergeant's beaming countenance.

"Yes. That's why I keep him. That, and the fact that Clancy's hasty blundering sometimes shows me what not to do! I believe he'd die before he'd double-cross me, and that's the best thing I can say of a coworker. Strange, too . . . we have nothing in common—except our trade!"

While he spoke Smith stood in the shadowy, overgrown path, turning over and over, in his hand, the black, false mustache Clancy had given him.

"Does that tell you anything?" Gittles asked.

"I'm trying to isolate it. I've a hazy remembrance of having seen one like it recently. If I can place just where, it might . . . help a lot. Doc, I'll not go with you down to the camp. Eating isn't nearly so important as beating this case. See you later."

"My embonpoint is a matter of years of careful culture," said Gittles, patting his rotund stomach. "I'll cater to it, if you don't mind."

"Not a bit. Sorry I can't indulge in a good hot meal myself."

He watched the little coroner stalk down the path, regretting instantly that he had not asked him to find out about Love's condition before he left.

"Well, I'll talk to one of the three, anyway," he told himself. "It's got to be done."

Catching sight of Gittles around a turn of the path, he called:
"Oh, Git!"

"Yep."

"Would you just as soon step in and see Love before you go? Perhaps I'd better see him as soon as possible."

"Right-o. I'll take a look see and let you know."

Satisfied, Smith turned around and took his way toward the south end of the house.

"Now for it," he said grimly.

XI

A car swung into the drive, stopped at the porch, and Randall got out.

"Say, fella, don't you detectives ever eat?" he called.

Smith stopped.

"Sometimes we do," he said grinning. "But to-day I guess I don't. Sorry, because now that you have mentioned it, I'm as hungry as a bear."

Randall opened the back door of the car and disclosed a tray of steaming food.

"Better get in and sit down. I'd have been here sooner, only I've been running my legs off looking after things. Izzie called up and I've had a hell of a time with him. You know Mr. Cohen, don't you?"

"I do!" said Smith around a piece of chicken, smiling broadly. "Sympathy!"

"Man, I sure need it! He nearly had a fit when I told him about Hoxton . . . God . . . what an awful mess!"

"It is . . . just that!" agreed Smith flatly.

"Is there . . . have you . . . found out anything . . . who did it?"

"Not yet. You mustn't expect miracles, Randall. It takes time to work out things. By the way, you can tell me something."

"I'll help all I can!"

"I know you will. Was Broox, by any chance, an untidy eater?"

"Lord, no. Fastidious!"

"You're sure?"

"Positive! Why . . . what's that got to do with . . . it?"

"I can't say yet," said Smith slowly. "I don't know myself . . . perhaps nothing. Here's another one. Was he fond of fruit . . . did he have any by any chance that last night, or bring any lunch up here to the house with him?"

"He was fond of fruit, but we didn't have any for supper that night and he didn't bring lunch with him. Nothing."

They were silent. Randall watched the detective eat for a bit, then his glance wandered toward the front door of the house. His face sobered and he turned away. Smith, watching, could see that Broox's death was not just a murder to this young man. It was a shock he was unable to shake off. He himself was so accustomed to looking at dead bodies, then putting them immediately out of his mind and getting at the responsible parties, that it sometimes surprised him when people continued to maintain the atmosphere of subdued horror that murders induced.

"The queer thing is, though, really, that a person should not feel as you do," Smith said, speaking his thought aloud.

Randall looked around and said:

"I beg your pardon."

"Nothing, son. I'd like to talk to Miss Love after I eat. Will you go around and ask her if it will be convenient?"

Smith smiled as Randall went eagerly. He waited until he thought he had allowed more than sufficient time to return, then got up and walked slowly around the house toward the south end.

It was the first time he had had a chance to do this, and the strange, jutting contours, apparently planned without rhyme or reason, puzzled him. He stood a long time by that side of the house where the wall was unfinished and the rooms exposed. He saw that the dust of years was accumulated in their corners.

What violence had shattered these walls and what strange state of mind had left them in this condition? He had a fleeting impression that this all might have been arranged for a motion-picture set. He had seen property-men make places look as old as this one. He could not bring himself to believe that any owner would so neglect a place . . . would not even gather up that moonstone as big as a butter pat which had fallen out of that bejeweled window! And would thieves and intruders have left it there, to gather the dirt of the seasons?

The whole thing began to assume the atmosphere of a hoax. Deeper than that was a fleeting impression that kept flashing across his consciousness, leaving him tingling with one of those intangible hunches which had heretofore proved of invaluable aid in unraveling knotty mysteries.

He had been looking off at a long, walled corridor that came from the central part of the house and connected with an oval building set apart, silent and deserted amid dead shrubs and rankly growing weeds.

"H'm," said Smith slowly, looking at the corridor. "Now I wonder why that should affect me like that. It's a lot simpler than some of the other queer things about this place. I wonder . . ."

He gave it up for the present and walked on. Soon his ear caught the low murmur of voices coming from inside the house from somewhere within the room whose window he was just passing. This window, he noticed, was like most of those in the old structure, high up, over the heads of the occupants, for he could not see them. But he recognized Randall's voice and another which he assumed belonged to Beatrice Love.

"Don't lie to me . . . for God's sake! Can't you see that all I want is to help?"

"That boy wants to help everybody," thought Smith, smiling faintly, remembering it had not been five minutes since Randall

had made him the same fervent offer. But now there was pleading in the tones. Then the girl's voice:

"I am not lying. I do not know! I only . . . fear . . ."

"But fear what? What is it? Can't you even tell me that?"

There was a moment of silence. Captain Smith did not give a
thought to the fact that he was eavesdropping. He moved closer,
so as not to miss a single word or inflection.

The girl's voice again:

"I do not want even to say it! It may be all foolishness, and then
. . . how disloyal I would feel, even to have thought such a thing!"

Smith strained his ears and his whole seven senses to detect
any deeper, unspoken significance in her words. Was her fear
really as foolish as she maintained, or did it have some double
meaning? Before he could answer his own question, if indeed he
could at all, a new voice rose high into the argument.

"Why don't you tell the truth, Bee? You know Aloysius is an
idiot! You know he acts like a lunatic the minute he gets a gun in
his hand! If I hadn't stopped him he'd have shot the stomach off
our landlord night before last, and you know it!"

"Alicia!"

"Well, it's the truth!"

"I know . . . but you say things . . . so . . . so . . . people get
such queer impressions!"

"Listen, Bee Love. I say things just like I always have, and
like I always will. And I don't care what kind of impressions
people get, or who gets them! I'm not going to go posing around
here like a select school for girls just because there's a batch of
detectives prowling around! Did Humpty-Dumpty tell you when
your brother will come back to his natural state of idiocy?"

"The doctor said that Mr. Smith might be able to talk to
Aloysius to-morrow morning," replied the girl called Bee, somewhat coldly. "The fact that my brother is your husband might
induce you to speak a bit more respectfully of him," she added.

The other woman laughed. Smith recognized it as a genuine expression of amusement.

"Bee! Bee! Still carrying around the old inhibishes? Because a man is my husband, am I to deny his most conspicuous failings? You know Aloysius is an idiot . . . and so do I. What I mean is, just the kind of an idiot to get mixed up in an insane affair like this! The wonder is he didn't do it a long time ago!"

Silence again. Randall and Bee were evidently talking in low tones to each other, for Smith heard the murmur of their voices. Then the other voice exclaimed: "If that damned detective is going to come, I wish he'd get here and get out again!"

And again Bee reproved her with, "Alicia!"

Smith thought it was high time to present himself, and this he was about to do when he saw Ryan approaching and waited for him. "Hello, Chief! I was looking for you. I've got those prints. They're down to camp. And a love message from Rosenthal."

A grin accompanied the handing over of a telegram from the president of Superior Films.

"Poor old Rosey! I'll bet he's sick to his stomach!"

"You'll be worse than that when you see what he says!"

Smith opened the envelope and read:

Captain of Detectives Smith
With Superior Films Company on Location
Camillio Santa Clara County Calif

Cohen would like to know when you will be through with the extras stop would appreciate wire from you giving some idea of your findings stop he also expresses desire to visit camp and check up expenditures and developments please advise stop regards

Rosenthal

Ryan was still grinning when Smith finished.

"Here's the low down on that, Chief," he said impudently; 'Izzie iss driving me crazy! Already I am sick to my stummick! Vot haff you found out? If you don't get busy and tell me some-things, I vill send Izzie up there to help you find the murderers. I feel like murdering him myself right now. Oi, that fellow!'"

Smith laughed.

"Very good, Ryan. Very good! When you get tired of working for me, I'll recommend you to Rosey for the talkies! Send a wire to him, and tell him to sit tight for another twelve hours."

"How about sending back those extras? Want to say anything about it?"

"I do not! Simply don't mention the subject! That's the most non-come-back-at-able way of stalling, my son! Wait, though . . . put a postscript to that wire. Tell him if he sends Izzie up here, there will be three murders, and for him to take some bicarbon-ate of soda for his stomach."

"Yes, sir," said Ryan, grinning again.

"And, Ryan, some time back I sent Clancy down to Lake's with a bunch of shoes. I was going to let them wait a while, but I want to look at them soon as I get a chance. Take 'em to Skeets and tell him to lock them in the prop box. Wrap them up care-fully, separately, and see that nothing is lost from the bottoms."

"Right-o, Chief. How's she going, anyway? Personally the damned thing's a ring-around-the-rosey to me."

"Rotten, so far," agreed Smith. "Beat it now, son, and get that wire off before that jibbering monkey jumps up here. Every time I see Rosenthal handle that fellow Cohen without choking him, I am reduced to a state of speechless admiration!"

Ryan grinned.

"Like I am at you and Clancy!"

"Every man has his talents, Ryan," said Smith shortly, for he brooked no inter-office backbiting. "I suspect Cohen serves

Rosenthal in much the same way I find Clancy invaluable. On the way to Lake's office stop and get some lunch. I expect you're hungry."

"I'll tell the world. My stomach thinks my throat's been cut! Shall I come back here afterwards, or what?"

Before Smith could answer, the door to the Love quarters burst open and a woman walked out. Smith's first realization was that she was strikingly beautiful, and his next that she reminded him of an aeroplane! Her brows had the same level uptilt to them as the wings, and she herself had the same suggestion of standing ready to swoop straight up, or straight down, without any decorative maneuvers with which, manlike, he credited the entire female human family. There was a breeziness about her voice when she spoke . . . free as the north wind of coquetry, and as biting.

Smith's tardy realization was that she must be Love's wife. Certainly she was not the one spoken of as Bee . . . Yes . . . those were the same clear, sarcastic tones whose unflattering remarks were so unevadingly accented by a ringing, bell-like quality.

"Are you that Captain Smith for whom everyone's been stepping sidewise?"

Smith bowed.

"I am Alicia Love, and that poor sap lying in there with his entire lid blown off is my husband, Aloysius."

Somewhat prepared by his eavesdropping for the amazingly graphic exaggerations peculiar to this woman, Smith still wondered curiously how on earth the wife of the wounded man could speak in this fashion . . . when, as yet, her husband might be near to death, or . . . to the gallows! Swiftly she was talking again, answering his inanely murmured:

"Oh . . . I see . . . you are Mrs. Love."

"Yes, and I'm not proud of it! But that doesn't mean that I'm going to sit down and weep, and let a bunch of unimaginative pavement-pounders arrest Aloysius!"

"But my dear woman, no one has attempted to arrest your husband!" He did not stop to interpret the difference between pavement-pounders and detectives . . . hadn't time to, in fact.

"I suppose you did not send that little bald-headed coot in to see if you could talk to Loish. I suppose you merely intended making a social call . . . afternoon tea . . . or something like that. And do you suppose I do not know that everyone within ten miles of the scene of this tragedy will be considered a possible murderer? Aloysius . . . a murderer . . . rot! Why, the poor shrimp hasn't nerve enough to be one!"

"Really! You don't seem to have a very high opinion of the masculine half of your domestic partnership!" said Smith, beginning to be annoyed and also a bit bewildered.

"Has *your* wife?"

A loud guffaw from back of them punctuated this pert rejoinder. They turned to see Clancy, who had come up unexpectedly.

"Who's that baby elephant?" Alicia Love demanded immediately.

Smith was entertained by the way Clancy's grin was absorbed in a flush of indignation.

"That is Clancy, one of my assistants," he said chokingly.

"He looks like it!"

She paused for a moment, and Smith saw she was filling her lungs for a lengthy attack. Before he could think of anything to forestall it, she opened fire.

"Now don't protest your intelligence! It won't do any good! Just tell me, if you can, what you three have been doing all day! Has anyone been arrested? No . . . of course not! Right now the murderer . . . a fiend . . . might be roaming around loose in that insane old pile . . . waiting to spring out at any one . . . to murder them! Of all the fool . . . the *brainless* ways of going at things! A hundred murderers could be hiding in that house *this minute* . . . a hundred against you three!"

"I really think you are exaggerating a bit, my dear lady!"

Smith's voice was quite polite, but his gray eyes were glinting.

"Can a horrible thing such as happened in there *be* exaggerated? What matter if a hundred men . . . or one . . . did it? A fiend who could do that once, could, and would, do it again!"

"Certainly," Smith agreed. "Believe it or not, you know, we are trying our best to locate the murderer . . . or murderers!"

"And the best way you can find is talking to a man who's on the point of brain fever! *I'll* tell you all you want to know about my husband."

"I'll bet she will!" Clancy muttered to Ryan. "Lord, let's fade . . . the boss is in for it."

They started oozing out of the picture, but Alicia stopped them instantly.

"You stop right where you are! Every one of you is going to hear this! I'm not going to be made out a liar later!"

"I assure you—" Smith attempted coldly, but was overwhelmed before he finished.

"You want to know about Aloysius. Well, I'll tell you . . . and I'll tell you the truth! He's a fool. God knows what he did with his gun. I haven't been able to find it. I suppose you have it locked up as proof positive he shot this man Broox! That doesn't make any difference, and it doesn't *prove anything*. I admit he had a gun. His sister knows it. He started out of the room we were in to follow that dog Calamity. That dog's name ought to tell you something. He's always getting into trouble. My husband is crazy about him. Every time I see him with that pup, I'm glad we never had a baby. Now listen, Mr. Detective, my husband *did* start out with a gun last night. Probably he shot something with it. But he's not a murderer, and he didn't have any reason for killing that man Broox, anyway. . . ."

"Mrs. Love, will you be kind enough to tell me how long you have been in this house?"

"Too long to suit me! Last night we got caught in the storm and came in here for shelter. The car's coils were wet. Bee and Aloysius thought they heard noises and kept dashing in and out like maniacs. I went to my cot and went to sleep. I got up this morning, and Aloysius had disappeared! Alicia said he went after Calamity. That fool dog had been prancing around that nutty room we were in ever since we came, looking stiff-legged and pretending he smelled burglars.

"I can't tell you when my husband left, nor how, nor where he went, because *I don't know!* Maybe Bee can, but she's acted so silly about my talking about the thing at all, that I haven't asked her. All I know is that Aloysius went after Clammy, and that he had a gun, and that he was brought back this morning with his poor lonely seven hairs shot off, and . . ."

Smith was surprised to see that her sea-blue eyes were swimming in tears her pert remarks belied.

"So . . . you *are* afraid, after all . . . that your husband may be found guilty?" he said quietly.

"I'm not afraid," she denied instantly. "How can one be guilty when he doesn't mean to kill anyone? And what right has a fool director roaming around a deserted house at midnight, anyway? He ought to be shot!"

"If your husband had shot your landlord the other night, would you have made the same contention?"

She looked at him and the quick angry color swept into her face. "So . . . *eavesdropping! You would!*"

"Certainly," he admitted frankly, then, his tone sobering:

"Being a detective isn't so much fun . . . or so easy, you know."

He smiled with that well-known intimate expression in his voice, eyes, and mouth. Alicia caught herself smiling back, but as quickly checked herself.

"Mrs. Love, I'd far rather have you on my side than against me. Surely you must know I do not wish to pin this on your husband, but . . . just as surely you must understand that if I find clues leading us to suspect he killed Broox, or Hoxton, or both . . . I will follow them down! Justice demands it . . . and my profession! Why don't you put that clever brain of yours to work to help solve this mystery . . . unless you are afraid . . . of running into the murderers . . . or something."

"I'm only afraid of he-cows, intoxicated automobile drivers, and fools! That's why I'm afraid for Aloysius. Give that man a gun and put him in a place like this, with a lot of strange creaks and groans, and he'd go into action like Custer's cavalry!"

Smith laughed. He was beginning to enjoy this woman's appalling frankness, even if he did wonder to what extent it could be trusted.

"Would you recognize your husband's gun if you saw it?"

"I don't want to recognize it. Throw the thing away . . . it'll only be the sixteenth pistol I've gotten rid of since I married him!"

"But . . . but . . . my dear woman, can't you realize that this is a different matter? This is serious!"

"You're right it's serious! What *you* can't realize is, *how* serious! For the rest of my natural existence I have to live with a man who's a hero!"

"A hero! I'm afraid I don't follow you!"

"You wouldn't . . . but any wife would! If that poor boob of mine escapes hanging, he'll have that kitchen cram-jammed with fiends, all trying to overpower him and carve him to bits! Before he's told that story twice, he'll have himself leaping around like Douglas Fairbanks doing a *D'Artagnan*, laying out varlets right and left!"

"Maybe it won't be so bad, after all," smiled Smith, anxious now to terminate the interview, for he had accidentally put his hand into his pocket, where it encountered the black mustache.

"If you find out anything you think would help, please let me know. And now, will you excuse me?"

"Certainly. Run along!" she said listlessly.

For the first time Alicia Love's voice was not a triumphant denunciation! She remained standing, watching the three men walk away, and if she dashed the frustrated tears from her eyes with a quick, impatient gesture, they did not see her!

"What did you come back so soon for, Clancy?"

"Morrill's sitting in his tent painting pictures. He asked Skeets not to let anyone bother him," said Clancy in disgust.

"Painting pictures! H'm . . . is he an artist?"

"I don't know. I'm just telling you what he's doing."

"Well, go back and hang around. When he gets through, try to slip in and get a peek at what he's been up to," said Smith.

"And, Ryan, remember those boots!"

"Right, sir! I'm on my way!"

Smith turned back to the house, the look of the hunter on his face, and his right hand closed about his revolver. He opened the big front door and went through the ballroom, directly toward the kitchen.

"Unless I'm much mistaken," he muttered, "that's where I saw it!"

XII

"Stick 'em up!"

Smith jabbed his gun barrel in the guard's ribs. He was not taking any chances. As he did so, he thought, whimsically, that had Morrill been a witness, he might have reversed his opinion of Clancy's not bearing resemblance to him.

Obediently the guard's hands went over his head, but not without a curse, and a menacing stiffening of his torso against the gun barrel. . . .

"What the hell do you want?" he snarled.

"Not much . . . only . . . this!"

With the last word Smith caught the man's heavy black mustache and ripped it off.

"Ha! I thought so!" he exclaimed triumphantly. "Now rub your lip if you want to . . . but don't start anything!"

Glaring, the guard rubbed his lip vigorously and sneezed. Smith waited calmly until he had finished. When he spoke, his voice was as hard as nails.

"Now come clean!"

"Say, you make me sick! What a hot dick you are, spending your time taking make-ups off a picture company! You didn't think I *grew* that thing, did you? If it's crêpe hair you're after, go down to camp and peel the beards off about five hundred o' those guys. They're playing ex-soldiers, mister, and they ain't supposed to have beauty parlors in the trenches! You could add a ton to that little bunch of hair if you wanted to! I hate awfully to disappoint you," he added with nasty-toned sarcasm, "but your ignorance is sure the biggest part of you!"

"Yes," said Smith softly. "And you might be interested to know, if need be, I would do . . . just that . . . rip the false hair off of every one of those thousand extras . . . to find out where *this* . . ." he reached into his pocket and drew out the bunch of hair Clancy had given him, "came from! To find . . . another . . . just like it, my man! But I have not had to go to that trouble. I have what I want right here!"

"I told you if it was false hair, you come to the right place. I c'n match you again!"

The guard reached down into his own pocket, ignoring the increased pressure of the gun muzzle as he did so, and pulled out a third false mustache, exactly like the other two.

Smith took it and looked at it steadily. He was thinking intently. He had only glimpsed the men down at camp, but he could not remember having seen any wearing a mustache . . . beards, yes, and a growth of straggly hair on the upper lips . . . but not one with a defined mustache. The guard watched him out of sullen eyes, and Smith, surprising him by glancing up suddenly, thought he detected in them also the introspective look of rapid mental activity.

"He's concocting a story," he told himself, and allowed the man time to perfect it. The guard gave a short, contemptuous laugh.

"Why, say, mister, it ain't no crime to be wearing make-up. That's what we guys are up here for! I got on grease-paint, too . . . you never can tell when you're going to be called to work in a picture. Maybe the director says he's going to play golf, but if you go counting on it, he's back rarin' to go! After you've worked in one or two picture locations you know enough to keep your make-up on all the time. Go down and ask the rest of the guys!"

"Why did you choose to wear a mustache instead of a beard, like the rest of them?"

"So I'd stand out like a sore thumb, that's why, fella! Same reason Harold Lloyd wears trick glasses, an' a lot of flappers pull some fool stunt on Hollywood Boulevard, so's to get in the papers! It ain't talent they wants in pictures. It's fame! If I was to go down Hollywood Boulevard swingin' a skunk by the tail, I'd get locked up for it, sure, but I'd stand a better chance of gettin' a contract in a comedy company on Poverty Row than if I was carryin' posies. I got to earn my living, fella."

"I see," said Smith dryly. "Was it part of your publicity campaign to drop this mustache beside Broox's body?"

For a moment the guard remained silent. Whether Smith had surprised him or not he could not tell. What he did sense, though, was that the man's brain was shuffling decisions to admit the truth or evade.

"Come clean! It will be better for you in the end," he warned sternly.

"Well, then . . . all right. I *did* drop it in there! When I was helping to carry out that wounded guy! When I come back I went in and looked for it, but I didn't have time to find it before I heard somebody comin'. I figgered it wouldn't do me no good messin' around in that room . . . would look bad . . . and I wasn't goin' to let myself in for having the bracelets put on me, and bein' accused of . . . murder."

"I see. Do those mustaches drop off so *easily* very often?"

The man shot him a speculative look before he said:

"Depends on how old they are. If I was goin' to be in a close-up, of course I'd have put it on a hair at a time . . . make it right on my face. But in them long shots the old fashioned ready-made kind is good enough. Sometimes the glue gets old, and they don't stick. I ain't no Chester Conklin, that can just jab 'em at his mouth and hold 'em there by curlin' his lip around 'em."

"What is your name?"

"John Donovan."

"All right, Donavan. Stay here until you are relieved."

Without another word Smith turned away. His brisk bearing belied the discouragement he really felt. He had thought he had a hot clue . . . and yet he could not find a questionable angle to the man's story. He had seen enough of the making of motion pictures to know there was truth in what the man said.

Yet as Captain Smith walked down the hill from the old house to camp, he had the uncomfortable feeling that he had been hoodwinked. He thought back over his interviews with Alicia Love, with the man at the door, with Morrill.

He thought over the varied yet all equally ridiculous stories these three had told. Morrill with his ravings . . . his quotations and his visions of beautiful women. Alicia with her contradictions, her crisp wise-cracks. Donovan with his excuse of wanting to stand out from this crowd by means of a black mustache!

Smith felt that they were all three, and the uncanny house with them, poking fun at his stiff back as he marched down the hill. He did not enjoy the sensation. He realized that coldly snapped commands . . . the grim-jawed, steely voiced methods of the man-hunter . . . are ridiculous if they are not productive.

One human hunting down another . . . it was all a silly business in the eyes of the Lord, anyway, no doubt. A firm believer in the inherent instinct to kill, he thought that it was simply mere happenstance that he himself had not dealt the blow which had turned Hoxton's head into a pulp . . . that he himself was not desperately concocting fantastic stories to conceal his guilt!

So ruminating, he walked into a verbal conflict that raged from one side to the other of the main road between the tents.

Skeets Williams on the one side, waist deep in a conglomeration of army equipment, perspiring, worrying puttees and stacks of guns like an agitated terrier . . . and Randall on the other side, pad and pencil in hand, his weary nervousness at the breaking-point, but held in check so that only a good look into his brown eyes revealed his actual mental brain-storm.

Skeets straightened up, both arms bulging with a miscellany of articles, his shock of hair plastered, sweat-wetted, to his forehead. He shook his head and then raised one elbow to rub his nose.

"Listen, Randall, I don't give a damn what you say," he declaimed heatedly, "they's only nine ninety-nine!"

"There's a thousand!" Randall came back with somewhat of Abraham Rosenthal's imperturbability.

"They's only *nine ninety-nine!*" shouted Skeets, exasperated beyond endurance. Then, as Randall stared coldly at him, he started to sputter his reasons. Randall caught sight of Smith.

"Be with you in a minute . . . soon as I flatten out this dumb-bell," he said in a perfectly audible aside.

"Don't try to tell me my business, fella. My list says one thousand, and that's all they is to it. You got to dig up one thousand outfits, or pay for the missing! If you got any more to say, tell it to Cohen."

"Oh, my Gawd!" Skeets wailed at that. "Listen, Randall, honest to God, I started out with nine ninety-nine, and they's nine ninety-nine here! I'd rather lose a week's salary than to talk to Izzie. Can't I fix it up with you?"

"You can . . . not!"

They stood glaring at each other. Skeets was a good property-man. He had personally seen that every one of the men turned in their accouterments; had checked up all articles of their equipment, had examined everything to see if its condition matched up with the damage that might be expected from the field shooting—and no more!

The poor lad's back had a place in it that was pretty sore, from rising and bending, rising and bending, nine hundred and ninety-nine times multiplied by the number of articles in each individual outfit. This, together with nine hundred and ninety-nine questions, excuses, and demands from the mob of extra men. On the other hand, Randall had been having a hard time over the telephone with Izzie. Smith said curiously:

"Why the battle of the Marne?"

"The poor sap over there can't account for an outfit, and he thinks he's going to put one over on me."

"Say, I've took a lot from you, Randall, but you can't call me a liar!" yelled Skeets, immediately getting a bit white.

Smith felt sorry for the lad. He could see he was about at the end of his rope, physically. He was sorry for Randall, also earnest and honest . . . and worried.

"Why don't you check 'em again," he suggested.

Neither one answered, just turned a discouraged gaze on the collection. Then Smith remembered, and smiled.

"Calm down, boys. The missing outfit is on that guard up at the house."

"Oh, good gosh!" said Randall, relieved and a bit shamed simultaneously.

Skeets did not speak for a moment, then he burst out:

"But say, listen! I only had nine ninety-nine when I started . . . and I got 'em *now!* How do you feature that?"

"Skeets, I got to apologize," said Randall solemnly. "They sent a fellow out to take the place of that fellow they fired. I picked him up on Cahuenga. I clean forgot to tell you, what with everything else on my mind So you see, with that guy up there, it makes the thousand I got on my list!"

"That's all right, Randall," Skeets returned, immediately mollified. Then, starting to speak again, he stopped with a muttered exclamation, and stood frowning, evidently thinking intently.

Coming to a decision, he leaped over the pile of stuff and grabbed Smith by the coat lapels His hands were shaking visibly.

"Listen, Mr. Smith! I betcha I know who killed Mr. Broox!"

"Yes? Tell me!"

"That guy that busted him on the jaw at the studio before we left. I'll bet he went out to the pass, and made up a story about Hank sending him out there . . . gosh, Randall, you ought to know Hank better'n that . . . he wouldn't be that good to us! And then . . ."

"Just a minute, son. Let's get the story straight from the beginning. Better let Randall tell me." Smith patted Skeets's thin shoulder and turned to the assistant director.

"I guess Skeets knows more than I do," said Randall. "I only heard that one of the thousand men was fired, and then when I was out on the pass a man stopped us and said that Hank had phoned him to meet us there, and told him to get his outfit at the Western Costume Company, to match up what we'd rented of them."

"Yeah, and I'll bet Hank don't know a darned thing about it. I'll bet it's the guy who pretty near killed Mr. Broox! MacDougal picked him up and threw him out. Randall wasn't there, but I guess you heard about it, didn't you, Randall?"

"No, I didn't, Skeets. All I know is that Hank sings out just as we were leaving that we were one man short. Didn't have time to tell me why. Then that fellow stops me on the pass, and I just take him on. Gosh, I had so darned much else to think about I never gave it a second thought!"

Skeets turned to Smith, who was listening intently.

"This guy was an ex-soldier. He tells Broox that he knows him . . . and then he up and busts him in the jaw! Broox says that the fellow's cuckoo from shell-shock, and they throw him out, and nobody thinks any more about it, but I'll bet dollars to doughnuts . . ."

"Randall, did that man you picked up give you his name?"

"Yes. Let's see . . . it began with a D, I think."

"Was it John Donovan?"

"Sure, that's it! But how did you know?"

"Skeets, did this man at the studio call Broox by name?"

"Naw. Got him all mixed up with another guy named Jones he used to know in the army."

Smith and Randall exchanged significant glances.

"Skeets, would you know the man if you saw him?"

"Maybe. I ain't saying, because I was so darned busy, and they was a thousand of 'em . . . and . . . well, I wouldn't want to swear to it, but maybe I would."

"All right, Skeets. Now you go over to Donovan's tent. Can you locate it?"

"Sure. We got 'em parked in fours, and their tent numbers and names on a list."

"Good. You go over and search it. Tell his tent-mates to stay in camp. Soon as Ryan gets here from the village, tell him to take charge of them, and anything you find in Donovan's equipment or in the tent that looks suspicious. You'll find real bullets . . . take good care of 'em."

"He ain't got no real bullets. I only gave the extras blanks," said Skeets.

"You look, just the same. You'll find them," said Smith quietly. "Randall, have you seen Clancy?"

"Yes. He's sitting over there a little ways from Morrill's tent."

"Will you ask him to come here? . . . and oh, Skeets!"

"Yes, sir."

"Where's that bundle Ryan asked you to take care of for me?"

"In my prop box, sir. I'll get it right away."

"Thanks. I'll come along to your tent. I want to work in there."

"Make yourself at home, sir."

A few seconds later Smith looked up from a row of up-bottomed, muddy-soled boots. He was digging carefully at the sole of one. Clancy came and stood silently by the table, knowing better than to interrupt his chief just now. He knew that look on Smith's face.

"Clancy . . . go up to the house and get that guard . . . if he's there! Take your gun, and . . . *bring me your man!*"

"You betcha!"

Clancy slipped out. It was really amazing how silently and swiftly the big fellow could move when occasion demanded. Smith waited, content. He knew if Donovan was there, Clancy would bring him in. Of course . . . there was the probability that Donovan was *not* there. In that case it was merely a matter of tracking him down. Randall came in.

"Do you think you've got the man?"

"Look at your list, Randall, and tell me the name of the man that was scratched off . . . the one they threw out at the studio . . . if you can."

"Sure. Back in a minute."

When he returned, Smith was examining with great satisfaction a small piece of matted mud and paper he had just removed from a boot bottom. He began carefully picking out the paper and smoothing the bits open and flat with his thumb-nail. Randall looked over his list and found the canceled name.

"It's Duncan. James Duncan," he said.

"I thought it would be something like that," said Smith quietly. "When a man suddenly has to invent an alias, Randall, he invariably retains his real initials. I don't know why. Perhaps he thinks by sticking close to his real name he will throw the police off the track. It's been done so often, you'd think they would realize it is a dead give-away. But there is a stupid, an animal-like streak in criminals . . . or they would not be criminals. The James Duncan whose name you have down on that list, and who hit Broox at the studio that morning, is the John Donovan you picked up on the road. He disguised himself with a false mustache and gave me a nice little song and dance as to why he was wearing it. I have no doubt that we will find he has also stained his skin . . . perhaps dyed his hair. Anyway, he got by Skeets, who didn't recognize him. Not strange, though, in a bunch of a thousand men."

"Gosh . . ."

"When Serge picked up men to guard the body of Broox, this man put himself in his way so that he would be chosen as one of them. He maneuvered so as to be placed by the door. . . ."

"How do you know?"

"Combination of circumstances . . . very simple," smiled Smith. "He went into the room where Broox lay, just as soon as he thought he would not be seen. He was taking a big chance . . . and he knew it. He did not stay long . . . but he got what he wanted!"

"What did he want?" asked Randall eagerly.

"He told me he wanted his false mustache. What he was really looking for was his gun . . . the one with which Broox was shot! That's why he went back this morning. He knew the gun would be a dead giveaway. Something scared him away last night, so that he left it! See that piece of paper? That came off his boot. Now watch and I'll show you where it came from."

Smith took a folded piece of typewritten paper from his pocket. Carefully, bit by bit, he fitted the torn segments into the place where a portion of the sheet had been torn away. Then he looked up triumphantly.

"Matches, doesn't it?"

"It sure does! And I know where you got that paper! It came off Mr. Broox's script . . . the one he was working on that night up there."

"Correct."

"And that dirty — tramped on it when he went in there and killed my director!"

"He *certainly* tramped on it. You can positively identify this sheet of paper as belonging to Broox's script, if it becomes necessary, can you? Not that I think it will ever be necessary, inasmuch as I can prove that this piece from which it was torn was in that room when, and before, Broox was killed."

"I could identify it, if any of the type could be cleared up. Broox had the original copy. All the rest are carbons."

"Fine. That gives us double proof, if we need it . . . which we won't. I cannot exactly understand why the man would lose his gun, or drop it . . . but on the other hand, I know he was in there this morning . . . and the only thing not accounted for . . . at least the outstanding thing . . . is one missing gun. For some reason, or in some way, that man lost it . . . and went back for it this morning. He must have!"

"But, Mr. Smith, what did he want to kill Mr. Broox for? Gosh . . . everybody liked him . . . I never heard anything against him."

"You had never heard, until I told you, that his real name was Jones, either, had you, Randall?"

"That doesn't mean anything. Why, there's hundreds of men in pictures using fictitious names. Jones isn't a very high-hat tag to put after 'Superior Films Director,' is it?"

"I admit that . . . however . . ."

"Say, is Clancy going to bring that guy down here?"

"Yes . . . if . . . he's there to bring!"

The assistant director's face set into grim lines, and he clenched his fists at his sides.

"All I ask . . . is just to get a chance . . . just a *chance* . . . to work that bozo over . . . the dirty —," he said through taut lips. "The damned murderer!"

XIII

It took just five minutes for word to travel via underground that the red-faced, fat sergeant of police had been sent up to the old house to arrest an extra man named Donovan, who was on guard there. Little groups of ex-soldiers began to gather, talking, drifting toward the tent where Captain of Detectives Smith sat waiting.

"Huh . . . fat chance they've got of finding that bird there! D'yu s'pose he's goin' to sit on his behind and wait for 'em to come and get him? Not if I'm any judge of human nacher, he ain't!"

The speaker spat into the dust of the road and wiped his mouth with the back of his hand.

"Say, wasn't he in your tent, fella?"

"Yeah . . . and he's a hard egg! Sociable as a clam. Came up here with his make-up on, and too damned lazy to take it off! Wore it to bed."

Skeets Williams stopped stacking equipment long enough to yell:

"Say, you guys . . . didn't I tell you to stay put?"

Donovan's three room-mates, who had been edging along with the crowd, stopped and grinned.

"Keep your shirt on, kid. We ain't goin' nowhere!"

"I don't care where you're goin' . . . don't go!"

"All right, all right, sonny, if it makes you that nervous!"

"I ain't near as nervous as you guys are goin' to be if Ryan has to chase around to find you. You git back in that tent and stay there, like I said!"

It gave Skeets, property-man, a thrill to be ordering men around the way Randall, assistant director, did. Maybe Rosenthal would get wind of his part in solving this mystery and promote him! He started whistling happily as he worked.

"Hello, Williams. Where's my boss?"

It was Ryan.

"Over there. And say, wait till you hear what's broke! Anyway, you go over to that tent over there. They's three birds in there and you take charge of 'em. Wait a minute." Skeets dug down in his pocket.

"I found these here real bullets under Donovan's pillow. You take these bullets and those three men, and you dust over to my tent and tell Mr. Smith that outside a box of make-up, same's all extras use, with sixteen different kinds of thing-a-ma-jigs in it for type make-ups, they wasn't anything else that looked suspicious. And you tell Smith, too, that every ham actor in the game carries more false hair and wigs and stuff around than Lon Chaney ever owned in his life. So that ain't . . ."

He stopped, suddenly conscious of Ryan's twinkling eyes.

"Yes, Your Honor, and what next, Your Honor, sir?" teased Ryan, pulling his forelock. Skeets immediately got red and flustered.

"I wasn't trying to get smart, Mr. Ryan, honest. Mr. Smith told me to tell you, and I was just doin' it, like he said. But wait till I give you the low down! We got the murderer!"

Ryan's bantering mood disappeared. His brown eyes began to glow.

"Say that again!"

"Sure. Clancy's bringing him down any minute!"

"Who is he?"

"Calls himself Donovan. Extra man. Got him on guard up at the dump there!"

"H'm . . ." said Ryan, in Smith's best manner.

"And who do you think app . . . apprehended him, mister? *I* did!" announced Skeets in solemn, convincing triumph.

"Atta boy! Are you sure that's all Captain Smith told you to tell me. Every little thing?"

"Yep."

"All right. Thanks." And Ryan was on his way. Skeets resumed his whistling, one eye cocked for the return of Clancy and his prisoner.

Not one of the anticipatory audience made a move as Clancy herded his man to Williams's tent. But the accusing eyes of the crowd interpreted the shrieking silence unmistakably—

"Murderer!"

"Murderer!"

"Murderer!"

The man must have heard the soundlessly whispered condemnation, but did not look to right or left.

He kept his eyes sullenly, on the ground, even until he was halted directly in front of Smith.

"Gawd, Chief," said Clancy, "I never saw such a brassy bunch o' murderers!"

"Have any trouble, Clancy?"

"Naw! He was smoking a cigarette like he was sitting in his own drawing-room!"

"All right, Clancy. You got your man. Just stand by, now."

Smith leaned back in his chair and studied Donovan. He saw a countenance that matched . . . yet, with some indefinable difference, contradicted . . . the black, bristling mustache.

And while he looked, so did everyone who could crowd in front of the open-faced tent. There was no noise, no comment. Not a snicker or a cough.

Skeets was pale with suppressed emotion. He had never before been so close to a murderer . . . or to catching one! Ryan's eyes were riveted on Smith . . . making an indelible impression on his mind of his superior's every expression, every slightest muscular or nervous movement. Clancy stood with his elephantine legs spread apart and watched Donovan, praying the guy would start something so he could express his opinion of murderers in general by slamming him viciously on the jaw.

Serge, the cameraman, alone seemed utterly indifferent. But that was Serge's way. From such lazy indifference he might literally jump into the middle of a situation as though he had been sitting over it like a cat over a rat-hole!

Donovan's eyes took cognizance of the newspaper covering the objects on the table. His mouth twitched.

"Your name is not John Donovan . . . but James Duncan," said Captain Smith quietly. "Isn't that so?"

"What of it? I ain't the first to take a stage name."

Snickers relieved the tension of the crowd. Donovan chewed his lip savagely. Somebody called sarcastically:

"Me and John Barrymore!"

"Close that tent-flap, Ryan," said Smith immediately. "Get Williams in here first, though."

While Ryan was doing this, Smith continued to study the man. Finally he lifted up one half of the opened newspaper and drew out a clean towel and a jar of theatrical cold cream and handed them to Donovan.

"Remove your make-up, Duncan," he said. "I imagine you get that Oriental slant to your eyes by pulling them up with fish skin? Peel it off. If you have putty in your nose, take it out. Let's get a real look at you!"

Donovan sullenly smeared on the cream and wiped it off, removing the saffron-hued grease-paint with it.

"That ought to be shade about number fifteen, making my deductions from Juvenile-Hero-Flesh which I know to be number four," said Smith.

"Any ham'd know that. Only it isn't fifteen, wise guy!" snarled Duncan.

"I don't happen to be a ham. That's why I'm proud of my knowledge concerning theatrical makeup. It is a subject, I have found, that holds universal appeal . . . because it is the next thing to the footlights . . . and the camera! Play-acting is the most fascinating game in the world. You may not know it, Duncan, but that is why criminals find a certain thrill in disguises and aliases!"

Duncan did not answer, but went to work on his nose. Smith's eyes lighted.

"H'm . . . so that *was* a false proboscis! I thought so. You overdid it a bit, Duncan. It is not likely a man of your set-up and facial bone structure would have such a tremendously broad, flat nose!"

Duncan sneered.

"You're not so smart as you think you are. I've seen all kinds of noses on all kinds of faces."

Smith smiled, watched him remove the false nose, and dig two balls of putty, the size of two peas, from his nostrils. Through each ball was stuck a length of straw, about a quarter of an inch long. Smith knew these openings gave Duncan all the air he had breathed since he set out from Hollywood.

"It's amazing to me, Duncan," he observed, "how much you fellows will suffer . . . for your . . . ah . . . art!"

Duncan did not answer, but busied himself cleaning off the last bits of his false nose.

"That's good enough. Now take off that wig," Smith ordered. "Give it to me," he added, as Duncan obeyed.

"Ah, I *see*. So that's the way you fellows change the shapes of your heads! See this, Ryan! Not a wig that fits the head, but a wig on a head—a form of its own . . . a lump in it. Very clever. I must admit that changing the shape of the head does more to change a person's appearance . . . than . . . a false mustache."

He studied the man in front of him, shorn of all aids to disguise, with curious interest.

He saw the man's skin was pallid . . . pasty . . . that there were pinched lines deeply indented from the nose to the mouth . . . that there was a look such as only one experience puts in a man's eyes! As the years slipped by, and the world conflict slid farther and farther back into the pages of history, Smith found it more and more difficult to meet that look in his fellow-man's countenance! He found it more and more difficult to justify the suffering that had bred it with the fast-fading, doubtful glories of war! His first impulse was to put out his hand, touch the man's shoulder humbly, and say: "I'm sorry, old man."

Instead, he said, quietly:

"Shell-shocked. Gassed?"

"Yes."

"Williams, step up here! Is this the man who assaulted Mr. Broox at the studio?"

Skeets licked his lips nervously, and his Adam's apple slid up and down his thin throat.

"Yes . . . yes, sir. That's . . . that's him," he said, feeling as though he were putting the noose around Duncan's neck. Somehow, the pride in his accomplishment seemed to have faded out.

"Certain, Williams?"

"Yes, sir!"

"All right. Now Duncan, alias Donovan, where did you first meet Captain Jones?"

"In France. I was in his company."

"And from your tone, and your elaborate disguise, effected in order to follow him up here, I take it you had a grudge against him?"

"You're damned right I did!"

"Did you assault Captain Jones at the studio that morning?"

"I tried to kill him." Duncan stared defiantly at him. "They threw me out!"

"And when you did not succeed, you went to the Western Costume Company, or some other costume company . . . I can very easily check up on that, you know . . . rented a costume, and lied to Randall later on the road. He took you on. You came up here, waited your chance to get Jones, or Broox as these men know him, alone. When that opportunity presented itself, you did just what you had planned to do . . . you shot him!"

As he spoke, with cold finality, Smith's eyes turned icy. Perhaps in their gray gleam Duncan saw the glint of the handcuffs, the cold, gray walls of the prison, the stark scaffolding of the gallows, under a cold gray dawn!

"I didn't kill him! I tell you I didn't kill him!"

His voice rose to a scream, so suddenly, that Clancy let out a grunt of surprise. Those outside heard him, and their heads jerked sidewise with that little spasmodic twist as their staring eyes turned toward one another. Captain Smith did not move, made no sign that Duncan's abrupt and startlingly emphatic denial had impressed him. His calm voice went on, implacably:

"If you did not kill him, then why did you go back to get your gun . . . to remove incriminating evidence?"

"I didn't. I told you why I went back!"

Smith's face became more stern:

"Duncan, *where is that gun?*"

"I don't know! I couldn't find it!"

"So . . . you did *try* to find it? Now, see here, Duncan, you'd better stop hedging and come clean . . . it will be far better for you."

Duncan did not answer and Smith slipped his hand under the newspaper on the table and drew out six bullets.

"Those were found under your pillow, Duncan," he said. "It was a bullet like this that killed Captain Jones."

He rolled the paper back farther and revealed a boot. "Yours, Duncan! And the sticky clay packed into a cake on the heel contained bits of paper torn from a piece that was one of Broox's script sheets, and which this morning was lying on the table of the room in which he was killed! You were in that room, Duncan, not only this morning . . . but last night!"

He stopped . . . waited. The ex-soldier gnawed his lips; beads of perspiration sprang out all over his pale face.

"Duncan . . . why did you kill Captain Jones? What did he do to you?"

Silence! Duncan's fists slowly doubled at his sides, the sullen expression on his face gave way to one of malignant hatred. He started to move, and immediately Clancy had him by the collar.

"None of that . . . you!"

"Clancy!"

"Aw, let me work him over, Chief . . . he's just spoiling for a beating. Maybe he'll come through clean, then!"

"Clancy!"

"All right," Clancy grumbled, and in a last aside to the man beside him: "Talk fast, feller!"

Still the man would not speak. He looked about him, as if seeking some way of escape, found none in the expectant, eager attitude of Clancy on the one side, the quiet, watchful stand of Ryan on the other, or the calm, searching gaze of the cold-blooded man behind the table.

"Duncan," said Captain Smith, "I'm giving you every chance to have a square deal. All your actions are against you! I could put you in jail right now . . . and . . . what is more . . . most likely send you to the gallows, on what evidence I have against you!

You aren't helping your chances a bit by refusing to talk . . . and . . . my man . . . I'm only going to warn you once more . . . you'd better come clean! You planned the whole thing, didn't you? You came up here with the sole purpose to kill Captain Jones, didn't you?"

"You're damned right I did!"

XIV

Duncan almost shouted the words in hysterical abandon. Smith gave out a soft, sighed "Ah," then leaned back to study the look of pride, perverted, degenerate pride, that accompanied Duncan's confession. As he talked on, Smith sensed the boasting in his voice; was fascinated by the way in which the man seemed to pour forth his damning words unmindful of their implication, of their results to himself. Indeed, all thought of self seemed to be obliterated by the pulsing hate he had for the man who had been his superior officer.

"You're damned right I planned to kill him! And he had it coming to him! The only thing I'm sorry for is that I didn't get to finish him!"

"Oh, but you *did!*" interrupted Smith calmly. "He's *dead*, you know!"

"Yeah. I *know!* You ain't tellin' me nothin'. Didn't I see him lying there? And it's just like you guys to try to make me the fall guy . . . and let the fellow who did it go free. That's the best thing the police does!"

He rounded off the remark with a string of curses. Foam began to gather about his twitching lips. Clancy raised his eyes significantly at Captain Smith, but the latter shook his head.

"That won't get you anywhere, Duncan," he said. "Not if you stood there and described in detail the imaginary murderer and told me just how he did it! No, my man, the spotlight of suspicion points at *you*, and that spotlight will stay on you until it is proved you are innocent . . . or . . . until you have paid the penalty!"

"It can stay on me till hell freezes over, and the devil slides around on his tail, but it can't prove I did it. You sit there like you was God Almighty on the Throne of Judgment, which you ain't, 'cause if you was you wouldn't have to be asking me questions about what happened! You'd *know!* And you *don't.* And I'm wise to what'll happen next, if I don't come through! I ain't no fool!"

"Then why don't you come through?" suggested Captain Smith softly.

"And that's just what I'm gonna do! I'm gonna tell you the truth, and give you a *chanct* to believe it! Which you won't admit, even if you do . . . 'cause why . . . 'cause you've already said I'm the guilty party, and it hurts one of you guy's pride somethin' fierce to take back your word!"

He stopped, wiped his mouth with the towel Smith had given him. His hands, his whole body, in fact, were shaking spasmodically. Smith felt a twinge of pity, but he knew this was no time to display it.

"I'm listening, Duncan!" he prompted quietly.

"All right. Here it is! I hated the guts of that guy! Did you ever try to stand *at attention* all night long, with your belly sticking to your backbone, and a guy over you with a loaded gun with orders to shoot you if you didn't stay that way? No, I'll bet you didn't. Nor you ain't gone around the country with a dishonorable discharge hangin' over you, neither!"

"And what did you do to *him* . . . *first?*"

"I didn't treat him like Jesus Christ . . . that's all."

"All right. Go on!"

"I swore I'd kill him if both of us ever got home alive. Never the day of all the years since have I forgot it! What he done to me over there gave me the T. B. . . . They put me in a hospital when we got home and wouldn't let me out. While I'm in there, my wife dies . . . and my kid . . ."

He stopped. No one spoke. Here was something irrevocable! A human drama begun and finished, and no one could change the pain-twisted mask of tragedy for the laughing face of comedy!

"So . . . when I sees him that morning . . . I went at him! I was a fool. I sh'd'a waited until I got some kind of weapon. When they threw me out, I did just what you said, and I come up here with the intention of findin' a chance to kill him. Then that night he and Hoxton and Morrill goes up to that old barn. I followed. . . ."

"How did you get by the guards?"

"That pair of yaps? Say, mister, I've gotten by *real* guards in my time! Well, it looked pretty. I could croak him and it would be laid onto one of them other two guys. Everybody knew Hoxton was sore at him, anyway. They went into that big front room . . . and then I lost 'em, because the light which was shining through the window from his lantern all at once goes out. I was lookin' in, tryin' to figger out where he'd gone, when somebody takes a shot at me. I ducked for cover and waited.

"Nothin' else happened, except once a couple of folks came snoopin' around the front end of the house. They had a dog, and for a minute I thought I was going to be caught sure. Then they went away. I sneaked back up to the window, and I sees the light again. Pretty soon the front door opens and somebody goes out. I sneaked a look in the other window, and I sees Jones in there alone. While I was watching, he goes over to a nutty looking hole in the wall and disappears. . . . Then I went around to the front and inside."

"Could you see?"

"No. Only when it flashed lightning, but I knew where he had gone, and I followed. I knew I had him alone and I was satisfied. I sneaked up them stairs leading to that room where all them instruments are. I had to light a couple of matches on the stairs, and if you look, you'll find 'em there somewheres. When I got into that music room, or whatever it is, there was a door leading downstairs again. There was a light down there, and I knew that was where Jones had gone. So . . . I went after him."

"Could you see him from where you were up there?"

"No, I couldn't. But I could see his light, and I knew it was him. I got out my gun . . . and . . ."

He stopped, looked around, but no one spoke.

"Go on, Duncan," said Captain Smith finally.

"Well, right then I made my big mistake for which I'm damned sorry!"

"Yes, Duncan—it's always a mistake to kill," said Smith.

"Aw, I don't mean that! I told you I didn't kill him! D'you think I'd be sap enough to admit wanting to if I had? I made my mistake in wantin' to let him know who was going to kill him! So, as I steps down the last stair, I takes off my mustache and coughs. When he turns around I had my gun on him. He didn't know me right off, with my wig and my makeup, so I up and tells him a little ancient history. Pretty soon I sees he remembers and knows who it is that's talking to him. He starts advisin' me what a fool stunt I'm pulling off . . . and I gets so interested talkin' back at him, I don't see he is edging up on me. He tells me the reason he claims not to know me at the studio is so's not to make trouble for me! That sounded good coming from him! I tells him a few more facts—which again was a big mistake. I'd ought to have shot first and talked afterward. If I'd'a shot him when I hit the kitchen and saw him standing there looking at them yellow cups . . ."

"Yellow cups? What are you talking about, Duncan?"

"Cups! Yellow goblet-looking things. They looked like they was gold. I'll bet some of them guys that was in there before you came copped 'em, 'cause they wasn't there when I looked in there this morning."

"Listen, Duncan," said Smith, with a wearied air. "I've heard a lot of funny tales since I came up here. But your last remarks are about the funniest! Please stick to the truth and don't invent things. You don't do it convincingly."

"Calling me a *liar* now, ain't you? Well, listen, bo, was *you* there?"

"No, of course I wasn't, or you'd never have killed him," said Smith tartly.

"Well, then, if you want to tell this story you go ahead! If I tell it, I'm gonna tell what happened!"

"All right, but stick to the truth!"

"You're mighty right I will. When he sees me he sets that goblet down . . . with the others. They was a bunch of them settin' on that sort of table. He sets it down beside a couple of candles . . ."

"Wait a minute," said Smith sharply. "I thought you said Jones had a lantern?"

"Sure he had a lantern! Also they was a lot of candles and all burning. I was so interested tellin' him what I was gonna do to him, I didn't use my head. So when he yells for me to look behind me, I falls for it. Then he jumps me . . . !"

"And you shot him . . ." added Clancy with flat finality.

Duncan whirled on him snarling.

"No, I didn't shoot him, you big flat-footed sap!" And to Smith, "If you want the rest of this story keep that yap's trap shut. . . ."

"Never mind, just proceed," said Smith sharply.

Duncan debated a moment whether to relapse into sullen silence, and then thought better of it.

"He jumps me, and grabs the hand in which I had my gun. Then we had it, all over that goofy place. I don't mind telling you I tried my damnedest to twist the gun around and shoot him. But I couldn't do it. That guy was stronger than a bull. Finally I thinks I got a chance at him and I pulls the trigger. But just as I do, he jerks his head sideways and I miss him!"

"Where were you when that shot was fired, Duncan?" demanded Smith sharply.

"Well . . . we was over *toward* the north end of that room. Then he knocks my gun out of my hand and picks me off my feet and slams me on the floor . . ."

"How do you mean? Hit you?"

"No. He just jerks me off my feet and throws me end over end, and I bring up in a heap in a corner, and the floor drops out from under me! And that's all I remember until I come to, and find myself in a boxed-in hole under the floor."

"That sounds pretty fishy, Duncan."

"I don't care if it does. That's where I was, and I had one hell of a time getting out!"

"Oh, you got out of there?"

"I'm here, ain't I?"

"Oh, yes," said Smith, "and your gun isn't here! So I suppose you know where it is? You haven't told me about that yet. And I'm *really* interested in that gun, Duncan!"

"So was I! That's the one thing I can't account for! The guy who killed him must've taken it with him!"

"And yet you go back there this morning in the hope of finding it?" said Smith softly; "slipped *up* there, didn't you, Duncan?"

"No, and I haven't slipped up *nowhere*," Duncan snarled. "Course I went up there to look for it, and my mustache. I thought I might not'a been able to see 'em last night by just lighting matches."

"But I thought you said there were candles burning, as well as that lantern?"

"And they was when we was fighting When I started to climb out of that place, the room was blacker'n a cat's back! I listened and didn't hear nothin' and finally I climbed up out and lit a match. Then I see Jones lyin' there with a hole clean through him. First off, I looked for one of them candles, but they wasn't there. So I goes about lightin' matches, tryin' to find my gun. I knowed if it was found there, I'd be in for it. If I'd'a got to kill him I wouldn't'a minded!"

"Yes . . . very pretty, Duncan. What else did you find?"

"Well, the next thing I know I stumbled over another feller. I lit a match and recognized him as a guy I hadn't seen since the war. His name was Love."

"Oh, you knew Love too?" said Captain Smith significantly.

"Yes. And that don't mean a damned thing, neither! I didn't know he was there. First time I seen him since we was in France."

"So . . . Love was in France . . ."

"Sure he was. Say, you don't know nothin', do you? So was his sister! And you can put this in your pipe and smoke it; a lot of fellers made fun of Love. And he's sure a goofy guy, but he knew how to treat men white and they stuck by him. . . . So, when I see him there, I figgered as how he and Broox had met somehow and had shot it out. . . . So I went on huntin' for my gun so's to get out of there . . ."

"Wait a minute. Why would Love and Broox shoot it out? And why would Love's men stick by him? Did they have trouble over there?"

Duncan's face grew sullen and his mouth closed tight. Clancy stepped forward and poked him in the ribs.

"The chief asked you a question, fella. Answer him!"

"That's their business," said Duncan, "and none of mine! I ain't blackenin' no girl's name, leastwise as fine a kid as that little nurse! I'm just tellin' you this: if her brother shot the dirty heart out of Jones, why, he figgered Jones had it coming to him . . . that's all! Now, if you ask me any more questions about 'em, I'm shut up like a clam."

Smith, after a look at the man, knew he meant it. "All right, Duncan. So, after finding your gun, you beat it, is that it?"

"I never found my gun . . . nor my mustache. I've told you that a dozen times. When I couldn't find 'em, I beat it, you betcha!"

"Where is it? I'm speaking of your gun. . . ."

Duncan gave Smith a look of supreme disgust.

"Say, feller, can't you understand English? I told you and told you, I didn't find it!"

"Not this morning?"

"Not last night . . . nor this morning. I don't know where the hell it is. I wished I did!"

There was silence for a moment. Finally Smith said:

"Now about this hole in the kitchen floor. Tell me about that."

"It's there, mister. I c'n take you right to it."

"Suppose you tell me where to find it."

"So . . . that's it, eh?" said Duncan, staring levelly at him. "I'm pinched, eh? Well, I'll do just that, anyway. Now what d'ya think of that, even if you don't believe it's there. D'you know where they's a couple of two-by-fours, looks like, sticking up out of the floor over at the north side?"

Smith nodded. He had wondered about those two braces.

"Well, you look under 'em. They's some sort of trick elevator there."

"If Broox and Love were shot after you fell in there, why didn't you hear the shots?"

"Didn't I tell you I was knocked out!"

"Yes . . . you *told* me that . . ."

"And you can believe me or not, I don't give a damn!"

"How many shells did you have in your gun when you started?"

"She was full. If you find my gun, you'll find one shell shot, that's all."

"The costume company made you sign a slip for your equipment. Where's the duplicate?"

"I got it right here."

Duncan searched his pockets, then handed the slip of paper to Smith, who read that his gun was Series X 8548926.

Smith put the paper in his own pocket, and then leaned back and looked steadily at Duncan.

"You've told a wild tale, Duncan. You've tried to alibi yourself. This morning you deliberately lied to me. What happened was that you killed Broox, wounded Love, went back upstairs, where you met Hoxton just returning, and you put him out of the way to keep him from telling on you! Then you ditched your gun. You forgot about the mustache until this morning . . . that much of your story rings true. You tried to get it and you failed.

"You made up that stuff about the goblets, because, regardless of your inference as to one of the men taking them, that is not at all likely . . . they are not there, were not there when Randall discovered his director's body this morning. You stuck here in camp, thinking that was the only way you could remain undiscovered."

"That's what I get for telling you the truth," snarled Duncan. "Go up there and look for that elevator; you'll find my finger prints all over the damned thing!"

"You might have been hiding down in that hole first, before killing Broox, you know!"

Duncan looked startled, then fell to cursing. "Sure, sure, pin it on me!" he yelled. "I wisht to God I'd never told you about that hole!"

He began to cough, his breath coming in choking sobs. There was an uncomfortable silence from the others until he finished.

"Do you know what time it was when you assaulted Jones in the kitchen?" Smith then asked tentatively.

"No, I don't. Must've been near midnight. I got back to camp at twelve thirty."

There was a silence. Smith sat, frowning, making notations in his little red note-book. He looked up at last.

"Well, Duncan, I've got to hold you," he said, and to Ryan, "Take him down to Lake and tell him to lock him up until further orders."

Ryan took Duncan's arm, none too gently. Smith stopped them.

"Just one more question, Duncan. Did you, by chance, see anything of a beautiful woman up there last night?"

"No, I didn't. I suppose you are trying to pin something else on me . . . abduction, or rape, or . . . something I never even heard of . . ."

"No . . . I'm not trying to pin anything on you. I'd give a lot if I could figure out how much of your own story is true . . . and find your gun! When I do, I'll know more than I do now . . . maybe."

Utterly discouraged and dog-tired, he stared off at the somber outlines of the monstrosity that housed the secret of the dual tragedy.

"Well, that's over," said Clancy, with beaming satisfaction. "Not so tough a case, after all. . . ."

"Over!" retorted Smith, showing heat. "My God, Clancy, this thing's just begun."

XV

Apparently Larry Randall was an ordinary young man, only ordinarily good-looking. He had nice brown eyes and a frank, nice face. He was well setup, and his mouth and chin were pleasantly firm. He had gotten through high school creditably, and from then on his book reading consisted of the "pulps" . . . detective and wild western magazines . . . and the various motion-picture gossip sheets. He liked his work, and he did not ride a hobby. He was not "cultured" in the cosmopolitan sense of the word, and he did not want to be. What was not apparent, and was extraordinary about him, was a cleanly fineness of heart and soul and body, and the innate potentialities of a loyal, tender husband and father! Of this, of course, he was utterly unconscious. But Beatrice Love had looked into the faces of many men . . . had looked at their bodies, dressed and stripped. She knew men. She had learned that homely old saying, "Handsome is as handsome does," and she recognized in Larry Randall an absolute lack of all those traits that break a woman's heart. She was looking at him, and thinking these truths about him, all the time he stood in front of her, his eyes a bit grim and his face muscles tensed, saying:

"You didn't fool Smith! He knows you lied to him!"

She did not answer.

"When Smith came back, and I got one good look at his face
. . . I . . . well, I knew things were looking bad for your brother."
He turned away from her and walked up and down. What right
had a man with a wife and a sister . . . and maybe a mother . . .
to kill? Just to ease his own sense of importance . . . to get even
. . . to show himself the victor in a quarrel! He knew that Beatrice was clenching her fists to keep herself from breaking into
tears . . . he knew that she was desperately trying to protect her
brother . . . lying . . . pretending . . . guarding . . . and all the
time shuddering at the thought of him swinging from a rope . . .
at Alicia in disgraceful mourning! A rage filled him. He wished
that Love had been shot down dead!

He went back to her and stood in front of her.

"Listen, Beatrice . . . nobody should sacrifice himself for another . . . when the other is wrong! Don't you see that you aren't
helping to make the world any better? If a man commits a crime,
he ought to stand the punishment. If a criminal always had to
pay the price . . . why . . . he'd think a long time before he'd break
the law."

"I am not sacrificing myself. No one has accused me of the
murder . . . and I do not think I will be accused. And as for the
world . . . well, I'm afraid those nearest and dearest to me count
for more than humanity in general!"

"Oh, I know I sounded preachy . . . it's just because I . . .
because I . . ."

He stopped, confused, but she did not help him. Just sat
there looking at him with that stilled, watchful look that she had
had ever since she had seen her brother with that wound in his
head.

"What's the use of hedging?" Randall burst out feelingly.
"Won't you tell me . . . *did* your brother kill Broox?"

She started to speak, and then sighed and kept her silence.

"You told Smith that you didn't know Broox . . . but I think you did. In fact, I know . . ."

"I told Mr. Smith that neither Aloysius nor I knew a motion-picture director named Broox!" she interrupted steadily.

"Oh, that's so silly! You're trying to get by with a play on words! Don't you suppose he saw through that?"

Perhaps, if he made her angry with him, she would throw caution to the winds and tell him all about it.

"You lied to Smith, and he knows it! That's why he took you to the undertaking parlors and made you look at my director's body! And you turned white and nearly fainted when you looked at him . . . and even then you said 'no' when he asked you if you had ever known him. Beatrice . . . you can't fool Smith! He's too clever! And don't be too sure that you won't be suspected! Morrill swears he saw a beautiful woman walking down that hall toward the kitchen, and . . ."

She stopped him with an impatient gesture.

"But that's so foolish! I'm not beautiful . . . and I was not in that part of the house that night!"

He felt she was telling the truth. He felt also that he was not getting anywhere, but he kept doggedly at it.

"Why did you get white and almost faint when you looked at . . . Captain Jones?" he asked.

She raised her head quickly at the name and caught her breath. The moonlight, showing fitfully now and then through small clouds, made her eyes as limpid as the light in a cavern under the sea . . . and with the same golden-green glow.

"You are . . . beautiful . . ." he said slowly, looking at her loveliness. "You are . . . beautiful . . . and you . . . know it! *Darling!*"

For a long moment they gazed at each other, struck into throbbing silence by that last impetuous endearment. To them both came the realization that they were really seeing each other for the first time. . . . Beatrice rose and came a few steps toward him.

"Why . . . Larry! *Larry!*" she cried, and her voice was a silver chime of happy surprise and delight. It was as though she had long been seeking him, and suddenly he had appeared to her . . . her love, that she had known forever!

He opened his arms and she went into them. He folded her close and looked out at the world over her beautiful golden head . . . in his eyes the triumphant, eternal masculine challenge:

"This is my woman! Let her be!"

And after a while she began to talk, his arm about her, her head against his shoulder.

"We both knew Captain Jones. It was before Alicia and Aloysius were married. She knows about it, though. We were in France. I lied about my age and got over as a war nurse. Loish and Captain Jones and I were drawn together from the start, because we felt the same about the war! We were there because our country was in it, but the frightful cruelty . . . the uselessness of it depressed us! The suffering was almost more than we could bear . . . just to witness! I do not think that any one of us ever felt that excited sense of patriotism that blinds people to the wickedness of it all. Then . . . Captain Jones and I were at the front. It's hard now to believe that we could have been in a dug-out, with shells falling all around us . . . with . . ." she stopped talking and shuddered, "the things that can never be put into print, happening. . . . We were alone. We were worn to the break-ing-point. It seemed like the end of all Creation. It seemed there wasn't any way out, ever . . . any escape from the bursting shells, the frightful mutilations . . . the *war!* I think we both came near to losing our reason. Captain Jones stood up and shook his fists at God and screamed:

"'Stop it! *Stop* it! You are the only One who can stop it! Why don't You?'

"And the tears were running down his face. All the time we could hear wounded men moaning . . . all the time . . . and then he looked at me, and cried:

"'There's one thing beautiful and clean left in this madness . . . my love for you! We'll have one hour of something that isn't murder and blood and dying screams . . . and terror! I'm going to kiss you, Beatrice, and I'm going to do it with my ears shut to . . . that . . . out there! I'm going to forget it, just for an hour . . . or I'll go mad!'"

Beatrice stopped again and Randall did not speak. She felt his body tense with sympathy . . . she felt him listening to the horror of it, and suffering as she and Captain Jones had suffered, at the knowledge of it.

When she spoke again her voice was low and steady.

"Captain Jones was, as you know, Larry, a big, strong man. I had seen enough of life to know that the thing he asked was perhaps the thing that would save his reason. He was tottering on the brink of insanity. I looked at him and knew that there would have to be some relaxation of his tremendous emotional strain, or he *would* actually go mad. I was sorry for him. My heart ached for him, because I knew how the war had gotten him down . . . just like it had me . . . but *I* didn't have to go out again and *kill!* But, Larry, I didn't love him! I liked him. I admired him . . . but not . . . not love! He thought that I was still thinking of what people would say. That I refused because of convention, and . . . a natural reluctance to—" Beatrice laughed a little grimly.

"As if conventions . . . social conventions . . . mattered when men were murdering each other! But I couldn't make him understand. He simply went crazy . . . and, oh, he was to be pitied! It was just like those big trees out there, blasted and torn to pieces by dynamite . . . his body was like that . . . in the grip of his passion, and not only his passion but his mental suffering! I want you to pity him, Larry . . . not condemn him. . . ."

"Go . . . on . . ." said Randall thickly.

"I am going to tell you the truth, Larry . . . I do not know what might have happened had we been left alone. Don't you see, he had no standards left! And he loved me!"

"Please don't . . . don't drag it out so . . . what happened?" Randall said huskily.

"Nothing happened, dear . . . nothing! We were saved from ourselves and . . . Captain Jones was sent to hospital. He had brain fever. I had to tell my brother, because he kept asking me why I did not go to see him . . . he called for me . . . but I knew it would only make things worse. I wanted him to forget. My brother swore he'd kill him if he recovered, and we all returned home. That's all, Larry. We haven't seen him from the time we sailed—and he was still in the hospital in . . . until . . . we came here. We didn't, of course, know he was going to be here. If Aloysius shot him, he met him unexpectedly, and . . . just . . . shot . . . oh, the stage was all set for it! He had his revolver, and . . ."

"I know . . . as your sister-in-law said, your brother is . . . a fool! He'd shoot first and think afterward," said Randall bitterly.

"You must not hate him like that! I do not *know* he did it. But of course I cannot help worrying . . . but Larry, that man Duncan, or Donovan, you told me about! Why, it's plain he was lying! Didn't he *threaten* to kill Captain Jones?"

"Yes. He admits it. The funny part of it is, he admits everything, except actually shooting him! I don't know what Smith thinks of his story. I can't make him out myself. I know he's a bad egg. You can tell that just by looking at him."

"He must be. Captain Jones was a stern officer . . . yes, but he was never unjust! Larry, don't say anything to Alicia! She's so amazingly truthful, even about her nearest and dearest . . . if she knew that Broox was Captain Jones, she'd blurt out something that would make it worse for Aloysius!"

"She's the queerest woman I ever met! She acts as if she hates him!"

"That's just her way! She's the kind that gets angry and sarcastic when she's scared to death. Why, she'd cut off her hand for my brother, really! He's her sweetheart and her husband and her baby . . . the way she talks, you'd think she didn't want a baby, but I've found her crying her eyes out when some friend of hers had one! She *adores* Aloysius! Life would just be nothing . . . if anything happened to him. It would be the end for her!"

And now, without warning, Beatrice began to cry. The hot tears ran down Randall's shirt front, and that very fact brought a dismal comfort to her. It was the first time she had cried down a man's shirt front, and it was the first time Randall had held a sobbing woman in his arms. Back of their worry and fear, both of them experienced a little thrill at this. Once Randall hugged her close, and said:

"God, I'm glad that neither one of us . . . did it! After all, darling . . . after all, we've got each other and our lives before us!"

And then, a thought striking him, he exclaimed quickly:

"Say, you aren't going to have any fool ideas about . . . well, about not marrying me . . . if . . . if . . ."

"No . . . Larry. No . . . that's mid-Victorian, as Alicia would say. But of course, I never could forget that Loish . . . oh . . . and Larry . . . they'd . . . *hang him!* Oh, I can't . . . stand . . . thinking about it!"

He tried to comfort her, and his brain worked over and over all the facts he knew about the murders. One way it pointed to Duncan. Another to Love. Another it looked like Morrill . . . and then again it looked as if it might have been Hoxton that shot both Broox and Love. He set his teeth and groaned, "God, it *can't* be her brother!"

Captain Smith knocked at the door of the Loves' quarters. It was opened by Alicia. Her face fired with instant, protective antagonism.

"So . . . it's prissy-pry himself!" she snapped. Smith began to feel sorry for her. She was like a mad little girl, knowing herself powerless, yet spitting out childish insults in a vain hope of vanquishing the enemy. His experienced eyes saw the pitiable terror, and appeal for help, that showed through her defiant glare.

He smiled and bowed.

"If it gives you any pleasure to call me that . . . it is!" he said. "May I speak to Mr. Love?"

She scowled.

"Did the doctor say you could?"

"For five minutes only, and under the supervision of his sister. He said she'd know when her brother was getting tired."

"She would . . . if she was here, but she's gallivanting around like a love-sick heifer with that young picture man. Of all things! After all the men that Bee Love has had propose to her, and then . . . and then she should fall for that simpleton! What's the idea of the breeches and puttees, and the bland and open countenance, anyway? He looks like a Y. M. C. A. instructor!"

Smith laughed. Silently he admitted that Alicia Love's comments were pat, if not always flattering.

"Randall's all right. He's a good chap. Don't be so hasty, he . . ."

"So's our cook a *good* woman," said Alicia bitingly. "Why, good heavens, do you know that Bee was proposed to by a *count?*"

"No . . . I didn't know it. However, don't worry over lost titles. International marriages aren't successful, generally, I understand."

"As if any marriage would be successful with Bee Love acting like a doddering idiot! She's lost her wits! She sits mooning over Loish's hand, and pretending to herself it's that goody-goody boy's! It's positively nauseating! I never saw Bee Love so . . . maudlin!"

"Mrs. Love, aren't you going to ask me in?" said Smith determinedly.

"Not if I can help it," she admitted immediately.

"Oh, come, come, now! That's not the way to act! Be a nice little girl and . . ."

"Shut up!" she snapped furiously. "Don't 'nice little girl' *me!* I simply abhor cajoling men! I'd rather you'd swear and boot me out of the way!"

As she said this last she braced herself with one arm across the door.

"Mrs. Love, you're acting very foolishly! And you're only gaining a few moments! I don't want to be rude . . . even discourteous, but . . . I'm *going* to talk to your husband! And I'm going to do it right now!"

He removed her by the simple method of taking her arm in his steely grip and holding her aside. She gasped and cried:

"Do you want to kill him? He isn't well enough."

"I'm not going to kill him. Doctor Gittles knows his business!" Smith said coldly, and walked across the large room to the cot on which Aloysius Love lay. He stood looking down at that part of his face which was visible between the bandages. Yes . . . from what he could observe, Love was just that kind . . . an impulsive, quick-tempered, erroneously gallant idiot! His wife was right! Most of the time such men get through life without doing anything particularly erratic. Now and again a man like that acts out his unreasoned impulses . . . and . . . there is a tragedy . . . and yet . . . Smith knew . . . the so-called criminal might only be a *D'Artagnan* misborn.

Certainly this man was not yet out of danger. His face was not only pale, but pinched and blue. Smith bent and took up the lax hand. Aloysius's eyes fluttered and closed again, but Smith knew he was awake.

"Looks like you had a close shave, old man," he said kindly, "but you're on the mend. I'm Captain Smith . . . no need to be alarmed. Just want to ask you a few questions. If you don't want to talk, I'll not bother you." He watched the wounded man closely as he spoke . . . purposely assuming an unhurried, casual manner. Love made a weak effort to smile.

"That's . . . all . . . right. . . . Ask away."

"All we know is that you were after your dog, and left this room somewhere before midnight. When we found you, you had that hole in your head, and were lying in the kitchen of this house . . . quite a ways from here. Can you tell me what happened?"

"Clammy . . . darn . . . little . . . fool . . . but he . . . was right . . . kept barking and fussing around so I . . . couldn't sleep." Love stopped and breathed deeply for strength, then went on, "I opened that door . . . there . . ." He tried to rise to point, but Smith pressed him back.

"The door right opposite the foot of your cot?"

"Yes. Leads into . . . long hall . . . lots of doors in it . . . Clammy beat it . . . like a streak . . . I called . . . tried to stop him . . . no use. Then I heard voices . . . sounds of . . . fight . . . opened a door . . . and . . . that's all. . . ."

"You mean that when you opened a door to the kitchen where we found you, something happened?"

Again Love tried to smile, and motioned to his head.

"That . . ." he said significantly. Smith stood for a moment looking down at him. Then he asked:

"There's only one door to that kitchen, Love. It's a timed trick thing. How did you open it?"

"After . . . I lost . . . Clammy . . . he led me . . . a merry chase . . . don't know . . . where I did go . . . I just . . . opened a door and that's all . . . can remember. Don't know about door . . . being timed."

"And the instant you stepped into the kitchen you were shot?"

"Guess so. . . . Fell down guess. . . . Woke up here."

"Love, wasn't it that you walked into the kitchen, recognized the man there, shot him . . . and got shot in return?"

Love's eyelids fluttered. He took a breath. Lifted his hand and made a wavering motion. Alicia, who had stood with her eyes riveted on his face, made a little exclamation of concern.

"Oh . . . can't you see he's not strong enough!" she cried indignantly, but Smith disregarded her protest. He bent closer, watching each breath that Love drew. Picked up his hand and kept his fingers on the weak pulse as he talked.

"We found your gun. There was one shot gone. It matches up with the bullet that killed Broox!"

Love said, "Licia . . . tell him . . . about . . . shooting Ahern. . . ."

"I *did* tell him I told you . . . you heard us talking about it . . . that 'Loysius shot at our landlord! He didn't hurt him. I suppose he didn't clean his gun! He never does!"

Smith tried another way, hoping to surprise some unguarded comment from the wounded man.

"Do you have any idea who shot you? Somebody evidently tried to kill you."

But Love said only:

"I wasn't there long enough to . . . recognize anyone . . . I think I told you that. Wouldn't want to get an innocent person in bad . . . so . . . rather not . . . say. Don't know who shot me. . . ."

"All right. Answer this, then, please. Did you have any reason for killing . . . *Captain . . . Jones?*"

"Oh!" gasped Alicia, and stared, white-faced, at Smith.

"*Did you?*" Smith persisted. Alicia threw herself bodily between him and the cot.

"Stop! Stop! Do you want to kill him? Can't you see he can't talk? You've worn him out! I should think . . . I should think you'd be ashamed of yourself!" Her voice broke into sobs.

"Step aside, please," said Smith firmly, and took her arm. She writhed in his grasp, but held her ground, sobbing wildly now in a paroxysm of terror she made no effort to control.

"Oh . . . just wait until he's well! Don't . . . torture him now! He doesn't know what he's saying! Oh, don't you know he nearly died! He might die . . . even yet! I suppose it's an everyday . . . affair . . . for you to . . . see people all shot . . . but it's the first time Loish has come home with his head blown off! I'm so afraid . . . he's . . . going to die . . . oh . . . haven't you *any* pity?"

Tears were pouring down her face and running into her taut and trembling mouth. A sound from the sick man made them both turn.

"Yes, darling! I'm right here . . . what is it . . . tell me, honey . . . tell Licia . . ." she was on her knees beside him, her wet cheek against his, her lips against his bandaged chin. . . .

Smith left her there, sobbing and crooning . . . begging him to get well.

As he walked away he realized that, after all, she had beaten him. He never could hold out against a woman's truly heart-broken tears! Well, it was just a loss of time he could not help. He was not going to clear up the mystery by throwing Love into brain fever, that was one sure thing!

XVI

As Smith approached the beautiful front door, he saw Clancy's corpulent form mincing along like a male *Little Buttercup*, bobbing up and down like a fat duck on the waves as he went from tiptoe to tiptoe. In this manner he disappeared into the house.

"Now what!" exclaimed Smith, and out of consideration for whatever game Clancy was playing, stepped back into the shrubbery. He heard the door open, but this time it was not Clancy who came out. It was Morrill. He wore no hat, and his customarily neatly brushed hair stood up in a peak in the middle of his forehead, making him look comically like *Snookums* of funny-paper fame.

He came out on a trot and disappeared around the corner of the house. As soon as he rounded the corner, Clancy also emerged, sneaked to it, and then off at right angles, and dodged into a clump of shrubbery, where he crouched, peering out at the side of the house which was beyond Smith's vision. He was, of course, watching Morrill, and Smith could see his round blue eyes popping as he squatted there like a fat bear in hiding. Soon Morrill came trotting back and went into the house again, and once again Clancy started to follow him, but was stopped by a soft whistle from his chief.

As Smith walked into sight and advanced to him, Clancy threw out a fat hand and hissed:

"Sssssh!"

"What for?" asked Smith, who was naturally a quiet-spoken man and hated to be shshed!

"He'll be out again. He's been doing that for the last half hour. Sssssh! . . . here he comes!" Clancy pulled his superior out of sight, and, as before, Morrill disappeared around the corner beyond their sight.

"What is he doing, Clancy?"

"Damfino! You know that picture I told you he was paintin'? Well, just as I'm certain that bird has lit—settled down for a nap or somethin', I see him peekin' out of the tent . . . rollin' those pop-eyes of his all about. Then he ducks back, and pretty soon comes out with a package under his arm. I know he's not trying to bury any of the remains, because the bodies was intact, but he was lookin' suspicious, so I followed. When he gets up here, he hunts around and gathers up a lot of old junk, boxes, and boards, and stuff, and gets up on it. Then he pastes that picture smack up against that there Tiffany window in the ballroom . . ."

"The broken one?"

"No. The other just like it. He climbs down . . . takes a header on his snoot when the boxes fall over. Then he beats it inside. When he's in there he prances around the ballroom lookin' at that picture . . . and say . . . what d'ya think? It looks as big as all outdoors! He spouts a lot of poetry at it, and then dashes out again. He tries to get the picture off the window-pane, but it's stuck, see? So he takes out his handkerchief and starts making spit curls all over it, to get it loose. Then he moves the boxes back and pastes the picture on them, and dashes in again. About that time I guess you showed."

"Well, let's go talk to him."

"Aw, let him alone, Chief! You don't know *what* that guy's tryin' to pull! Give him rope to hang himself!"

Ignoring Clancy's beseeching countenance, Smith walked up to the door and opened it. Morrill was standing in the middle of the ballroom, looking at the window, with his head cocked on one side. He seemed distinctly pleased with what he saw, although it was an amazingly hideous countenance, with bristling hair, and a mouth that grinned in behemothan ferocity. He jumped and wheeled about when Smith purposely slammed the door.

"I thought you were different, but you're just an ordinary door-slammer! My father . . . who was a gentleman . . . said that every slammed door was a wooden damn!"

"I thought I was being quite decent! Clancy, you know, has been *sneaking* up on you!"

Morrill smiled.

"The fireplace was a close fit," he said with a little chuckle. "Your estimable bond-slave secreted himself in there while he watched me! I helped him all I could. I was burning with a desire to gaze upon this descendant of Patrick Cotter, peering out at me . . . but I refrained from seeing him at all. . . ."

"Patrick Cotter?" said Smith curiously.

"Patrick Cotter was a famous Irish big man. He lived in Bristol. A cast of his huge paw is preserved in the College of Surgeons."

"I see . . ." said Smith, simulating an interest he did not feel.

Morrill burst into an enthusiastic harangue.

"I am very much interested in giants and elephants. I read about the former and collect the latter in bronze, jade, and ivory. Many people confuse the giants of mythology with the giants of actual history. Many people believe that giants were all confined to mythological tales! However, I assure you, there have been

over half a hundred real giants. Anak, father of the Anakim, and
Anak, whose real name was Joseph Brice, born at Romannchamp
in the Vosges Mountains; Andronicus, grandson of Alexius Com-
nenus; Bamford, now buried in Saint Dunstan's courtyard; Blacker, born at Cuckfield, Sussex; Bradley, born at Market Wheaton,
in Yorkshire; Brusted, Busby of Darfield, Chang of Fychou; Cotter, Daniel, Eleazer, who lived in the reign of Vitellius; Franz,
the French giant; Funnum, Gabara, the Arabian giant, Gilly . . ."

Smith broke into the rapid flow of names with upraised hand
and voice.

"Have a heart," he cried, laughing.

Morrill stopped a moment and looked at him solemnly.

"Perhaps you are more interested in elephants? Marvelous
creatures! The symbol of tolerance, eternity, and sovereignty!
The world, you know, stands on the backs of eight elephants . . .
the Achtequedjams. I have a lovely group . . . lovely, but not so
lovely as that group I saw once in China—carved from imperial
jade of feutsui shade, so called from the brilliant plumage of the
kingfisher, ah, a heavenly green joy!"

"Yes, yes," said Smith impatiently. "I've often admired the
color myself."

Morrill gave him a faintly amused and slightly apologetic
smile.

"You are thinking of green . . . the color? I was speaking of
jade . . ." he said.

Smith's eyes narrowed. What was Morrill pulling now? Was
he stalling, trying to divert his mind?

"I was speaking of jade . . . and green also," he said coolly.
"They're the same, aren't they?"

"Jade is as improper a term for green as orchid is for lavender or mauve! There are many colors of jade! It does not confine
itself to one, any more than do orchids. So many people are
deceived by the obvious and generally made mistakes of life! Now

this group of mine It is not green jade . . . it is of a pink shade, commonly known as rose! I found it in the far interior of China, near the Turkestan border . . . whence, I was told (and for once I do not believe it was a lie) that it had been carried when the empress dowager fled.

"I have also bits of lavender, so-called amethyst, bright red and yellow, apple-green, lettuce, and pea-green . . . and one . . . one very, very tiny piece of white, flushed with pink . . . the rarest of all!"

Smith started to speak, but Morrill went on, unhearing.

"All things are like that. There are the commonly known facts about them . . . like your reference to jade-green . . . and then . . . there are the esoteric truths . . . and it happens that this is so . . . even in murders!"

"Just what are you trying to get over, Morrill?" said Smith sharply.

Morrill turned guileless blue eyes upon him . . . smiled and shrugged disparagingly.

"I? Nothing . . . just rambling in my talk. Perhaps trying to justify to you my coming back here . . . delving again into the occult messages of this house . . . even though I shiver and quake with fear! Yet something drives me on. I feel that there is, indeed . . . a *mystery* here! I am not presuming even to counsel you, my friend, but . . . I earnestly beseech you to take account of the *strange happenings* in this house! But we were talking of jade . . . and perhaps you are not so interested in it as I thought. But if you are, I should like you to see an exquisite bit I have, camphor jade . . . a tiny world supported on the back of Mah-Pudman . . . the grand old elephant who stands upon the back of Chukwa, the tortoise. But perhaps you are *not* interested in elephants? I am intensely fascinated by them."

Smith had known other small men with a passion for elephants. He had also known huge men, with pygmy brains to have it. As for Morrill's brain, he was by this time quite sure the man was not what he at first seemed. His conversation just now showed a knowledge of things not generally known. At least, if nothing else, he must be a student of sorts.

"Some day, Morrill, after this beastly business is done with, I'd like to see your collection . . . if you will allow me."

The little actor's face beamed,

"I shall be delighted. I should also be glad to tell you anything more, now . . . that you cared to know about those subjects, and others akin to them. . . ."

"Thank you . . . not now, Morrill, not now," said Smith hastily. "But now let's get down to brass tacks. You told me that the face outside the window, at which you shot, was tremendous. The one you have put up out there certainly is! You called it a . . ."

"Chalbroth. The stem of the giant race."

"Exactly. Well, I see that you have rigged up a contraption there to convince or deceive me. What are the dimensions of that picture out there? Just about billboard?"

"No . . . no, indeed!" protested Morrill. "I drew that face to normal human dimensions. I was very careful! I borrowed Serge's tape measure and applied it to the cook!"

For a moment Smith looked at the window, through which the huge countenance glared. Then he looked questioningly at Morrill. He was frankly puzzled.

Morrill threw out his slender hands apologetically.

"I admit to my shortcomings, Captain Smith, and also I admit to my talents! After thinking over that apparition, I decided to convince myself and yourself . . . of either its genuineness or its fallacy. I drew the face. I set it up outside. I came back here to see why, and from what angle, an ordinary sized face could assume such proportions. Had it remained an ordinary sized face, I should have known that some hoax was played upon me. But it did not. Behold it!"

"What's the answer, Morrill?"

"My sluggish memory awoke a moment ago and bespoke to me concerning the existence of optical glass. That window, which must be worth a fortune, has for its central pane . . . an oval some three feet long . . . the finest Belgian optical glass, sir!"

"Which would so magnify any object as to give it a seemingly gigantic appearance?"

Morrill bowed his head in assent, saying:

"And now, Captain, the other half of the problem presents itself! *Whose face* was it that I saw outside?"

"I can clear that. I have just had a confession from a man who says he peered in that window the night of the murder!"

Morrill looked decidedly startled.

"Mercy! Mercy!" he exclaimed. "Will he need plastic surgery?"

"No. You didn't hit him."

"I am relieved!" Morrill began walking toward the door. "Sir Giblets will tell you I was chasing a petticoat this afternoon," he murmured.

"What?"

"The beautiful radiance . . . the amazingly shining and iridescent countenance of the goddess I saw walking down that corridor . . . remains with me . . . so that I must go peering into the face of every woman I see. Once I thought I had her, sir. I did, indeed! But she insisted her name was Beatrice Love, and that she had never been in that ballroom, or near it, until this morning! However, she was very beautiful! I think I frightened her a little, and that she thought me a madman . . . like your Adam . . .

"'Not that Adam that kept the Paradise, but that Adam that keeps the prison.'"

Smith laughed.

"When you resort to Shakespeare, Mr. Morrill, sometimes I can follow you. 'Comedy of Errors,' eh?"

"Correct! and is this not?"

"It is. Rather, it is *now*, but I'm a bulldog, as well as a watchdog, Morrill. I'll keep at it until I clear it up."

"And I am not beguiled by your beguiling manner, Captain Smith! I know you will keep at me, also, until it is cleared up! But to return to our subject. After gazing upon the lovely face of Miss Love, I once again thought I had found my vision. I saw another woman. . . . However, I *did* think she was in strange garb . . . but beautiful creatures sometimes appear in disguise. I peered into this woman's face . . . and . . . behold! She was Sycorax."

Smith looked mystified.

"The witch-mother of Caliban. . . . you remember?"

But Smith's bantering mood had left him. His eyes narrowed with his thinking look.

"Did you honestly see such a woman, Morrill . . . or are you telling me monkey-tales?"

"I swear it on the seven Bibles . . . Eddas, Five Kings, Koran, Tri-Pitikes, Vedas, and Zend-Avesta . . . as well as our own, sir."

"Where was this woman?"

"While Adam was sneaking and hiding from me, she was sneaking and hiding from him . . . and watching us both. Previously I had had my little affair with her. I believe she is outside in the shrubbery somewhere, right now!"

Smith turned to Clancy, who had kept silent for an unusually long time. When his chief got in one of these "high-brow" conversations he kept his mouth shut and tried his best to look wise, but only succeeded in looking sulky, like a great fat baby.

"Clancy . . . go out there and find this woman and bring her to me!" ordered Smith sharply.

He sat down on the veranda steps and waited. Soon Clancy came, and hobbling in front of him was one of the most pathetic, and at once repulsive, figures that Smith had ever encountered.

Old . . . older than time itself, she seemed, and the dust and debris of ages coated her, from her mud-caked, misshapen old

shoes, to her hoary head. Smith saw the scalp, incrusted, showing through the sparse gray hairs . . . and turned quickly away.

When he met her rheumy eyes, lashless and ravaged by tra-
choma, a sickening pity welled up in him. The old woman stared
back at him silently. He thought of a rattler in the blind season
. . . just such eyes . . . dull and cloudy-looking, and underneath the film he was conscious of a black and beady brightness,
fixed on him with hypnotic steadiness. The flesh had long since
left the facial bones, and the skin, bilious and scaly, hung in
grease-coated pouches.

When Clancy had pulled her around to face him, she had
nearly fallen, but caught her balance on her withered, twisted
limbs with a grimace of instant, snarling hatred.

Now she stood, speechless, leaning heavily on a gnarled club
clutched tightly in one withered, shaking talon. Her hair was a
mat of dead ashes . . . stringing out in horny tangles down her
scrawny neck. For the rest of her . . . rags . . . just a bundle of
filthy, tattered old rags, one upon the other. A shapeless sack,
holding together a brittle bunch of bones!

"Let me see that club," said Smith to Clancy.

Obediently, yet not attempting to conceal his disgust at the
contact, Clancy reached for it. Smith thought again of a blind
rattlesnake striking out malignantly at an enemy it could sense
but not see . . . even her eyes seemed to burn red as Clancy twisted the club out of her clawlike hands.

Smith studied the club painstakingly with his pocket mag-
nifying glass, spending a long time over its knobby, blunt end.
Then he handed it back to the silently waiting woman. She
clutched it savagely, leaned heavily upon it.

"Put her in that chair, Clancy. Don't keep her standing."

Smith looked down upon her for some moments. Then he
was unable to do so any longer, and closed his eyes against the
filth and horrible old age of the woman. All at once he wished

he had not had Clancy bring her. She was, doubtless, just some poor old creature . . . he had seen others, both men and women . . . who had grown old that way. It was unpleasant, of course.

He tried to reason out some way for her to fit into his shaping solution of the murders . . . and could not. He was unable to bring a question to form on his lips. He was completely at a loss as to how to approach her.

He might have asked her the ordinary questions, and, had she been talkative, that's what he would be doing. It was her silence . . . that seemed to be palpitating with the same unspoken, insidious menace as the old house itself, that nonplussed him. She seemed as unhurried as the progress of the planets in their paths . . . and her manner had the same aura of irrevocable fatalism! There she was, giving him back look for look, showing no fear . . . no curiosity . . . just a steadily emanating hostility . . . the more dreadful because of the witchlike being who impulsed it. He saw the slow pulse-beat of age in the deep hollow of her stringy neck and it sickened him . . . the palsied quiver of the head, fast growing too heavy for the decrepit, dried-up spinal bones to support.

He became conscious that her lips were moving . . . moving . . . with that aimless mumbling of the aged . . . the light was caught now and again by her saliva wet gums, over which the shrunken lips were stretched in a thin, tight line.

Mouthing sibilant, whistling aspirates . . . the heritage of old age . . . she seemed to be repeating over and over, some well-learned lesson . . . or formula . . . perhaps doggerel, summoned by her wandering mind from out the long-dead past.

"Poor, horrible old creature," thought Smith, and immediately she had the power to bring him thoughts that no ghastly cadaver had bred.

Death was release of the soul from bondage to the, more often than not, unlovely body. But here was life . . . a soul chained to its hideous receptacle . . . and it shocked him as no corpse had ever done.

God . . . here was it all . . . the beginning and the end of human existence . . . sitting there in her smelling rags . . . the mother and the bearer of men . . . the image of the Creator . . . warped and twisted and fouled by man's long efforts to prove to his God that the human will is paramount!

They were all jumbled up in his head . . . the things this frightful old woman inspired. Thoughts flared and died and flared again . . . yet over and through them all was a mesmerizing and stultifying depression.

In this revolting human thing was the answer the swigging Omar never found, and which wiser men than he would never find. . . .

Yet men went their ways, prattling of law and right and wrong, and praying on Sundays . . . gouging and scheming to gouge on Mondays . . . all to the end that they might leave behind them, down through the march of the worlds, a pathway strewn with its bags of old bones like this! What a monument to their heritage!

Smith was aware that Clancy was coughing and shuffling his broad feet. He would have to start asking the woman something. . . .

All at once he was tired of it all . . . what mattered how those two back there in the old house had met their deaths? What mattered anything, when life could go on in such bodies as this one before him. . . .

Clancy coughed again, louder. Smith straightened . . . sighed. He forced this strange mood from him. He was the trained man hunter once more.

"What is your name?"

He had to repeat the question twice.

"Scraggs!"

The word was scratched out of her, sharp and high. Smith
knew she was unused to speaking loudly enough for others to
hear.

"Your first name, Scraggs?"

"Scraggs . . . Scraggs. . . ."

"Yes. I understand. Your name is Scraggs, but what else? What
did they call you?"

"They do not call . . . they whisper . . . whisper. . . ."

"Nuts!" said Clancy hoarsely.

Smith gestured him to keep quiet, but not before the old
woman had flashed about on him, jerking around with a sudden-
ness and violence that should have torn her neck sinews loose
and let her old head go bouncing about the floor. Her black eyes
gleamed hatred. Clancy backed up a step or two.

"I'm shut!" he exclaimed.

So Clancy felt it too. . . the force of the creature's hatred.

She brought her eyes back to Smith. He wished she would
stop staring. If she would only blink . . . those eyes were beginning to make him uncomfortable.

"They whisper . . . whisper . . . sometimes they go mad, and
start the thunder . . . then their faces are made of fire. . . ."

Back of her Smith saw Clancy's round blue eyes popping with
eagerness to get over his thought as he did a ring-around-the-
rosie with one finger on his head.

"Who is it that whispers?" Smith asked.

"He! He! He!" the old woman cackled, bending almost double over her club . . . choking . . . coughing and spitting before
she got her breath again. "He! He! He! Tillie won't tell. Up forty-
seven steps ten feet . . . we'll fool 'em, Tillie! Looks like a door
. . . but it isn't . . . Tillie Scraggs, you damned old fool, you've
spilled it! Wipe it up! I'm dying, Tillie . . . ha . . . ha . . . dying
. . . say you'll do it or I'll twist your neck off . . . Tillie, you old
horse-face . . ."

Smith got to his feet.

"Take her away, Clancy," he said quietly.

"Sure—no use wastin' your time . . . she can't talk sense . . . but Lord, I'd rather resign than touch her!"

As he stepped forward, she raised her club menacingly.

"Hey, you old cuckoo, none of that!"

Clancy gripped the skinny old wrist and tore the club out of her grasp. Immediately she began to weep . . . mumbling and choking, the saliva drooling from her mouth.

"Oh, here . . . take it, but quit *that!*"

Clancy thrust the heavy stick at her hurriedly. As they moved off, Smith took out his handkerchief and with a feeling of distaste wiped his hands, remembering that he had held the club in them.

XVII

Smith walked wearily to Williams's tent, hoping he could catch a few moments' relaxation. No sooner had he got the idea, than Randall came in.

"I just got a wire from Mr. Rosenthal," he said. "He'll be in camp to-night. I thought you'd like to know."

"Thanks, old man," said Smith. "And don't worry so much. When he comes I'll talk to him."

Randall heaved a sigh of relief. "That'll help a lot! I'll have to dust myself and see that the cook puts up a good meal. See you later."

Smith slumped back in his chair and sighed.

"I like Rosey," he muttered, "but I'm so dog-tired I wish he hadn't gotten that idea until morning."

However, knowing Rosenthal, Smith felt certain the portly and very much agitated producer would arrive fast on the heels of his wire. He gazed wistfully at Williams's cot.

"I guess I might as well forget you," he said to it, and sighed again.

Ryan stuck his head in.

"Say, Chief, Rosenthal's coming. Did Randall tell you?"

"Yes, thanks, Ryan. Tell Skeets to dig up another chair, then bring me all that finger-print data. Then you fellows clear out and let me alone, will you?"

"Right, Chief. How's she look now?"

Smith smiled a tired smile. "Rotten, Ryan, rotten!"

"It'll work out, Chief," returned Ryan with a cheeriness he did not entirely feel. "They always do for you."

"I hope so, Ryan . . . but it's a mess. Run along now, and when Rosenthal gets here, I'll talk to him alone."

"Sure. I'll keep them all away. Well, good luck. Nothing you want me to do, special?"

"Get a little rest if you can, Ryan. Heaven knows what'll turn up. Better grab a snooze while you can.

"I sure will, if you don't need me."

"No . . . go ahead . . . and grab a couple of winks for me while you're at it, too."

When Ryan had gone, Smith forced himself back to his problem. For an hour he sat there, oblivious of everything save the mass of clues, finger-print photographs, his little red note-book. Soon he heard the roar of an aeroplane overhead, and realized Rosenthal had arrived. He pushed the mass of data away with a petulant frown. . . .

"Not a rational story in the whole lot," he growled. "A fine story to tell Rosey . . . a fine tale . . . bunch of damned hallucinations!"

However, Captain Smith's calm eyes looked steadily into Abraham Rosenthal's round brown ones. Then he stepped forward and laid a slender muscular hand on the executive's shoulder. Neither spoke. They enjoyed a friendship so warm, so close in understanding, words were unnecessary.

"My friend, you look tired," said Rosenthal at last, forgetting his own load at sight of Smith's haggard features.

"And you, my friend, need not tell me you are sick to your stomach," returned Smith, noting the baggy pouches under the brown eyes, and the strained look of the fat, customarily genial face. "Here, try one of these."

He held out a cigar and grinned boyishly as Rosenthal recognized it as one of his own private stock.

It was an old joke between them that Smith's brain worked better under the stimulus of Rosenthal's rare weed. The picture magnate saw to it that he was always well supplied.

"So, you vant I should help you think?" said Rosenthal. "Vell, let me tell you, I haff done nothings else but think! My Rachel tells me not to come home until I can act like a human being, so I come up here."

He sank into the chair Smith designated, waited courteously for Smith to light his cigar before biting the end from his own. At last, puffing vigorously, he sank back with a long sigh and fixed his eyes expectantly on the other.

"There it is!" said Smith, gesturing wearily toward the table. Rosenthal let his eyes run over the odd assortment. Smith catalogued them, touching each lightly with a long, lean finger.

> Love's gun
> Morrill's gun (found beside Hoxton's body)
> One exploded shell
> Sheets from Broox manuscript
> One sheet, with piece ground off by a muddy heel
> Duncan's boot
> Missing pieces from sheet (above), found on Duncan's boot heel
> One black mustache
> One bit of candle wax
> One candle
> One empty fruit salad can
> One preserved cherry

"Huh," grunted Rosenthal. "Vat do they all mean?"

"I wish I knew, Rosey!" Smith returned. "Suppose I go over the whole thing!"

"I vish you vould."

"Right-o. . . . Here it is."

Then for an hour there was the steady hum of Smith's voice, with occasionally a groan or a painfilled protest from Rosenthal. Having completed his account, Smith sat back.

"And there you are, Rosey," he finished.

For a long time Rosenthal sat silent, brooding. The pained look in his eyes had deepened; his face remained filled with the horror Smith's graphic recital of the tragedy had brought there.

"It . . . iss . . . awful!" he said finally.

"It's a mess, Rosenthal," returned Smith. "A nightmarish, horrible mess! Nothing makes sense, and every one of these tales is far-fetched! Yet . . . in every case, I have found just sufficient corroborative evidence to give credence to the tale, or at least part of it! Somewhere they depart from the truth—they must . . . ! But which ones, and where, is the question! We've got to assume that one of them is the murderer . . . a fiend . . . masking cold-blooded fiendishness under a cloak of alibis and half-truths and sheer fiction so cleverly woven together as to leave me entirely at sea. . . . Yet . . . I tell you . . . the answer is *there*. I'm sure of that, if I could decipher it!" He waved his hand again, wearily, at the evidence on the table.

"It iss all vild . . . impossible . . . !" exclaimed Rosenthal. He stared at the table, frowning and lost in thought.

Again silence settled down between them. At last Rosenthal roused himself from his morbid brooding, got up, and leaned over the table. One by one he poked the various clues with a fat finger, as if he would force the truth from it.

"Vat has *that* to do vid the murder?" he asked. "That looks silly."

"Doesn't it?" agreed Smith. "I found that in the sink by which Broox was killed. How did it get there? Broox took no lunch up to the house with him that night. Yet next morning that little red bit of fruit in edible condition was resting nicely in the sink above his dead body! Who put it there? If that cherry could talk, Rosenthal, I believe it could give us the true story of the crime!"

"Haff you traced down efferything to find out who could haff had that cherry?"

"I've done the best I could. The cook disclaimed having cherries in any form. That lets Duncan, Morrill, and Hoxton out!"

"But vere did that fruit salad can come from? Sure, that cherry came out of there!"

"I found that can in the Loves' quarters! More, I learned that Love has a habit of having a bowl of fruit before going to bed. He did that the night Broox was killed!"

"And that man Love vas found in the kitchen, and his gun vas shot?" Rosenthal shrugged expressively. "I don't know vy he'd be carrying that von piece of fruit vid him, but there it iss! He did it!"

"If I admit that Love killed Broox (based on the presence of that cherry), then *who shot Love?* Broox had no gun . . . of that I'm pretty certain. . . And we found none beside his body!"

Rosenthal thrust out his fat lips. Smith knew from this that the president was thinking deeply. Finally he stuck out a fat hand.

"Giff me vat *you* think," he said. "Take effery one who vas mixed up in it, and tell me vat *you* haff decided. . . ."

"Well," said Smith finally, "we've got to look at this from three angles. First: Who had a reason, regardless of how vague, to want to kill Broox and Hoxton? Second: Who had the opportunity? Third: Who did do it? . . . meaning, which one of our suspects' actions matches up with the facts as we know them. Let's take the Love family first—we have to begin somewhere.

"They were on the scene. Love and his sister both had sufficient motive to want to kill Broox. Love had a gun. I've an idea the sister has one also . . . of the same caliber. Mrs. Love let slip to Ryan that Love and his sister often practiced target-shooting. The story of Love going running about that house trying to find a dog seems preposterous. . . ."

"Haff you seen the dog?" demanded Rosenthal sharply.

Smith shook his head.

"Then maybe they vass lying. . . ."

"Perhaps, about the dog's getting away and their going after it. But . . . they had a dog, all right, when they landed at that house. The dog is missing."

"How do you know, iff you haff not seen it?"

"Because, Rosey, I checked it up. There were a lot of dog hairs in the back seat of their car. Dog hairs sticking to the edge of one of the fireplaces in their quarters, where, evidently, the dog had leaned to scratch himself. The dog is either an Airedale or an Irish terrier . . . judging from the hairs. . . ."

Smith opened his red note-book and showed a little wad of reddish gray to black hairs.

"So we have Love and the sister with a motive to kill Broox. Love, actually found in the kitchen . . . and no sign of the dog . . . which they called Calamity, by the way."

"Huh! I should think they vould! I should call him vorse things than that if I could see him! Five hundred thousand dollars that dog hass cost me! Calamity . . . mine Gott!"

"I'd like to set eyes on that dog myself, Rosey . . . for another reason, however. But getting back to Love. He *could* have shot Broox. He *might* have killed Horton first while trailing Broox to the kitchen . . . taking our premise as the supposition that Love knew Broox was there . . . which he could have known. He might have recognized him as the man he'd been wanting to even scores with ever since the war . . . just as Duncan did! But there's no evidence that Love was in that music roam. On the other hand, I followed his trail from their quarters to the kitchen . . . through a maze of confusing corridors, and ending through a panel in the kitchen . . . one of a set of thirteen . . . which proved to be a door. His finger-prints were on it. I found his footprints all the way, with the exception of the one long, main corridor, which is free of dust. I lost the dog's myself, so it is easy to understand that Love did. It was some place near a goofy stairway that had forty-seven steps and only went ten feet, then ended in a trap-door! So, if Love did kill Broox, we'll say . . . he didn't kill Hoxton . . . because he didn't do it after he shot Broox. Didn't have time, according to Gittles. But . . . Alicia Love was asleep, she says . . . all the time. Beatrice Love, having also seen Broox, recognized him, might have followed her brother, fearing what he would do! She came by way of the music room . . . got turned around, or lost . . . and heaven knows, that's easy enough in that maze of hallways and trick openings . . . she might have discovered Hoxton, knew he witnessed the murder of Broox by her brother, and struck him down! To support that theory, we have the statement of Morrill that he saw a beautiful woman carrying candles. . . ."

"But he saw her in the hallvay downstairs . . . not in that music place," interjected Rosenthal.

"She might have been both places, and . . . here's the significant thing, Rosey . . . I found faint prints of a woman's feet in that music room, and . . . no candles anywhere else but in the Loves' quarters! What do you make of that?"

"Oh, vell," said Rosenthal with a shrug of his fat shoulders, "there iss nothing to it! She killed him!"

"Someway, I cannot believe that . . . that girl did it! Too brutal, Rosey! Too unmercifully fiendish! The head was mashed to a pulp . . . some other motive kept the blows hammering on

Hoxton's skull . . . some motive besides just removing him . . . the gratification of some long smoldering hatred . . . or some overpowering determination to exterminate him . . . utterly. . . ."

"But . . . dose footsteps!" Rosenthal insisted.

"Yes . . . I found them . . . I'm not dreaming about that! They're there!"

Rosenthal leaned back and gestured with finality.

"Can she explain vy she vas up there?"

"Denies it . . . well, let's go on, Rosey. We'll take Duncan. The man admittedly went there with the firm intent to kill Broox. He says so. He had a gun of the same caliber as the one which *did* kill Broox! He admits shooting it . . . but insists that his was not the fatal shot! Give me the answer to that?"

"His story iss simply crazy! He iss crazy . . . to tell it, and then say he did not shoot Broox! Part off his story iss the truth, and the rest iss a lie! He did it!"

Smith smiled.

"You just got through incriminating Love and his sister," he reminded.

"Oi . . . oi . . . sure . . . I forgot. Vell, it looks now more like this fellow!"

"His story *does* sound fishy. I was so damned sure I had the deadwood on him! But, by golly, Rosey, he was down that elevator shaft! He had a deuce of a time getting out. I found blood on the thing, around the catch, and he showed me where he tore his nail, trying to pry the catch open! I found one of the buttons off Broox's clothes down there too . . . and, what's more significant, an empty shell!"

"Vell . . . vere did it come from? Who shot it?"

"We found the shell that could have come from Love's gun. Love's gun had one shot missing. Of course, with more scientific and expert work, we might positively identify that shell as having come from Love's gun . . . but we haven't had time. I want to clear up everything here on the scene first. So . . . the shell I found down the elevator must have been from the bullet that laid out Love . . . but if Broox shot Love, where is his gun? It's a cinch he could not have gotten rid of it after shooting Love, unless we discard the coroner's findings that Broox was killed and Love wounded almost simultaneously! He wouldn't have time! He couldn't have moved after he was shot!"

"No . . . but . . . maybe he shoots Love . . . realizes, if it iss found out, it vill ruin his motionpicture career . . . throws his gun away . . . hides it . . . then right avay gets shot himself."

"No place to throw it. The only window is too high . . . no crack or cranny . . . I've looked. He'd have had to go clear out of the kitchen. . . ."

"Vell . . . mebbe . . ."

"Nope. Well, on the face of it, we could suspect Love, and we could also suspect Duncan. But I'm not . . . even after his story . . ."

"Vy not?"

"Because the man would be proud of the fact of having killed Broox! He's downright sorry he didn't, he hated him so vindictively! And . . . he had no reason for killing Love. He knew him . . . and knew Love had a reason for killing Broox . . . that way he'd be more likely to make him his ally than murder him! Hoxton he might have killed for self-preservation . . . but if he did, and then manufactured this story . . . why, he's as cunning as a fox and Richelieu combined, and, my God, the man would have to have superb nerve!"

"By the way, Smith, ve better explain vy Mr. Broox vas not generally known as a captain. Looks very queer, unless you understand, as I told you before you came up here . . . it vas because he vas, at heart, a pacifist . . . he vanted to vipe out his military career."

"That's not worrying me. I remember, but I'll tell the reporters, or they'll make something shady out of it," said Smith reassuringly, and Rosenthal nodded, satisfied.

"And then, besides all these other conflicting items, there's that cherry!" said Smith in disgust. Both men looked at it as though it were a little red devil incarnate. Rosenthal, whose mind was beginning to whirl confusingly with these tangled tales, started to talk at random, spinning a tale no less fantastic. He said:

"Vell, here's vone vay! Maybe Duncan and Broox are fighting, and Love valks in, and Duncan shoots him right avay, because he wants to get rid off Broox, and he doesn't vant this other fellow around. Mebbe Love iss carrying that cherry and it rolls on the floor . . . and mebbe Duncan picks it up and throws it into the sink, to remove the evidence. . . . Oi, no . . . that's crazy . . . vat does he care about a cherry wen he leaves Love right there on the floor! Oi . . . vat a mess!"

Smith did not answer, but sat silent . . . frowning. Sometimes it clarified his thought to talk things out. Sometimes it only injected more confusion!

"Look here, Rosey . . . if Love came in carrying a candle (I found candle grease on the table, and candles in Love's apartment) and Duncan shot him, what happened to the candle? . . . and there'd have been grease on the floor, or on Love's clothing. There wasn't. Nope, I don't think Duncan shot Love. . . ."

"Say, Smith, wen Hardell vas killed, and you kept trying to tell me vone off my people did it . . . oh, vell, you said they might, or could, or something, I vas positiff none off my people did do it. You laughed at me! Now vat do you do? Effery time I get an idea you say 'no!'" exclaimed Rosenthal petulantly, and added, out of fairness, "Just like I did!"

"But not for the same reason, my friend! Your negatives were based on sentiment. I'm not warmhearted in the way you are! I've been at my profession too long. This thing makes me *mad* . . . and it makes your heart ache . . . *really* . . . I know! I'm just saying 'no' because of cold-blooded conviction that the action of the suspect, and the crime, do not fit! If I could get sufficient evidence, for instance, that that beautiful girl was a murderess, well . . . right away that is the way I would think of her . . . not, any more, as a beautiful girl . . . understand? The reason I cannot bring myself to believe Duncan killed Broox is because I do not believe the man has the mentality to build such an elaborate structure of evidence . . . both incriminating and misleading at the same time! That would take a master-hand . . . a daring, experienced killer! Or it would take insanity. Duncan is not insane . . . although the poor fellow's in mighty bad shape . . . shell- shocked, gassed . . . just another of those unlucky devils who went through hell . . . and have got to drag it out to the end. If he had shot Broox, he'd have gloated, openly, over it!"

"Mebbe . . . mebbe . . . until he remembered his own neck!" snorted Rosenthal.

"Say, Rosey . . ." Smith leaned forward, "what the devil do you make out of that story of his about disappearing golden goblets?"

"Pish!" exclaimed Rosenthal flatly. "Right avay I vouldn't belieff vone thing that man tells me! Golden goblets! Vere are they? He iss a liar! Who effer heard of golden dishes in a deserted house, Smith! Vat iss the matter vid your reasoning? Vouldn't they haff been stolen right avay . . . gold? Vould any vone let gold lie around in a deserted house? No . . . they vould not!"

Smith grinned.

"Looks funny, I'll admit . . . but someway I can't forget 'em. Well, let's go on. Now take Hoxton. He had a grudge against Broox. He's the sort would have done it either way . . . bashed his head in or shot him. He might have done it, too . . . but if he did . . . then . . . who . . . mangled *him?*"

Again there was a silence—and no answer from either of them.

"Which brings us to our most interesting possibility—*Morrill!*" said Smith.

"Oh . . . *no* . . . *no* . . . *!*" protested Rosenthal immediately.

Smith grinned, but the grin immediately metamorphosed into a grim, sardonic grimace.

"Our most interesting possibility," he persisted.

"Morrill was also on the job that night. Morrill had an abiding, festering hatred for Hoxton, who had ragged him unmercifully. It would have been easy for Morrill to have gone back up to that house, after Hoxton returned with him to camp. The men who were on guard thought their duties a joke, and told me so. Morrill then located Hoxton and killed him. More than that, Morrill would have killed Hoxton in just that way. He was afraid of Hoxton's huge, powerful bulk, bitterly resentful of the fact he himself had been cast into such a diminutive mold. He would have taken no chances with Hoxton, but would have bashed his head in, and done the job thoroughly! More, Morrill has the brains to have covered his tracks thoroughly. Oh, I assure you, there are many interesting possibilities surrounding that little actor! He's been insidiously suggesting weird possibilities, trying to throw me off to the track of some woman . . . painting me vivid dreams of a beautiful houri, whom, he claims he saw going down a corridor with a candle! Morrill has seen the two Love women . . . knows they are both beautiful! Someway, that little devil knows they had candles. . . . When he saw I wasn't so hot about his immense malignant creatures, and his whispering lemures, as he called them, he switched to this wild tale of beauty! When I didn't seem so hot about the Love woman either, he tried to palm off an old crone on me."

Rosenthal became excited.

"Crone . . . a real vone? You haff not mentioned her before."

"Oh, just a poor old soul in rags that hangs out up there about the outbuildings of that place. Old as hell, dirty as the devil, and as malignant as a rattlesnake. Crazy as a coot, to boot!"

"Maybe she . . ."

"Rot!" said Smith. "You haven't seen her. . . ."

"Sometimes seeing people makes it so von cannot form a true picture off them. You told me that yourself! Since then, ven some actor or actress iss touted to me, I do not see them! I haff Izzie and my casting director talk to them, then I find out vat they think. So . . . I haff safed myself lots off money. . . ."

"This old hag is out . . . no reason . . . just a bit of Morrill's ragging. The man is actually getting a great kick out of deliberately annoying me! He takes my time raving about a lot of artistic things, spouting poetry, all of which underneath pack a barb . . . and a lot of double meaning. Dammit, if I could dope out how and why he would kill *Broox*, and *Love*, I'd arrest him this minute! He's shrewd as hell . . . that baby."

"But I thought you said Hoxton had Morrill's gun?"

"Certainly! *Also*, Hoxton's gun reposed nicely in Hoxton's gun belt in Hoxton's tent! What was to prevent Morrill using it, then cleaning it and loading it again?"

Rosenthal pounded the table with his fat fist. "Mine Gott, Smith, it iss too mixed up . . . my brain is virling . . . I can't make no head or tail to noddings!"

Smith's own disgust showed in his tone.

"The whole thing is a *mess!* But I've come to the conclusion that Morrill or Duncan is guilty, or both . . . unless I believe parts of Morrill's wild tale and parts of Duncan's, and put them together and start all over, discarding everything, and go searching on the wildest, weirdest, and strangest murder quest one ever engaged in! If I do that, then I've got to dig into that weird house up there with a fine tooth comb, find that missing dog, and . . . several other things. . . . But . . . that theory's unbelievable."

"Vat iss unbelievable?"

Smith looked the president squarely in the eye.

"I'd rather not say, Rosenthal. But . . . you know how I depend greatly on impressions . . . intuition?"

"Mess."

"Well, I've a hunch there is something up there . . . something I have entirely overlooked! I've a notion to follow my hunch . . . I'll tell you this much. When I find that dog and Duncan's missing gun . . . I'm going to be a lot nearer the solution of these murders. If . . . I cannot get something more concrete that points more definitely toward Morrill."

They were interrupted by the abrupt entrance of Clancy, a puffing Clancy, whose little round blue eyes were hard and filled with excitement. Ignoring Rosenthal, save for a gruff grunt, he commenced.

"Say, Chief, wait until you hear what I got to tell you! I told you that little wart was guilty, didn't I?"

"Go on, Clancy," said Smith sharply. "Get to it!"

"I'm gonna!" retorted Clancy. "Listen, what d'yu think I found out?"

"I'm *waiting*, Clancy." Smith's tone was sharp.

"Huh . . . uh-huh." Clancy, brought up by the tone, grunted, swallowed, then straightened.

"Right, Chief. Well, I was watchin' his tent like you said, and I see him movin' back and forth, and occasionally spoutin' some sort of rigamarole. I watches his shadder and finally I sees something that gets me interested, so I busts in. What d'yu think this rat was doin'?"

"I couldn't possibly guess," said Smith sarcastically, "if you mean this for a guessing contest. . . ."

"Ugh . . . no . . . oh, no . . . well . . . I'll tell you. He was standin' there in front of a mirror with a long-haired, woman's wig in one hand and the prettiest, daintiest, little woman's shoes in the other. He had his face all made up and was tryin' that damned wig on, and cavortin' around in front of that mirror, with his hands on his hips, takin' little mincin' steps and talkin' in a high, squeaky voice, just like a woman . . ."

"Hold on, Clancy, how many hands has that fellow? A moment ago he had a wig in one, shoes in the other, the next minute he's got his hands on his hips. . . . How come?"

"Yeah, that's just the way it was. I peeps in the tent first and he don't see me. He's got them things in his hands, then he puts 'em on and does what I tell you. I steps in, quiet-like as you please" . . . Smith knew just how quiet Clancy could be when he wanted to . . . "and up behind him and thrust my mug over his shoulder. Boy, howdy, didn't he jump though . . . and look guilty!

"'You dirty little murderin' wart!' I says to him. 'So you're a woman, just like I thought all the time!'

"'I am, buffoon,' he comes back at me, pert as hell. I damned near smashed him, only I thought I'd let him talk and hang himself, 'I am, buffoon,' he says. 'I was many wimmin in my former life . . . you wouldn't understand the heights to which true artistry can ascend.' 'Mebby not,' I says, 'but I know how far they let murderers drop, mister, when they breaks their necks.' That stops him for a bit; then he goes on, 'Your master might understand,' givin' me a nasty grin out of that nasty mouth of his'n. . . . 'Your master might. . . . You might run to him with a message from me, seeing you are such a faithful hound of Mount . . . Mount' . . . wait a minute. I wrote it down. . . ."

Clancy fumbled with his big black note-book, jabbed at a page with a heavy thumb, and read:

"'Hound of Montargis,' he calls me. Then he utters—

"Fair ladies, masked, are roses in their bud,
   Dismasked, their sweet commixture shown,
   Are angels veiling clouds . . . or roses blown."

Clancy closed the book.

"Then he yaps at me, 'Tell that to your master! Tell him it is a cryptogram . . . and that I think he's clever enough to read it.'

Huh, if that guy's an angel, then I'm the King of Siam, harem and all. . . ."

"Then what, Clancy!"

"Huh . . . ain't that enough. Don't that pin it on him? He's guilty as hell, and makin' a fool of us, and havin' a grand time doin' it. But if you want some more, I'll give it to you. Who made those footprints in the hallway . . . the music room? He did!"

"I know . . . I remember now . . . he vas a female impersonator before the var," breathed Rosenthal, his round eyes popping.

"Keep still a minute," said Smith sharply.

Both Clancy and Rosenthal sat silent, as Smith busied himself with pencil at the table. There was a deepened frown on his face as the minutes sped by. Finally he let his pencil drop and sat, with eyes closed, as if asleep. Clancy, however, knew he was not asleep. He knew that at last his chief had caught something . . . something which had clicked into its place in the picture puzzle of the crime he had built in his brain. Clancy held a fat finger unnecessarily to his lips to enjoin Rosenthal to silence—his chief was not to be disturbed.

Captain Smith snapped out of it abruptly. His chair legs hit the ground, his eyes, now bright and glowing, gleamed out at them. His face had become stern, hard, uncompromising. He thrust out a long, lean finger at Clancy.

"You get back on the job. Keep your eye on Morrill. Don't go near him, but . . . don't lose him. Don't talk to him. Keep entirely out of his sight and way. Let him go where he wills. But . . . follow him . . . and don't stop him . . . short of murder. . . ! Get going! Send Ryan here."

When Clancy had gone, Smith turned to Rosenthal.

"I'm going up to that house, Rosenthal. Sorry I can't stop and chin with you."

"But . . . but . . . can't you vait till morning? . . . I don't like that house, from vat you haff said off it. . . ."

"No . . . Rosey . . . I've a hunch . . . I missed something there to-day. I'm going back to see if I am right. . . . Got to be done!"

"I vill go also! I vould not haff you in danger. . . ."

Smith shook his head.

"No, Rosey, you stay here. *This is my job* . . . what I'm being paid for . . . I'll take Ryan . . . so you need not worry. And any-way . . . if what I expect to happen . . . does happen . . . I'll shoot first . . . never fear!"

XVIII

"You stay here, Ryan," Smith said as they crossed the veranda to the front door of the gigantic, Stygian building. "Keep in the shadows, and keep your eyes and ears peeled. If you see anybody, keep out of the way. But if you think anything's wrong, come a-running!"

Ryan wanted to ask a dozen questions:

"How do you know anything might happen? What do you know? You expect something? What is it? What's your idea, anyway, in coming up here tonight?"

Instead he said only . . . for he knew this mood of his chief's: "Right," and posted himself in the black angle at one side of the big door.

Smith went inside, treading softly. He did not expect to surprise anyone. Rather, he wanted to be alone, and he had come with that purpose in mind. He was in one of those strange, exalted moods which came to him at times when he was nearing the denouement of a knotty case . . . when his whole system was keyed to its highest pitch of mental and psychic sensitiveness. He snapped on his flash and played it along the wall until he saw the fireplace, and the lotus bud that opened it. Then he ascended the stairs to the music room, snapped off his light, and seated himself on the organ bench.

The room was without windows, so that now he was in black, thick silence. He could not even see suggested outlines of the musical instruments grouped about. He tried to picture who had played these . . . but no physical forms resolved themselves in his imagination. He felt differently about the organ . . . then thought that of course it was because of Hoxton's having played it. But was it Hoxton? Morrill had admitted a desire to produce similar tremendous volumes of harmony! He had said he could not do it . . . but . . . how much of Morrill's story was true? The actor had flung sayings with double meanings at him just once too often . . . and Smith felt that it had been Morrill's whimsical messages that had started him up the hill to-night and induced this psychic mood!

Many explainable sounds were about him now. . . . His ears interpreted these, and his brain eliminated them . . . the scurrying feet of rodents inside the old walls . . . the protesting groans of old timbers . . . the eerie, soughing, disquietingly human-sounding voices of night winds in chimneys and hidden crannies. After he had isolated these, he relaxed and gave himself up to that receptive state which Clancy called "The chief's séances!" Putting himself into the vibration of others who had been here before him, the natural and expected thing would have been for him to turn to the keyboard and let his fingers stray over it, but instead he swerved around, facing away from it . . . motivated strangely.

"Now *what?*" he asked himself, and immediately threw out of his mind all conscious questioning. It was a moment before he succeeded in doing this. Then he felt that his attention was being drawn definitely one direction. He switched on his light and found himself staring at the spot on which Hoxton had been found. His first reaction was one of impatience. Of course! He was carrying that mental picture! Then across his vision flashed a downward, violent stroke . . . and again he became impatient.

Dr. Gittles's word picture of Hoxton having been attacked from behind . . . that was all! It gave him nothing new.

He turned off his light again. With every sense he possessed, he strove to throw out of himself any consciousness of the tangible clues, the fantastic stories, the speculative theories of the murders. It was some time before he succeeded in doing this, and when he did, the strain on him had produced a drenching perspiration and a trembling all over his body. He fumbled for his handkerchief to wipe his brow . . . moving cautiously, trying to prevent the small act from injecting itself as a disrupting and disorganizing vibration.

And then he felt himself attracted, as before, to where Hoxton was found. He sat there . . . seemingly a long, thin, indolent shadow . . . in reality an acutely sensitive plate on which impressions might be recorded!

All he got out of it was the same flashing movement through his mind's eyes . . . a downward, violent stroke.

Nevertheless, he got up, walked across the room, and looked down the stairs back of the spot where Hoxton had been found.

"Doc's idea is that the murderer came up those stairs. Well, maybe he did . . . but that only leads back to the other clues. Nothing new. . . ."

Dissatisfied, he went across to the stairs leading to the kitchen and descended. He settled himself on the table, turned off his flash, and put himself again into the receptive state as before. . . .

Ah, this was coming clearer! Broox . . . bending over his script right here at this table . . . Duncan coming in just as he had said . . . the fight . . . their struggling, panting bodies weaving and straining in the various parts of the room . . . the thin, war-ravaged face of Duncan . . . Broox fighting grimly, realizing himself in the grasp of a—at least temporarily so—madman, who was determined to kill him!

Smith saw it all. His years in the Orient had not been without fruit. His hours at the feet of one of the masters had given him powers at which his fellowdetectives would scoff, but which he valued beyond cost!

He could almost hear the venomous cursing of Duncan—the gasping breath of Broox. . . .

He jerked up abruptly.

Clearly a picture had come to him . . . the look of triumphant hate on Duncan's face, the slowly raised revolver, a flash, the vibration of the heavy discharge.

Smith straightened, was off the table, had switched on his light. Most carefully he measured the distance from the elevator to the chalked outline of Love's body. Back to the elevator he went, calculating rapidly, calling to his mind his knowledge of the ejection force of a Colt's forty-five. Carefully again he measured off distances; stood in the spot he had designated, again called up a mental picture of this room as he had seen it the morning after the murder.

"Of course," he said at last sharply, in a tone of disgust at his own obtuseness. "Of course! What a fool not to have thought of it sooner. Of course. It's as plain as a pike-staff! And . . . that accounts for Love . . . as sure as God made little green apples. . . . The man told the truth . . . and so did Duncan. . . . My God! . . . where is this thing leading?"

With his mind quickened, and every nerve tingling with that peculiar thrill which comes to people on the point of discovery— an invention—a creation—he went back to the table, and again sat immobile in the darkness.

But now his face was grim; the long lines bordering his mouth had deepened. In his eyes was wondering, dawning horror!

"Dastardly!" he muttered, and felt the menace of a strange, death-dealing horror stalking through the blackness of the room.

Oddly his sensitive perceptions were heightened instead of diminished by this sensation. And again, oddly, he was attracted, not by either of the spots on which the two men, Broox and Love, had been found, but by a part of the walls above the chalked outline. Close his eyes as he would, each time, unfalteringly, when opened, they centered on that east wall, that strangely modeled door gaping wide on its broken hinges.

"Duncan says he came down those stairs . . . yet *someone* came through that door. . . . Who? Who, if not Duncan?"

Abruptly and regretfully he realized he had lost his psychic mood. It had departed the moment he had started to measure those distances . . . the moment he had combined logical reasoning with his occult sense! Yet he could not throw off the thought . . . that door . . . and somebody entering this chamber of horrors through it! Memory prodded him.

"*Morrill* . . . of course!"

Almost on a run he traversed the winding passage to the ballroom and sat, a bit breathless, in the high-carved wooden seat where Morrill had sat, praying that his metaphysical powers had not been switched off entirely.

In the dark he sat, waiting, slumped down . . . relaxed. . . . In a semi-doze he slipped into the reactions of the actor and was possessed by them . . . hearing, faintly, Morrill's words describing how he had felt when, the night of the murders, he had spent those fear-filled hours here.

He could feel the actor's ingrown hatred of Hoxton. He could feel an impulse also of murder . . . the desire to exterminate a fellow-man! Smith was certain that Morrill, sitting here that night, had felt the *impulse* to kill! And then that impulse was submerged in a quaking terror of the place, and the night, the imagined crouching creatures, gibbering in corners, squatting and scraping toward him! He could hear their breathing, and feel their horrible ghoulish eyes . . . their slavering, greedy lips. Spacing through it came the vivid flashes of lightning, the rumbling vibrations of thunder. . . .

For a time, because of his sheer physical exhaustion, Smith permitted this. He knew he had merely succumbed to Morrill's highly colored and highly dramatic presentation of his experiences that night. Finally, a bit ashamed and disgusted, he shook the spell off.

"Morrill's confounded cowardice has committed itself to me . . . that's all—I'll never get anything sitting here except this crazy, craven vibration . . . or . . . My God! *Now* what?"

Like a twanged wire his nerves jumped to attention, his ears to listen. . . .

From the music room came a weird, dirgelike march of chords . . . broken and wandering . . . almost stopping . . . then blasting out again in inharmonious, erratic procession! Without melody, without rhythm, without any recognized music form.

As he raced across the room toward the fireplace, he heard Ryan coming into the room on the run. Without a word they took the stairs, flung open the door at their head, both flashlights on.

No one . . . emptiness!

The organ gave back to them a silent mockery. "Now what the hell!" demanded Smith sharply. Yet subconsciously he realized the music had stopped as they had raced up the stairs.

"You sure you heard it?" he demanded of Ryan.

"God . . . yes!"

Smith crossed rapidly to the instrument, touched his sensitive fingers to the bench.

"Somebody's been here," he said grimly. "This seat's *warm!* Too hot for a spook—or a rat . . . or . . . toad . . . whatever played that organ was human flesh and blood!"

"Look—there!" said Ryan.

Smith's burning eyes followed Ryan's pointing finger. There, to the left of where Hoxton's body had fallen, a section of the wall gaped open.

"So . . . that's what was attracting me a while ago," said Smith softly. And to Ryan, sharply, "Let's go!"

Both leaped to it, only to come to an abrupt, sliding stop.

The sound of a shot echoed and reechoed throughout the empty rooms.

"Fix that thing so it can't close and follow me," ordered Smith sharply, and was off toward the stairs leading to the kitchen.

Gun ready, he took the steps in a bound, regardless of the risk of a broken neck. Flash-light on, he landed in the kitchen, his mind rocking with the thought that he had reached the end of his quest. And again amazement halted him.

His light played in a rapid, thorough search of the room. Nothing! Then—

"Oh, my God!" he muttered. "You poor little tike! You poor little innocent devil! Who got you? Who . . . got . . . *you?*"

For there on the table, bathed in the light of his torch, lay the Loves' dog, still twitching, while from his shattered head poured forth his life blood in a welling, flooding pool.

Crossing over, Smith bent down and examined the dead animal. It had been, undoubtedly, shot with the same weapon that had killed Broox; there was the place where the bullet had entered the wall.

"Now who would do such a deed as this?" said Smith grimly. "Kill an inoffensive dog? You were rightly named, pup, Calamity! I would to God I knew where you had been, how you got here, and why, you poor, hungry, thirsty little devil. . . . That's it," he said, "thirsty!"

He lifted the dog's bloody head, played the light on his muzzle. A gleam came to his eyes.

"Now, I wonder . . ." He thrust out a tentative finger, touched the wet hairs of the dog's mouth, rubbed the finger against his thumb, noticed that whatever the dog had been drinking was sticky. He played the light over the table, let it rest a moment near the edge.

"Candle drippings . . . still soft . . . unhardened. . . ."

And then in the sink he found it . . . a round, red cherry, gleaming there, mocking him . . . smirking at him, by God!

Smith swore with feeling. He felt like swearing. He felt that he had been made a fool of—not a dastardly, horrifying murder this—but a cruel and petty thing to lure him on to a fruitless climax. To plant here this jeering thing, this red cherry, all was the work of a peevishly vindictive mind!

He let his eyes go back in pity to the dog. Then he noticed something he had overlooked before. The dog's body was strangely humped up and seemed to lie unnaturally. He lifted the body, and then let out a soft sighed "Ah."

Was this another travesty, or did it explain part of this nightmarish puzzle . . . this golden goblet?

Whoever had played the jest on him had heard Duncan's story! Not only knew of these strange clues he had found, but had imagination enough to make diabolical use of them to confound him further!

As he heard Ryan coming down the stairs, he tried to decide who might have done this. The Loves—with their candles and their fruit salad; Morrill—with his keen mind . . . his sly, classical innuendoes . . . his hysterical dramatics!

"I got that door fixed, I guess, Chief," said Ryan. "And say, there's the mates to those woman's footsteps Morrill showed us down below . . . in there, fresh made in the dust of the floor. What happened down here?"

Smith stepped aside.

"Look at it! Then you tell me!"

"Oh, say, that's a dirty trick," exploded Ryan.

"That's just what it . . . *looks* like," agreed Smith. "It's damned unthinkable," he added grimly, "but that Love family had better be able to give an account of themselves for the last—" he paused and glanced at his watch. "It's eleven fifty-five . . . they'd better know where they've been for the last half-hour! H'm . . . that's funny, that's exactly the time Broox and Love got theirs. . . . H'm . . . that's queer. . . . Now, I wonder . . ."

His face became cold, implacable, stern.

"This thing is worse than a joke, Ryan! It's horrible! You stay here. And don't leave . . . under any circumstances . . . until I get back!"

XIX

All was dark, apparently, in the Love quarters. Smith pounded loudly on the door. No answer. He shook the door and called. He was not sparing anybody's feelings. He heard a movement within and then:

"What is this anyway? Who is it, and what do you want this time of night?" It was Alicia Love's sarcastic voice.

"Open this door . . . don't stop to argue with me!"

"Oh, it's Sherlock Holmes himself," came her tart rejoinder. "Well, Mr. Snoop, do I stop to *dress*, or do you prefer me in my unmentionables?"

"Open this door . . . *now!*"

She did. And she was in unmentionables, very sheer ones too. Smith turned his flash on her, and then swiftly away.

"Where have you been since eleven o'clock?" he demanded.

"Where all good little girls should be . . . in bed!"

"Where's your sister?"

"She's a good little girl also!"

"I want to talk to her. Please call her."

She stepped aside.

"Since you've seen me practically undressed, you might as well come in and look over the rest of the exhibits. My husband, what's left of him, is there in that cot. Bee's is over there."

Smith walked to the side of the room opposite where Love lay, still in his bandages. The cot was there, but Beatrice Love was not in it.

He turned a hard face to the woman behind him. "If she's in this cot," he said sarcastically, "will you please come and locate her? She's evidently shrunk, since I last saw her!" At the same time he ripped back the blankets.

Alicia Love took one look, then turned wide, surprised eyes on him. For a moment she was speechless, then the color dyed her cheeks, and she exclaimed:

"Well, good heavens, what's the idea, anyhow, bursting in here like a madman in the middle of the night? If you're going to arrest any of us, couldn't you at least have the decency to wait until morning?"

"I said, 'Where's your sister-in-law?'" Smith snapped tersely.

"Well, really, where would she be at this time of the night, if she isn't in her bed? You can answer that question just as well as I can!"

She stared angrily at him, and while under his level eyes the blood flamed to her face, she held her pose. Before he could speak, she drew a deep breath and burst out:

"Say, listen, you get out of here! I guess you can put someone out there to see we don't run off, carrying this fool barracks under our arms! I don't know what's the matter with you, but you look mad enough to bite nails . . . and you go right out there somewhere and bite 'em! I hope they choke you!"

She marched to the door and threw it open. Smith stood still, his chin hardening.

"Go on," she ordered, and stamped her bare foot. "I expect Beatrice will get back in a moment. I'll tell her about your courteous call, and . . ."

Smith broke in on her.

"When she comes back you can tell her this! I want to see her the first thing in the morning, and tell her I said to get up early! She'll have to do a lot of explaining to me as to where she's been to-night!"

"Oh, for heaven's sake," Alicia drawled in exasperation, "I suppose we won't dare turn over in bed without telling you why! I think you're crazy!"

Smith lost his temper.

"Madam, I don't care *what* you think! That isn't what's worrying me just now!"

With that he marched out, albeit feeling a bit foolish.

As he approached the kitchen he heard Ryan's voice—

"I don't care what your reasons are. You stay right here until Captain Smith gets back."

Smith stepped into the room to find Ryan confronting the girl he had just been seeking. She had a gun in her hand.

Smith's eyes went to that immediately. Unless he was much mistaken, it was an army Colt's, 45 caliber.

"Where have you been, Miss Love?"

She turned.

"*Oh*, it's you. *Why* did you shoot our dog? Poor little fellow, how *could* you?"

"We didn't shoot him! He's right where we found him. You have not answered my question!"

"All afternoon I have been hearing Clammy whining! I tried to locate him, but I couldn't. Then, tonight, I heard him barking . . . oh it was awful . . . he seemed to be inside the walls somewhere. He'd come close and I'd hear him . . . and then he'd seem to go away, and I'd not hear him. Finally, after Alicia went to sleep, I couldn't stand it any longer! I got up and tried to find him. I found a corridor leading straight out of our room. I can show it to you. It has a trick door, like so many places in this house, and that's where Calamity had been, right there behind it, sniffing and begging . . . calling me . . . poor little fellow, trying to tell me he was there!"

She stopped and her voice broke. "And . . . I was too late. . . . Oh, for shame . . . to shoot a little dog!" Her eyes blazed at Smith through tears.

"I didn't shoot him," Smith said again, and to Ryan, "How did she get in here?"

"She came right through that door," said Ryan, and turned to point, then stopped with a blank look. "Why, the damned thing's closed. . . . It was right there, that panel right next to where her brother lay!"

"Well, we'll locate it later," Smith said. "It'll keep!"

He advanced toward the girl.

"Let me see that gun."

She allowed him to take it without protest. He released the clip, saw the magazine was full, sniffed at the barrel, but found that also was clean.

"H'm," he said, and to her, "When did you shoot this gun last?"

"I don't know. Not for weeks, anyway."

"But you had it to-night. Why?"

"Oh, but don't you understand? I told you about Calamity."

He was silent. Someway her clear gaze, through brilliant tears, held a steady clarity that impressed him. He had noticed, too, that she carried a flashlight instead of a candle.

"Please tell me," she said, "who could have killed our dog?"

"Miss Love," Smith said earnestly, albeit a bit testily, "neither of us shot that dog. I'd like very much to know who did!"

"Who do you *think?*"

Then he faced her squarely. "What I think is that somebody has played a mean, contemptible trick on me. Look here . . . can you tell me if that fruit salad juice your dog was drinking, and which was in this goblet, came from your quarters?"

She shook her head, eyes wide at sight of the golden cup.

"I'm sure it didn't. We opened the only can we had the night my brother was hurt. He wanted it. . . . Oh, Mr. Smith, I know this thing is *frightful*, and you are having a hard time getting the truth. . . . There is something about it . . . I . . . I . . . hesitate to say, for fear you will think me foolish . . . but . . ."

"Say it! Maybe I have the same feelings myself!" he encouraged.

She looked into his eyes, and in her own was a convincing sincerity.

"First . . . I have finally decided . . . because I too had fears at first . . . that Aloysius *is innocent!* I will tell you now I *did* think he might have shot Captain Jones! I *did* lie to you! But, you see, I couldn't tell you I had known Captain Jones, until I was sure myself that Aloysius didn't do it. And I am *now*—"

"What makes you feel so sure?"

"Nothing definite . . . only . . . it has come to me, and I know he's innocent, just as much as I know we are standing here! Something . . ." she shivered and drew her shoulders up, as if seeking escape from the place, "something . . . strange . . . *terribly strange* is here! I didn't shoot Calamity! You didn't, and Mr. Ryan didn't . . . but . . . there he is! Shot! Who did it? And what for? It must be the same person . . . fiend . . . !"

Ryan came toward them, a shell in his hand. "And it's the same caliber, Chief," he said.

"It's from the same gun!" said Smith slowly. They looked at one another with puzzled eyes, and in Beatrice's there was a growing terror.

"Oh . . . oh . . . I'm afraid! Can't we leave this place to-morrow morning, Mr. Smith? Please!"

"Certainly. You could have left at any time, except for your brother's wound."

"He's well enough." She became conscious of her negligée, and drew it around her. "I guess . . . I . . . better be going back," she said, in a little-girl scared voice.

"Ryan, you go back with Miss Love and . . . you've got your revolver?"

"Yes."

"Well . . . just stay there within call until morning, will you? It's a long grind, old man, but you can sleep in to-morrow."

"Oh . . . thank you," breathed Beatrice.

"Well, that's that," said Captain Smith, after watching Ryan and Beatrice Love pass around the corner toward the Love quarters. "If I believe that family, then who have we got left? Well, I'll soon know if it's Morrill," he muttered. "I can't believe Clancy's let him go that far, but . . ."

Smith found Clancy sitting sprawled on top of Williams's piled boxes of equipment, across the company street from Morrill's tent. Clancy was a believer in bodily comfort, whenever possible, and now lay back in somnolent, sleepy-eyed ease.

He did not hear Smith until his chief stood over him. Like a hippopotamus coming up out of a reed-lined pool, he reared to his huge feet.

"Where's Morrill?" Smith demanded.

Clancy pointed toward Morrill's dark tent with a thick thumb.

"Sure?"

"Yeah," grunted Clancy. "Sure! Also positive. Went to bed two hours ago. Why . . . what's up?"

"Tell you later. Sure about Morrill?"

"I peeked in about ten thirty. Dead to the world and snorin' peacefully."

Smith stared off into the night, frowning deeply.

"Well . . . that's that . . . then . . . and now . . . what have we . . .? Think I'll just have another peek to be sure, Clancy," he said finally.

"Go right ahead," said Clancy generously, "if you wanta. But he's there, brother. What's up, Chief? You've been running!"

"Never mind. No time to talk. Let's check up on your man!"

"All right! All right!" Clancy lumbered out after Smith, who was taking rapid strides toward Morrill's tent. Smith lifted the flap, listened a moment for the man's breathing, flashed on his light. When he turned back toward Clancy his voice was sharp, his face bleak.

"Your man's flown!"

"Naw, he's *there*, I tell you."

"Take a look for yourself!"

"Huh," Clancy grunted. "My God, he's gone, ain't he? Now can you beat that!"

"I can't even tie it!" said Smith ominously. "When did you look in here last?"

Clancy shivered at the tone of his voice. "Why, at ten thirty, and he was curled up on that cot sleepin' just like a baby . . ."

"Yes, Clancy. Playing possum! See that slit in the back wall of the tent? That's how he got out without your knowing it. Can't you do anything I set for you . . . and do it right?"

"How did I know he'd pull anything like that? What happened? Has this little guy . . . ?"

"Never mind! You get out and find Morrill! Rout out the camp if necessary . . . but . . . but . . . *find him!*"

"Are you looking for me, gentlemen?"

Both men turned. Clancy let out a grunt.

"Say, you little weazel, where the hell you been?" he demanded blusteringly.

Captain Smith played his light on the little actor, then added his cold, sharp words to Clancy's. "Yes, Morrill, where have you been?"

"I? Why Captain . . . I have been nowhere and everywhere . . . I have been communing with the forces of the universe, listening to the great silent symphony of the whirling spheres. . . ."

"Where . . . have . . . you . . . been . . . Morrill? . . . *Answer me!*"

"Why, I assure you I have answered you. I have been sitting on yon hilltop amid the fern and bracken, gazing upward and outward into this glorious moonlit creation of countless suns traveling their countless orbits of millions of light-years, and speculating where in all that space are also traveling the souls of those two men so late departed! Are they wandering, lost? Or have they joined a celestial company—or is Hoxton roaring at minor, smaller devils in the roaring caldrons of hell? There is a tree there, Captain. I rested my back against its huge, ageless trunk! A tree that was old when our Saviour was born! I leaned against its rough bark and thought of those immortal lines of Joyce Kilmer's . . ."

"Morrill, I'm going to ask you just *once* more, why did you rip open the back of your tent and sneak away from camp? And I don't want *poetry*. I want the truth. . . ."

Morrill smiled. "You believe they are not synonymous? A common mistake, Captain. But more of that anon—when we have more leisure together. . . . As to my sneaking out the rear of my tent. . . . It was merely a little part of the game Sir Giblets and I've been playing. . . ."

"Say, that's three times you've called me that," Clancy broke in heatedly. "I don't like it!"

"Most fat people don't like it. 'Sir Giblets' refers to your portliness . . . an old English expression, my good man. . . ."

Clancy snorted.

Morrill continued blandly:

"For hours this fat behemoth has tiptoed to my tent at regular intervals with the ponderous tread of a mad elephant, and just about as much tact and elegance, and poked his fat proboscis inside to peer at me! I thought it would give him a bit of satisfaction to . . . *not* find me! So . . . I pretended to be asleep and snoring peacefully . . . to lull his dull brain into fuller quietude . . . knowing he would accept the simulation for the real . . .

then quietly I slipped out and away where his bumptious person would not obtrude upon my thoughts, which he is perfectly incapable of understanding, I assure you. . . . I climbed that hill . . . and sat as I told you. Perhaps, if you are keenly enough attuned to the infinite, if you would go there and rest your head against that tree trunk, you can verify my silent communion with it. If not, you perhaps will have to accept my word for it! I have been nowhere else, I assure you again, most sincerely!"

"Search him, Clancy!" said Captain Smith, having almost exhausted his patience forcing himself to remain silent while Morrill said his little piece.

"Not a damned thing," said Clancy, who had not hesitated to rough up Morrill considerably.

"Get Serge and go with Morrill up to that place of communion, as he calls it. You stay with him. Tell Serge to search everything for anything that will prove that he was up there!"

"You had better hope, Morrill, that in your 'communion with the infinite' you managed to leave some finite evidence! And . . . one more warning . . . from now on . . . were I you . . . I'd see to it that Clancy . . . or myself . . . or Ryan . . . know in advance . . . of your desires for communion with the infinite . . . or any other sort of communion that takes you beyond our physical recognition of your sentient presence. Take him along, Clancy. I'll get your report later."

A minute search of Morrill's tent resulted in exactly what Captain Smith expected . . . nothing!

Thirty minutes later Randall's sleepy chauffeur, Red, halted his car in front of Dr. Gittles's house and Captain Smith descended. After a monotonous and continuous ringing of the doctor's door-bell, the door opened and Gittles, frowsy-haired and indignant, dressed only in his nightshirt, peered out at him.

"Oh, it's *you*, Captain. Come in. What's happened?"

"I want you to give me the history of that old house!"

"Well, Godfrey's cordial, man, did you have to wear out my door-bell, and roust me up in the middle of the night? I told you to come down some night. But I didn't mean midnight . . . Lord, you fellows haven't any consideration at all, have you?"

Fuming, Gittles nevertheless was leading the way toward his library, where he turned on the lights.

"Wait till I get my pants! Cigars in that old skull, there. Help yourself. Back in a minute. Leg's colder'n a cadaver's. Don't be afraid of those cigars. That skull's been fumigated!"

He hustled from the room. Smith made a gesture of taking a cigar, and lighted one from his pocket instead.

"We owe a lot to the fellow that invented pants," said Gittles, coming back into the room, busily tucking in his nightshirt. "Without pants a man carries around a superiority complex which most people mistake and call an inferiority complex. With pants, he immediately rises above his bare shins and becomes the noblest creature in the animal kingdom . . . capable of great and glorious deeds . . . unless he splits 'em! Now, Captain, having spoiled my beautiful dreams, what can I tell you?"

"I want the entire history of that house, Doc! All you know about it. . . . Someone got the Love dog to-night . . . in that kitchen, someone who could, and did, play that damned organ . . . and somebody who left me that . . . as a souvenir!"

Smith took the golden goblet from his pocket and set it down on the near-by table.

"So . . . the spirits are still busy, eh! Well, well . . . and I thought all these tales of that place being haunted . . . were sheer moronic imaginings of our local dwellers whose primary reflexes had not reached a state of pubescence. . . . Well, well . . . so our ghost is still with us. . . ."

"Rot!" said Smith hotly. "Come down to rationality, Gittles!"

"Rationality?" Gittles raised his sandy eyebrows. "What is rationality?"

Before Smith could speak, Gittles answered it himself.

"Reasonableness . . . a reliance upon reason; the capability of being reconciled with the facts as they are known to exist. It precludes that we are all nooscopically inclined; *Ens rationalis*, as it were, with no possibility of any paralogism, no antilogy in our intellectual or cogitative faculties. It intends that we mortals, with noddles of bone set upon our spinal cords, said noddles filled with a substance which in its last analysis is nothing more than a hatful of mashed potato substance, must accept as fact only such intelligible manifestations of reason as would come under the head of empirical, intellectual, and material cognition.

"But somewhere, Captain Smith, unfortunately, *non obstante* in the sensorium or the *penetralia mentis* of the average *homo sapiens*, we are up against emanations that preclude rationality. And so, in dealing with such a thing as that rambling, goofy pile up there on the hill. You have got to dig down into the recondite etiology of a pneumatology bordering on transcendentalism . . . at least transcendental to all rationality. You will have to delve into thaumaturgism, and admit things which are positively absonant and unscientific and opposed to all rules of logic if you would trace back these crazy legendary beliefs of our simple folk; if you would attain the *fons et origo*, the *vera causa* of the mythology of that house.

"We will have to go back a few years and consider a most interesting energumen . . . a person *per se*, *mens sana*, with as peculiar a dementia as is possible to conceive; a dementia which should fall more properly into the classification of acute and eccentric hallucination, which in time undoubtedly became a delusitory monomania. . . . That goblet formed part of a peculiar ritual of that hallucination, just as that house, whose very

air seems to give out a miasmic atmosphere of goofiness, is itself
the monument to that unhappy delusion. Mark, I do not claim
that any of the things I shall tell you about it are allowable in any
cognitive view, from any rational process of the mind.

"The tale digs deeper than any rationality we are acquainted
with in our limited studies of the peculiar reasoning and imaginative processes of the human mind.

"Yet, undoubtedly, we must either accept the theory that an
inceptive delusion may be transferred on after death through the
medium of the unrecognized spirit world, by agencies which are
not materially existent and capable of physical performance, or
we must believe that unusual mental concentration upon some
delusitory dementia produces, in the rational minds of the receptive who contact such irrationality, the same illogical, delusitory
dementia! Do I make myself clear?"

"As mud!" said Smith flatly.

"Fine! Having gotten that off my chest, and prepared your
potato mash, so to speak, for a weird tale, and your having picked
the right and witching hour for hearing such tales, it is fitting
I get down to brass tacks and lay before you what I know, and
what the natives hereabout *believe* about that house wherein, in
the last twenty-four hours, two men and a pup have come to a
violent end. They were not the first . . . oh, no . . . there have
been others, Captain, according to local gossip. . . . Now, lend
me your ears!"

Two hours later Captain Smith returned to camp. A faint
lightening of the eastern sky brought to him a realization that
dawn was near. He would have enjoyed telling Rosenthal what
Gittles had told him . . . but his tired body made him realize that
he had spent almost all the last twenty-four hours without rest,
keyed to the highest pitch, straining every fiber of his mind and
being, in his effort to apprehend the fiend that had perpetrated
these ghastly crimes.

Clancy and Serge were waiting for him, with the report that they could find absolutely nothing that would corroborate Morrill's story.

"Well, let's all get to bed, then," said Smith wearily.

"And let that little squirt run wild?" demanded Clancy, gesturing toward the dark outlines of Morrill's tent.

Smith nodded.

"Yes, Clancy . . . nothing is going to happen now for some time. I'm going to sleep until ten. Don't let anyone disturb me, not even Rosenthal. If you are up before me, say that I'll have something to tell him then."

But the sun had risen before Captain Smith closed his eyes. Bit by bit he was fashioning his evidence into a ghastly pattern, a pattern as strange and unbelievable as the tale he had just heard from the little coroner's lips.

XX

"Vell? Qvick! Tell me! I am all goose pimples vid curiosity!"

Captain Smith looked up from a much-belated breakfast and into Abraham Rosenthal's avid brown eyes. He laid down his fork and leaned across the table as the head executive of Superior Films lowered his portly self into a chair across from him.

"Rosey," he said solemnly, "you'll just have to go ahead and goose-pimple!"

"You mean you von't tell me?" Rosenthal exclaimed, and his face settled into an expression of hurt disappointment, like a little boy whose hope of going to the circus has been blighted.

"But it isn't a circus, Rosey," said Smith whimsically, "it's *murder*, the most climactic word in the languages of nations. If it were a circus, I'd give you a ticket . . . but right now I can't even give you a tip! Too much depends on talking little and acting much!"

"Circus . . . circus! Vat are you talking about? I didn't say nothing about circuses!"

Smith smiled.

"Just some of my foolishness. But about telling you. . . ." He glanced toward the door of the cook tent, and brought his voice even lower.

"Rosey, you've got cause to be disappointed. I know you came up here hoping to help me solve this thing . . . hoping to hurry

it to an end . . . as we did before! But this time the theory I have
is even more far-fetched, on the face of it, than the wild idea you
got about Hardell's death . . . and . . . which proved to be the
right one! I hope *my* wild idea bears out as correctly!"

"But . . . can't you tell me just vone vord . . . vone vord?"
begged Rosenthal, his round brown eyes pleading.

"It can't be told in a word. It's a long story. I'd like to, but
perhaps I'm on a wild-goose chase." Smith's doubt brought his
words to a hesitant close.

"But that baby blimp vat married MacDougal's daughter . . .
vat's his name . . . Clancy . . . vell, that Clancy tells me you've
got it all solved!"

"He's jumping to conclusions . . . as usual," said Smith dryly.

Rosenthal automatically began conveying portions of ham
and eggs to his mouth, but in his eyes disappointment still smol-
dered. Smith was sorry. He felt a bit traitorous. He liked Rosenthal . . . admired him. He trusted him. He respected the picture
executive's mental processes . . . but he not only could not take
the time to tell him, nor could he risk the chance of his idea slipping out. Rosenthal said, in hurt dignity, reading his thought:

"Vell, I should think, Smith, you vould know I am not a blab
mouth by this time!"

"It isn't that. I'd like to have you read an essay by a man
named John Barry on 'The Idea' . . . this idea is born, you know,
into the world . . . and it travels about for a home. Nobody wants
it. Somebody finally takes it in, and then everyone else jumps up
and yells, 'Knew that ten years ago!'"

"Vell?"

"It's like that! I'm afraid to even send out spoken words into
the unnamed currents of the air, for fear they be caught and interpreted! I'm reluctant to even speak this thing in words . . . for
it all rests on a certain happening to-night, Rosenthal . . . and
it's like stalking a wary-eyed deer . . . ready to spring into flight

at the *smell* of an intruder! That's all I can say. But rest assured you'll be in at the last scene . . . if you want to witness it."

"Sure. Certainly! Ven does it happen?"

"To-night."

"Vat happened up at that house last night? Randall vas telling me somethings about some excitement, and then he jumps off like a crazy man, vid his breakfast half eaten. Villiams tells me he has got a girl up at that house! Mein Gott, I should hate to haff that fine young man mixed up vid a bad voman! I feel like firing him. I feel like firing efferybody vat does anything ve can't send out to the Sunday school papers," said Rosenthal dolefully.

Smith laughed.

"Don't worry about that girl. And as for what happened . . . somebody shot about four hundred ninety-nine thousand nine hundred and ninety-nine dollars off that five hundred thousand dollar dog of yours, that's all!"

"That Love dog vat vas lost?" exclaimed Rosenthal, his eyes popping. "Vell, then you haff the murderer!" he finished flatly.

For a moment Smith's eyes bored into his, then—

"That the way it strikes you?" he asked quietly.

Rosenthal shrugged his fat shoulders.

"Vell, I vouldn't like to implicate an innocent party, but . . . vat vould an innocent party vant to shoot a poor little dog for?"

"And with a forty-five bullet . . . the same kind that got Broox!" said Smith softly.

"Mein Gott!"

They sat looking significantly at each other. Then Smith drew out an object that had been bulging his coat pocket.

"They left you a little token, Rosey."

"Mein Gott! They already haff left me too many tokens!"

Smith set the object on the table in front of him. Rosenthal's face flashed into a look of surprise. He picked up the golden goblet in his fat, ringed fingers and turned it round and round.

"Gold!" he murmured through wondering lips. "Gold! Solid, I bet you! Vere did you get it?"

"Where I hope I'm going to get the murderer to-night!"

Smith got to his feet, leaned over and patted the other affectionately.

"Take a rest to-day, Rosenthal. You can't help, and I don't want you to even look like you know anything's coming off to-night. Ryan will tell you what to do and when to do it. . . . It might be just as well, if you have a revolver, to slip it into your pocket."

Rosenthal shrugged off the hand and shook his head vigorously.

"No! No! Already there hass been too much business vid revolvers!"

"All right . . . you'll be safe enough, I guess, anyway . . ." and Smith started off to meet Ryan and Clancy coming up the company street.

"Morning boys . . . had breakfast? Fine. Come on over to Williams's tent. I'll give you the low down. She busts loose to-night!"

Smith had been talking steadily for an hour into the amazed and slightly unbelieving ears of his two men . . . stopping Clancy's outbursts with a cold eye and irrevocable voice. Now he got to his feet.

"There's no need to worry. I've kept up my target practice. I don't like to boast . . . but . . . I'm what the wild Westerners call 'quick on the draw,' boys, as you know. . . ."

"But look-a-here!" Clancy burst out, red-faced with excitement, "if they get me, they only get a big hunk of beef without much brains . . . but if they get you . . . they get . . . they get . . ."

"Enough! You know I appreciate it, but this is my work! There's things about this I can't put into words . . . my crazy hunches . . ." He stopped to smile at them. "I depend partly on that talent of mine to help me through. Now listen, Ryan! If I do get it, you know what to do. My red note-book will give it all to you. It may take a lot of work, but you can follow out my outlines, and . . ."

"Whoever 'gets you' had better finish themselves while they're at it!" swore Clancy feelingly. "I'll just whittle 'em down to a match . . . that's all . . . and . . . then . . . . light 'em and watch 'em burn!"

This was Clancy's worst threat, and Smith knew that the big sergeant could, like an enraged elephant, go must on occasions.

"Keep your shirt on, old man," he said steadily. "We're a pack of calamity howlers . . ."

"Huh . . . *Calamity* howlers is right!" Clancy snorted, and they all grinned ruefully.

"The best thing you boys can do for me is to see that everything goes off right. No slips. There's the real danger. Follow instructions and I do not think anyone will be hurt. Now let's get down to brass tacks. First, I want to talk to Randall, Serge, and Williams. Tell 'em to come in singly, and . . . carelessly. Have Williams bring in some props to camouflage him. Randall can bring me my lunch tray. Serge can ask Williams for extra film, or something, and come to get it himself. I'll be in here making a complete report in my note-book for a couple of hours. Ryan, dust down to Lake's office and tell him I want him to meet me at that turn in the main road just below the house at . . . ten thirty to-night. Tell him to bring Pelley with him, and, if he can, a couple of others, armed. Tell him to let Doc Gittles know. He wants to be in on the wind-up—and we may need him!"

As they started out, he warned:

"Now, remember . . . not one word! Don't tell any of those fellows what they're wanted for . . . just tell 'em to be there! Clancy . . . get back to Morrill!"

Clancy made a wry face.

"Yeah . . . back to wet nursing that dirty little murderous wart!"

Smith offered him a consolation cigar. As he handed it out he said, "Can't show partiality. Here's one for you, too, Ryan."

They slipped out of the tent. Later Randall came in, eager-eyed and breathless.

"Say," he commenced excitedly. Smith told him to sit down.

"I can't tell you much, Randall. I want you to promise to do just what I say, and repress your natural curiosity."

"Sure. You bet! But just a minute, if you don't mind. My girl says you told her she could get out of there this morning, and—"

"Miss Love? Congratulations. You're a fast worker!"

Randall looked utterly amazed. Smith chuckled.

"You don't think so, eh? That's because it's the real thing. Time doesn't mean anything, then . . ."

"It's just like we've known each other always, sir. . . ."

Randall had an awe of this man, with his quiet remarks, his friendliness . . . his cold finality. He also had not shed his worry that Beatrice, or one of the Loves, might be mixed up in the murders . . . and yet there was something about Smith that stopped him from seeming too anxious . . . or asking questions. To himself, he said: "God, but I'll be glad when this is over! If Bee's mixed up in it, why . . . why . . . I'll just have to do what I can to help . . . and . . . that's that. If anything happens to her, it's curtains for me . . . that's all!"

"Somewhat of a fatalist, aren't you?" said Smith, breaking into his thought. Randall flushed.

"I . . . guess . . . so . . . but how did you know?"

"By your face. Don't worry, son. Now about the Loves moving. No . . . they can't go to-day. I promised Miss Love, but in the light of certain circumstances, I must break it . . . justifiedly . . . I can't miss one chance. . . . Tell her not to be frightened. Lake will have a man on guard there all the time, and Rosenthal has given me permission for you to be there as much of to-day and . . . to-night . . . as you want. . . ."

"Thanks a million!"

"No thanks. That's not a favor. That's an order. I want you to be there from ten o'clock on. . . ."

Answering Randall's look of bewilderment, he said only:

"From ten o'clock on you are to guard . . . Miss Love! She will not be, and is not to be, out of your sight . . . or touch. And Randall . . . do not discuss this with anyone . . . as Rosenthal says . . . 'Not vone vord! Not a vord to anyvone!'"

"Yes . . . sir," said Randall slowly, and, looking very much discouraged, went out.

"Can't help it, lad," said Smith to himself, watching him. "Please God, you'll look differently tomorrow."

Then he turned his attention to his revolver . . . cleaned and oiled it thoroughly . . . reloaded it.

"I wonder if I'm crazy," he asked himself. "And yet . . . there is that golden goblet . . . and that red cherry . . . and Duncan's wild tale . . . well, if I'm barking up the wrong tree, I won't bag my game, that's all. And that's that!"

It was at dinner that night that Smith watched Rosenthal with sympathetic amusement.

"You'll get acute toxicosis, Rosey, gulping like that," he protested softly.

Rosenthal did not answer.

"You're boiling over with bile like a spoiled child! It'll poison you!"

"I wish you would get a fish-bone in your throat," retorted Rosenthal heatedly, "so you couldn't speak for a month! I should pay you a big fee, and then you should come up here and find out about my murders, and tell me nothings!"

"Sit tight, Rosey . . . until to-night. . . . You may get a belly-ful!" retorted Smith crisply, and again lapsed into silence.

Ten-thirty!

Night, and black as a cat's back. The moon, a late one, and not showing even a tip over the almost indistinguishable mountain crest back of the strange house.

Four men slipped in single file, without speaking, up the drive . . . slid through the big front door . . . and then separated . . . walking with hands protectingly before their faces in the dark fastnesses of the weird building . . . finding their various stations . . . hoping devoutly they would not stumble . . . not even daring to mutter this hope under their breaths . . . hardly daring to breathe. . . .

Lake, Pelley, Gittles, and Serge.

Their dark shapes, flitting silently through the dark void might have been imagined, for immediately all was brooding, sullen, impenetrable blackness . . . as before!

Eleven o'clock!

A second phantomlike group slipping out of the shadows and into the house. . . . They followed Ryan, who went directly to the high-backed carved wood seat and guided each one into it. Rosenthal repressed a grunt of relief as he met its solidity.

There was no further movement from the latest corners . . . no sound, save their rapidly beating hearts, that could almost be heard . . . and no light to penetrate the thick gloom . . . dispel into nothingness the sinister imaginings of their brains!

Minutes seemed hours. Ryan had left them. Beatrice Love leaned noiselessly into the curve of Randall's arm . . . wanting to burst into tears for sheer comfort of his steely muscles along her quivering back.

On the other side of the fireplace Lake was flat against the wall, his lean, malarial length motionless as a black cardboard pasted silhouette. Only once he moved, when a stirring of the air

about him indicated the passage of another . . . and to his ears
came the almost imperceptible open sesame:

"Ryan . . . Lake. . . ."

Then the shadow passed up the stairs and was swallowed up
by the deep blackness of the music room.

In the kitchen, in the rear of the house, the door that had
been broken in still sagged open on its hinges. The door to the
music room stairs was closed, as it had been, but above, in the
music room, in an ell between the end of the organ and that secret door, revealed to Ryan and Smith last night, was the thin,
flat figure Ryan. In the kitchen the door to another secret passage, the one into which Aloysius Love had stumbled on that
fatal night, was wedged open about an inch, and to that inch-
wide crack was held a steady gray eye that now and again moved
away as its owner glanced down at the illumined hands of his
wrist watch. . . .

Eleven twenty nine. . . .

"H'm . . . pretty soon now! It'll either show me up as a fool . . .
or . . . we'll get that murderer!"

For fifteen minutes more Captain Smith held that gray eye
steady, focused on the sink and the table, while within him an-
ticipation warred with incredulity.

Then a bright pencil of light cut into the crack and across
his eye. Into his vision there began to be assembled an array of
golden goblets. They were filled with segments of fruits . . . and
now the figure preparing this strange midnight feast stepped into
view.

"Good God! . . . Morrill's houri. . . !"

Smith all but spoke his startled discovery . . . and pressed his
thin lips tightly as the figure, with radiant, strangely iridescent
face, and rich and flowing garments, moved out of his sight.

"The music room stairs . . . of course . . . it's working out . . . but . . . Morrill's beautiful woman . . ." He stopped to recognize the click of the stair door as it went shut.

"Now for it. . . ." he said grimly. He felt for his gun, and, that in his hand, stepped softly into the room of death and crossed to the table. A moment he spent bending there, verifying in reality the things he had imagined from such bits of evidence as a drop of wax and a preserved cherry. . . . Then, picking up a goblet, he turned, with his back against the table . . . and waited. . . .

He counted twenty slowly, then leaned forward . . . and nodded. Only the glow deepening in his eyes told of his tense excitement. . . .

For then, ringing out through the stillness, throbbing and dying to throb again came the broken chords from the organ he had heard the night before. . . .

Steady and calm the man waited . . . and at last slowly raised the goblet toward his lips. . . .

"Might as well drink this . . . now . . . a toast to the gods . . . for it's on their laps now . . . my life . . . or . . ."

He tipped the goblet up as the door from the music room began to open. . . .

As the chords of music came to the ears of those in the ballroom, Beatrice shrank closer into Randall's arms, stilling the exclamation that rose to her lips. Now she knew she had been right when the night before she had thought it was not only Calamity's thin whining that had aroused her!

Rosenthal was surprised into a startled exclamation.

"Quiet!" came the instantly hissed warning from Lake. In hypnotized silence they listened as the chords rolled sonorously about them in the air, vibrated even the walls at their backs where the reeds contacted it . . . so that they felt it through their bodies. It gave them a sweat of unnamable terror, this closeness to those unknown, murderous hands that moved the keys.

Then, when Beatrice felt she must scream aloud, and Randall's and Rosenthal's legs were tensing, prepared to spring, the music stopped. Silence!

Lake sensed the jumping nerves of those on the bench. He did not trust them. He ordered again, "Wait!"

Almost on the words came the loud reverberation of a shot! Another!

Hard on the heels of the second, Smith's voice, shouting:

"Look out, Lake!"

The sound of running feet, with a path from a flash racing ahead of them, and in front, and leading the light and the racing figure of Captain Smith, something dark that flitted with the fantastic ability of a spook through the room and vanished up the stairs!

Smith's voice, as he followed:

"Sit still every one. . . ."

And then his feet pounding up the stairs, the sounds of a scuffle, brief but fierce, and then Ryan's voice rising in triumph:

"Okay, Chief! I've got her!"

Beatrice twisted suddenly in Randall's arms and gripped his shoulders.

"Her? . . . Her?" she whispered distraughtly. "Who does he mean?"

"Hush . . . darling . . . hush. . . . I don't know." Randall's heart was pumping with wild relief. His own girl was there safe, in his arms . . . and that was all he knew . . . or cared!

Lake, who had been busy with his flash, now came forward with a Coleman lantern in his hand. Pelley walked in from the passageway to the kitchen with another, Dr. Gittles hurrying in front of him.

Lake said:

"C'mon, folks . . . Smith said as how we wuz to gather in the kitchen if he got the murderer . . . and I guess him and Ryan has.

He figgers, account of his having looked suspicious at a lot of you folks, that you got a full explanation coming . . . if you want to hear it. . . ."

With Lake herding them, wordlessly, wonderingly, a little fearfully, they passed down the long winding corridor to the scene of the murders.

XXI

Candle-light wavering silently and soft on the richly gleaming chalices of twelve golden goblets! The unexpected sight of them caused the little group to halt for one astonished, indrawn breath. Then the broad bands of light from the Coleman lanterns struck across that dimly lighted, weird old kitchen . . . flashed into rainbow colors as they hit the bejeweled robes of a figure standing motionless, face toward the wall . . . and held there by two deputies.

An extraordinary and fantastic scene, and stupefying to the people being ushered into it. No one spoke. As in a trance the little group huddled in one spot . . . staring. Amos Lake, lean and slouching, alone seemed to be unemotional . . . serene with that provincial serenity which refuses to be amazed.

"Sorry folks," he drawled, "we ain't got better accommodations."

No one smiled. Instead, they turned to watch with eyes anticipatory of new horrors a slow movement . . . the regular drip . . . drip . . . drip . . . and dull sunburst splash of blood upon the inlaid floor! Sometimes, when the figure under the gorgeous robes writhed, that blood was swung inward, and against the brocaded silk . . . went slithering slowly down it from the hand hanging there . . . what remained of it. Dr. Gittles stepped up, gauze and antiseptic ready, and commenced to work on it, and as he did so his short broad body came between the silent staring group and that slow dripping red.

"Well, you finished this hand all right, Smith!"

Gittles's matter-of-fact voice was like a succession of sharp little raps on the head. It brought the watchers out of their be-musement. Horror and repulsion, not to the injury, but the cause for it, made a piercing vibration in their brains, remained—wid-ened . . . soon would engulf them utterly.

"Had to!" said Smith shortly, answering Gittles.

Ryan stepped forward to the table.

"Let's see your own, Chief," he said, and made to take Smith's arm.

"Just creased me across the knuckles. It will wait."

Nevertheless, he let Ryan bind a clean white handkerchief around it, then picked up a Colt's revolver, balanced it in his hand, looked at it a moment, then his eyes went to that strange, silent figure. There was abhorrence and pity in his face. He laid the revolver slowly back on the table and faced his audience.

"The ways with which we detectives arrive at conclusions are often mysterious to the laymen," he began.

The deep-toned steadiness of his voice made Beatrice catch her breath in a little thankful sob. It re-created for her her nor-mal world . . . men and women and life apart from the tragic grotesquerie of the present.

"When possible, I like to let the people involved in a case witness the end," Smith continued.

He stopped to smile whimsically.

"Being considered a possible suspect for murder is not pleas-ant. It leaves a shadowed memory. I have had people tell me that the thing which helped to wipe that memory out has been the ability to sit in on the finale. . . . A finished thing can be put out of the mind."

He paused . . . let his eyes go to the sink, with its beautiful, and to the rest inexplicable, exhibits, from there to the quivering figure beside which Gittles was still working, slowly let his eyes come back to those tensely waiting.

"We have had here a triangle of crime . . . a three-sided tragedy. I assure you, at times it seemed to have innumerable planes, each one leading back and fitting, without solution, into another! I could go on indefinitely almost giving you ideas that leaped into my mind . . . theories like combinations of a jig-saw puzzle . . . that could be worked out as well one way as another! . . . when I stepped in here and saw . . . Broox, dead on this spot on which I am now standing . . . the chalked outline over there where Love had fallen . . . and upstairs the body of Hoxton!

"On snap judgment it appeared that any one of those three men might have done for the other two . . . that any two of them might have each committed a crime! For instance:

"Love, on his search for his dog, stumbled into this room. He recognized Broox on sight. They shot it out. Love shot a second before Broox, causing Broox's hand with its aimed revolver to jerk up, thus throwing the bullet high of its mark and along Love's cranium. That idea was strengthened by the testimony of Duncan, who stated that Broox had reason to fear an assault from Love. . . . But we could not locate Broox's gun, and with Duncan's advent into the triangle came another angle. Duncan had sworn to kill Broox. He had followed him up here with that intention. The mustache he was wearing was found near Broox's body, showing he had been in this room. I admit that I thought Duncan was guilty. Duncan's admission that he and Broox had had a hand-to-hand fight, substantiated by the condition of Broox's clothing, the shell from Duncan's revolver, and his finger-prints on the elevator all tended to make me think that Duncan was the murderer. Against that I had a strange tale from Duncan of these golden goblets and candles . . . and to substantiate this I found remains of fruit juices on Broox's vest, candle drippings on the table. Broox did not bring any fruit up here. There was no food in the place. Certainly Duncan would not bring any. Who then? The thought of another person involved began to come to me. Added to this was Duncan's very demeanor, his frank admission of his hatred, his sincere regret that he had not committed the crime!

"One question remained. . . . Why would Broox spill fruit juice on his vest? He was naturally a fastidious man! After turning this over in my mind, I came to the conclusion that the circumstances to make him partake of refreshment from an unknown hand . . . spill it . . . must have been unusual!

"From certain evidences I decided his fight with Duncan was real. His throwing of Duncan down the elevator shaft . . ." Smith pointed to it, "was real. I pictured him staggering back to this table, gasping for breath . . . picking up some container . . . one of the golden cups Duncan had told of . . . drinking from it. Duncan's story was strengthened, also, by the fact that I found a sheet of paper on this table that Duncan had walked on. *On this table*, I said. Do you get the significance of that? Would Duncan, *after* having killed Broox, stop to pick up a sheet and return it to the table? Not likely. Answer . . . Broox made an attempt to straighten his manuscript himself . . . but was shot before he finished!

"Duncan returned, you might say . . . so did I . . . at first. Duncan said his gun went off once during the struggle with Broox. Which led me again to believe Duncan's story . . . and to the deduction that Duncan it was who shot Love just as Love entered this room! For, remember, there was no weapon beside Broox's body . . . and Broox could not have gotten rid of it after he was killed. Instead, in the fight, when Duncan pulled the trigger in his attempt to kill Broox, he shot instead Love . . . and neither Broox nor Duncan, struggling for their lives, was even aware that Love had entered this room. . . Broox never, perhaps . . . and Duncan not until after he had climbed out of that elevator. . . . Checking up Love's story of what he saw made this conclusion the only tenable one accounting for Love . . . and his condition. But if I believed this, then I had learned something else most important. . . . The fact that Broox was killed too soon after Duncan's shot to discover Love!

"Yet the bullet that lodged in the wall there above Love's chalked body outline was of forty-five caliber . . . the same as killed Broox! . . . the type of gun Duncan brought into this room with him! Now do not forget that Broox did not have a gun . . . and that Duncan's gun . . . according to him . . . was last in Broox's hands. Also, according to Duncan, it could not be found.

"But, you might say, Duncan shot both Love and Broox and secreted his gun! I admit I entertained that idea. However, had I not discarded it, the shooting of Love's dog Calamity last night would have caused me to do so. Duncan was in jail at that time! So he is ruled out.

"Who, then, would shoot the dog, and for what reason? And who, having shot the dog, would leave behind them a golden goblet; just such a thing as Duncan had described? Either that deed was a perverted conception of a joke—or . . . the act of the murderer! Undoubtedly the latter, for who would perpetrate such a joke?

"Let us go back now to Hoxton. He was known to have a grudge against Broox. He could not have shot Broox after he himself was murdered, and, as surely, Broox could not have murdered him after he was shot. Besides . . . those two men were killed at approximately the same time . . . therefore, Hoxton was eliminated as the murderer of Broox. Again . . ." Smith threw up his hands. "All leaving us up in the air as to who killed Hoxton!

"Perhaps, you say, Love came into this room through the music room, and either killed Hoxton before or after shooting

Broox! This idea was exploded when I examined the secret passages leading from the music room and the one leading into this room. In this one I found Love's footprints, establishing beyond doubt that he entered by that passage. I did not find any evidence whatever of his having been in the music room. Doctor Gittles's testimony established Hoxton was not attacked by anyone coming up the stairs from this kitchen.

"One of the puzzling things was the finding of candles and an empty fruit salad can in the Love quarters—and none in the motion-picture camp!

"Did that red cherry and those bits of candle grease I found on this table the morning after the murder originate in the Love quarters? If so, who in that family could have killed Hoxton and shot Broox? What *one* . . . or what *two?* I found that Miss Love had an unusual affection for her brother. That he had threatened to kill Broox . . . on her account! Could she see her brother go to the gallows because of her? Then what had I? The idea that Miss Love might have followed her brother along that corridor . . . having seen and recognized Broox sometime during the evening, when she and Love were known to have been investigating the insistent barking of Calamity—could she have witnessed Love shooting Broox, and then have encountered Hoxton and struck him down to prevent his testifying against her brother? Not likely she would leave her brother wounded . . . and not likely she would leave the room by way of the stairs . . . and yet . . . she is a nurse. She could probably tell that Love would be *safe* to lie without care until morning, even though she was taking a chance, and perhaps she thought to baffle detection by assuming ignorance of the crime. To uphold this improbable idea were *woman's* footprints in the secret passage leading from the music room!"

Smith smiled, and his eyes sought the puzzled ones of those listening to him.

"You see, folks, every trail I made toward a solution was gummed up with conflicting clues and evidence! All could be traced down in time. For instance, I would have found that the woman's footprints were not Miss Love's, but" . . . and he turned to the robed figure . . . "we came to our climax before that was necessary."

Beatrice shuddered, faced with this horrifying suggestion; this calmly uttered idea that she might have fiendishly mashed a man's skull and shot another man down! Randall tightened his arms about her. In the pause, while Smith seemed searching for the simplest presentation of the conflicting angles of his story, she whispered:

"Who is it? Why don't they turn around?"

"Now we come to Morrill," said Smith, and paused. He saw their eyes seek each other with the startled mutual reminder that the little actor was not present . . . with them! Then they turned with one accord to that strange, robed figure. Smith went on, quietly:

"Morrill was not an ordinary type. I realized that immediately. I put myself in way of being criticized by my sergeant because I let him have rope . . . did not arrest him. You all know his fantastic story. Perhaps you do not know that I recognized, in him, a deep-rooted resentment against Hoxton, and against the army officer who turned him down when he volunteered. Could the officer have been Broox—otherwise Captain Jones? Not likely . . . but possible! Morrill's wild tale, embroidered with classical innuendoes, with which I decided he intended to confound me . . . fitted into one theory of mine. That whoever had done these heartless murders had a cunning beyond the average . . . a twisted mind . . . for, you see, that red cherry continued to pop up like a red devil every time I got around to its part . . . just a silly little thing like a small piece of fruit . . . but I could not get around it, or under it! It did not grow there. It was there! Somebody must have put it there? Why?

"Morrill, of course, is not physically fit to have laid out a man like Hoxton, but I had Doctor Gittles's word for it that even a woman might have done it, taking him by surprise, and from the fact that, when we discovered the secret passage out of the music room, we found it started by an immediate ascent of four steps. The blow was struck from there. That elevation would give the murderer sufficient advantage over the victim so that even . . . as Doctor Gittles said . . . a woman might have delivered the fatal blow."

Smith turned to Gittles. "I'll tell you now, Doctor, I was inclined to doubt that statement of yours until I found those stairs!"

Gittles snorted.

"To substantiate the idea that it was Morrill, I found that the actor had been a female impersonator . . . always an enigma to the ordinary man. . . . I immediately deduced that he was also a man who had masqueraded for years . . . hiding his real, vindictive, sinister self behind a manner of cravenness, but in reality calculating and cold, with the added advantage of his stagecraft! In short, a finished actor . . . really an artist . . . capable of assuming a difficult role and making it convincing! Clancy found a woman's shoes and a woman's wig in his tent. Saw him, in fact, putting them on. Clancy's idea was that Morrill came up here, dressed as a woman, paraded about, creating the hallucination of a haunt . . . even told me he had seen one himself . . . a beautiful woman . . . and that it was his footprints I had found in the secret passages! The shattered Tiffany window I at first thought was invented deliberately to further confound me . . . but . . . Duncan's testimony as to the window, and the shot at him, proved otherwise!

"All right, we'll say Morrill did shoot at Duncan, for Duncan was there. That part of his story was true! I still had the tale of the beautiful woman, and the footprints to prove or disprove!

"On the face of all this, a solution could be that Broox and Duncan fought. Duncan shot Love. Morrill murdered Hoxton and shot Broox, whom he apparently liked, to keep him from telling!

"As I said, the combinations of this triangle crime are apparently unending. I expect each and every one of you has still another one, backed up by what seem to you indisputable facts. But I will get on to the close. Ryan, let them look at the face," and he motioned toward the silent form. The two deputies revolved it as though it were a lay figure.

There was a gasp as the perfect, shining beauty of the countenance was revealed . . . the long and glistening hair beneath the gauze veil. Beauty so perfect and so radiant as to leave them staring foolishly, like people hypnotized. It was Beatrice who cried.

"Why . . . it's a *mask!* A Benda mask! I've seen them abroad and in New York!"

"You are right, Miss Love, although I did not know the artist. Morrill was right in his description of his heavenly houri! I came across that mask and those robes to-day, for I spent the entire afternoon in a thorough search of this house. They were hanging in a small, windowless room, at the end of that secret passage upstairs! I was convinced that those garments held guilt in their every shred . . . but . . . I did not know, certainly . . . who wore them . . . I . . . do . . . not . . . *know* . . . yet!"

Their eyes widened incredulously upon him. Smith looked at Rosenthal.

"My good friend, some time ago you gave me a glimpse into the making of motion pictures . . . into the make-believe land of the drama. It fascinated me as it fascinates all people. I find that I have a suppressed desire to be a director! I have found a great satisfaction in staging my climaxes in their most dramatic aspects! Sometimes the opportunity does not present itself. When it does I seize it! It lends fantasy to a many-times depressing profession. . . ."

"But Smith, I vould like to know who . . ." Rosenthal started impatiently, only to be stopped by the detective's upraised hand.

"Let me have my little drama, my friend . . . before we unmask this figure. I want you to consider another element . . . the history of this house!

"Last night I had it from Doctor Gittles. I will give you only the important facts. The owner and builder was a Mrs. Binchester. Undoubtedly she was eccentric. She had a belief, so it is said, that she would not die so long as the hammers kept sounding on this house. For over thirty years there was the constant rat-a-tat-tat of them continuously! She had the unhappy belief that there were many malignant spirits lurking to pounce on her. This impression was caused by an unfortunate occurrence, the San Francisco earthquake. The costly, magnificent dwelling she was erecting for her spirit friends was, in part, demolished. She interpreted this as a visitation from the spirits, and that they were angry with her for having lavished so much upon them. She abandoned the wrecked part of the house, and refused to allow anything to be touched. The debris, as you have all seen, lies just as it fell—covered with dust and containing many reclaimable treasures. From that time on her building program changed. Apparently she developed fear of the spirits. Therefore she tried to confound them by trick stairways, the rows of fireplaces with blind chimneys—elevators. She had a tremendous fortune, and was constantly in touch with the artists and craftsmen of both continents, so it was easy for her to obtain that beautiful mask . . . those coverings for her scrawny hands, with fingernails of mother-of-pearl! There is a popular story that she feasted these malignant spirits in goblets of gold . . . such foods as she thought would appeal to their esthetic tastes . . . honey and fruits! People about tell stories of the organ upstairs pealing out near midnight, and of glimpses through those windows of this strange woman walking with her candles, in her gorgeous robes!"

Smith paused as the eyes of his audience widened and remained speculative and aghast upon the prisoner. Then he shook his head.

"No . . . it is not she! That woman has been dead ten years. She had many servants. Among them Matilda Scraggs . . . now a bent and withered crone . . . palsied and enfeebled . . . just a filthy bundle of old rags swinging forward on a stick . . . mumbling incoherently . . . Doctor Gittles explained to me last night, in very technical terms"—Smith paused to glance at the little coroner—"which explanation I'll spare you now, how this or any person, associated for years with one such as her mistress, could, and might, take on the same brain kinks.

"When I had heard this story I found it fitted with the organ pealing at certain times . . . the golden cups . . . the fruit salad . . . Morrill's story of a beautiful woman! I had already seen and talked to Matilda Scraggs, who had lived on here alone, bound by a loyalty which, many of Mrs. Binchester's servants felt, was a result of her freely spent bounty. However, until I had heard the story of this house, I did not connect the lonely remaining servant with the crimes. Before we consider her, let me present to you the idea that life, as lived in this house—with its strange customs and long associations with a woman such as Mrs. Binchester—could reasonably have had a disastrous effect on a certain type of mind. I believe Matilda Scraggs has just such a mind.

"Presuming the guilty to be Matilda Scraggs, let me outline the action for you. The interlopers in the house on the night of the murders. Her insane, one-track mind intent on keeping faith with the spirits. Her attempt to do so unmolested . . . her coming in upon Broox, finding him defiling with his touch the sacred vessels of the midnight ceremonial . . . and, with the cunning that goes with insanity, her stealthy snatching up of the revolver (Duncan's) which lay on the table by him. Broox made an easy target, surprised, and, for the moment, motionless in his surprise, at the apparition of this radiant creature! She shot him. Then her going up the stairs to play the organ . . . part of the ceremony. We have Morrill's testimony, while he sat there in the dark ballroom, of unseen movement in the room, breathing . . . whispering . . . of her passing along the corridors with the candles . . . preparing the ceremony—

"How she knew of Hoxton's presence in the music room I cannot say. Perhaps she was wary, after finding Broox. Perhaps . . . and undoubtedly she had heard him playing the organ earlier in the evening . . . at any rate, she did not use these stairs to the music room, but went through that panel door to the passage which, I found this afternoon, connects with another panel, to the corridor leading into the music room. She came upon Hoxton, who was unsuspecting, and struck him down from behind. The weapon was this gun . . . on the butt of which still clings the gruesome evidence of its lethal use. Doctor Gittles will corroborate my statement that unbalanced persons, or persons with a fanatical mania, have superhuman strength. Last night, when the customary ceremonial was in progress, the little dog Calamity, which had been lost in this maze of trick contrivances, got into this room and lapped up the sacred fruit juices. It caused his death with" . . . Smith picked up the revolver, broke it open . . . "this gun! Here are four shots gone . . . one for Love . . . one for Broox . . . one for Calamity, and one for me! To-night I set the stage, and my actor walked into it. I had the advantage over Broox . . . I was prepared for anything! I shot the gun from that wounded hand—received this wound first. I had to let her shoot . . . first . . . and take my chance . . . to prove to myself . . . that my deductions were true!"

He held up his wounded, bandaged hand . . . and again besought their patience.

"Just one more angle before we pronounce Matilda Scraggs guilty . . . before we take off that mask! This thing could have been done by a person clever enough to make use of the common gossip concerning this place! It could have been done by anyone familiar with make-up . . . with feet small enough to make those dainty footprints . . . by anyone enough of a finished actor to play this part and then play another to confound me . . . in short . . . it could have been done by Morrill!

"I have not yet had time to compare those footprints with Morrill's woman's shoes. But of one thing I was certain. Whether my criminal was the one or the other, I dared not let another midnight pass, without putting my weird solution to the test. If nothing happened, if upon the stage here no other than myself appeared . . . then it was merely a question of tracing down and of isolating my clues, until I had finally traced to the end an ever-narrowing trail. I took a chance . . . and there . . . behind that mask . . . is the answer to all these tragedies!"

He stopped speaking, and silence clamped down. It was broken by Beatrice, crying:

"Oh, don't keep us any longer! Let's . . . get it over . . . with . . . !"

"Yess, yess, Smith . . . you've held the spotlight too long! Take that mask off!" Rosenthal ordered peremptorily. Smith made a signal of agreement to Ryan, who stepped forward. He had some difficulty removing the disguise, but at last did so. For a moment the black, lashless eyes glared at them. Then the voice broke through the long-held silence:

"Tillie, you damned old fool! Promise me. . . . I'll twist your neck . . . I'm dying, Tillie . . . they're after me. . . ."

Mumbling and choking, the old voice croaked on . . . finally breaking down to coughing, slavering sobs, whose unpleasant sound made them all look away, and mentally close their ears. . . .

"Cover her up again . . . take her avay . . . mein Gott! . . . I can't bear to look . . . vat a poor old creature . . . vat . . ."

Rosenthal stopped, unable to find words. The tears had come to Beatrice's eyes, and she silently accepted Randall's handkerchief.

From their loathing horror of the perpetrator of the murders had come now a loathing pity.

"She'll be put away in an institution," said Smith, "and the golden goblets can go with her. . . ."

It was early dawn when Rosenthal and Smith stepped into the waiting aeroplane for their return flight to Hollywood.

"Well, it's been a great night out, eh, Rosey?"

"Mein Gott! Say, vere vas that Morrill all the time to-night?"

"Sleeping like a babe! Great little fellow! He was trying to solve it all the time . . . even as far as dressing up and parading before his own mirror in candle-light, to see how easily he could be fooled! I shall go to see his jade collection as soon as I have time!"

Rosenthal sighed.

"Vat haff I done, my friend, that I should haff all these murders?" His fat face was unhappy in the dim light.

"Rosey, I've got a hunch. One of my famous ones! Your time of travail is over! Prosperity is before you. . . ."

"You really think that?"

"I do!"

There was a moment of silence, and then Rosenthal chuckled.

"That's a good fortune, my friend! I haff heard that it iss better luck to cross the fortune-teller's palm vid gold! I got something in my pocket. I vas taking it for a souvenir . . . but already I got too many souvenirs of this terrible affair! I got sad memories off Broox . . . so I giff it to you . . . close your eyes and hold out your hand . . . there, I cross your hand vid gold! I bet you not many Jews vould let go off gold vonce they get their hands on it . . . eh?"

He chuckled slyly as he closed Smith's fingers around a golden goblet.

"Thanks a lot—and I'm going to ask one more present. Give Randall a job. He's up in the air, with Broox gone . . . and he's . . ."

"Say, vat you take me for? Already I haff planned for him a svell wedding present. Just you vait! I'll make that Mrs. Loff's eyes stick out, so she don't effer throw up a lot off talk about European counts to him. In pictures ve can do anything!"

The pilot called back to them:

"All set? . . . All right . . . let's go!"

Someone Wearing a Benda Mask, 1925 (*Arnold Genthe*)

OF OPTICAL GLASS AND BENDA MASKS:
The Bizarre Secrets of the Edingtons' "Binchester House"
Curtis Evans

> "Vell? Qvick! Tell me! I am all goose pimples vid
> curiosity!"
> —Irrepressible Film Studio Magnate Abraham
> Rosenthal in the penultimate chapter of *The
> House of the Vanishing Goblets*

Only near the very end of *The House of the Vanishing Goblets*—
after local medico Dr. Gittles has divulged offstage to Detective
Smith (who belatedly bent his ear to the garrulous medico) the
strange history of this eerie house where two men have lately
died most violently—does the reader learn just how central the
legend of "Binchester House" is to the solution of the mystery
which Arlo and Carmen Edington have devised. The main suspects, estranged colleagues from the past and present of slain
director Ellison Brooks, were, it turns out, merely red herrings
all along, the real murderer being none other than the withered
old crone who in her pathetic rags briefly straggles across the
mystery stage in chapter XVI: Matilda Scraggs, a former servant
of mad old Mrs. Binchester, dead now for the last decade, who,
herself having gone insane in the devoted service of her late mistress, is determined to defend unto the death (preferably of the
interlopers) the secret and sacred services to the spirits which she,
Scraggs, still performs with clinically obsessive devotion. Like a

deadly Hall of Mirrors at a devil's carnival, the Binchester House most deviously had deceived, for a time, even the great Detective Smith (and with him, probably, the reader). The monstrous face at the window was merely the product of Belgian optical glass, while the astonishingly beautiful woman whom the actor Morrill descried wandering by night down a candlelit corridor was nothing but wizened old Matilda Scraggs herself, decked out in her mistresses' old robes and bewitching Benda mask.

The real-life Mrs. Winchester installed windows made from Belgian optical glass in her mad, mazelike house, of which the experience of touring has been described by one dazed visitor as rather like "wandering through the corridors of a schizophrenic mind." Another lost soul passing through Mrs. Winchester's mansion avowed upon returning to sanity and light that

> The Impression one retains is of a strong absence of color or a color like that of ectoplasm: even the Tiffany windows are mostly restrained and pale, while certain other windows made of large sheets of Belgian optical glass slightly magnify the palms and the shrubbery outside and draw into the rooms what can only be described as an intense pallor.[1]

Benda masks, an oddity of the Art Decon era, were the product of the imaginative mind of Polish artist and designer W. T. Benda (1873-1948). First fashioned by Benda in 1914, the masks, which the Pole meticulously sculpted out of papier mâché, attained popularity after the Great War in stage plays and dances and appeared as well in films. They were employed, for example, in productions of works by noted playwrights Eugene O'Neill and Noel Coward and in the notorious 1932 pulp horror Boris Karloff film *The Mask of Fu Manchu*, based on the novel

of the same title by English thriller author Sax Rohmer. The notion that Mrs. Winchester might ever have worn the masks while
communing with spirits roaming her Mystery House would seem
to have been strictly a fancy of the Edingtons' own creative imag-
inations, however.

ENDNOTE

[1] John Ashbery, "Mystery Mansion," *House & Garden*
(March 1987), 208, available at *John Ashberry's Nest*, at
https://ashberyhouse.yale.edu/poet/house-essays.

COACHWHIP PUBLICATIONS
CoachwhipBooks.com

THE
RUMBLE
MURDERS

Henry Ware Eliot, Jr.

MURDER TAKES
THE VEIL

MURDER AT
ST. DENNIS

SISTER SIMON'S
MURDER CASE

THE MARGARET ANN HUBBARD
MYSTERY OMNIBUS

COACHWHIP PUBLICATIONS
CoachwhipBooks.com

THE
SARA ELIZABETH
MASON
MYSTERIES

MURDER RENTS A ROOM

THE CRIMSON FEATHER

COACHWHIP PUBLICATIONS
CoachwhipBooks.com

THE
SARA ELIZABETH
MASON
MYSTERIES

THE HOUSE THAT HATE BUILT

⟫⟫⟫ ⟪⟪⟪

THE WHIP

COACHWHIP PUBLICATIONS
CoachwhipBooks.com

A JUDGE MASSIE MYSTERY

THE CORPSE IS INDIGNANT

DOUGLAS STAPLETON
and HELEN A. CAREY

COACHWHIP PUBLICATIONS
CoachwhipBooks.com

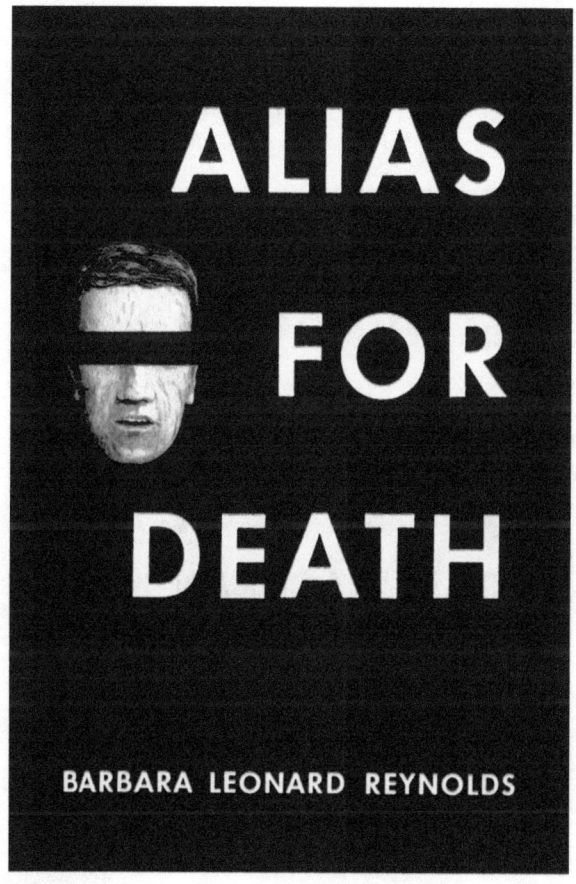

ALIAS

FOR

DEATH

BARBARA LEONARD REYNOLDS

COACHWHIP PUBLICATIONS
CoachwhipBooks.com

MOST MEN DON'T KILL

MURDER IN BLACK AND WHITE

DAVID ALEXANDER

COACHWHIP PUBLICATIONS
CoachwhipBooks.com

SAMUEL ROGERS

YOU'LL BE
SORRY!

YOU LEAVE
ME COLD!